LADY. VIOLET GOES FOR A GALLOP

THE LADY VIOLET MYSTERIES—BOOK SIX

GRACE BURROWES

GRACE BURROWES PUBLISHING

DEDICATION

**This series is dedicated
to my nephew, Jackson.**

CHAPTER ONE

Grief was besieging my household, though I had no intention of allowing that unseemly invader to once again breach my castle walls.

As a widow, I had endured the company of this same intruder for the two years of social banishment known as proper mourning. *Proper hell* would be a more accurate term. My husband had died suddenly, five years into a troubled marriage.

My regard for Frederick Belmaine in life had traveled a progression familiar to many veterans of the *advantageous match*. I'd started out full of schoolgirl glee to become Lady Violet Belmaine. I spoke my vows with a handsome, witty, urbane suitor, convinced that Freddie was equally pleased at his marital good fortune.

Little more than five years later, I buried him, long after I'd buried any dreams of a loving, devoted marriage. Freddie had been a hedonistic tomcat, though like most husbands in polite society, he'd maintained a tissue of separation between his selfish pleasures and his marital duties.

He'd been a perfect gentleman as far as his peers judged such matters, but within the privacy of our union, he'd been a far from perfect spouse. I'd genuinely grieved his passing nonetheless—he'd *tried*, we'd both tried—though as the months of black crepe, stopped clocks, isolation, and widow's weeds had trudged past, I'd also admitted to some guilty relief. Freddie had died far too young, cut down in the flower of young manhood, et cetera and so forth, but *we had not suited*.

My mourning was thus complicated, by anger, resentment, confusion, and by that damnable imp, guilt. What had begun as sadness and shock had transmogrified into melancholia and a paralyzing anxiety about even so mundane a challenge as leaving my house.

The prison I'd come to resent, the false temple to domestic accord, had taken me captive in truth. I began to dread divine services with more than usual foreboding. I made excuses to decline the quiet gatherings to which widows in second mourning were typically invited.

My maid, Lucy Hewitt, had been a staunch ally for the duration of this ordeal, and her casual mention of gossip—Lady Violet Belmaine was said to have become a recluse—had penetrated my misery deeply enough that I realized I had drifted into truly dangerous waters.

When all four of my brothers bestirred themselves to call on me within a single fortnight, I resolved to paddle back to safer shores. How exactly to do that had eluded me until I'd developed a closer acquaintance with Dr. Hugh St. Sevier.

Thoughts of St. Sevier were both painful and comforting, and I suspected they always would be. Hugh was French by birth. He'd come to England in childhood and been educated as a physician in Scotland. He'd crossed Spain with Wellington's army, serving as a medical volunteer, and when hostilities with the French had finally ended, Hugh had been a gentleman of substantial means and even greater charm.

The charm was deceptive, for St. Sevier was as formidable a fellow as any heavy dragoon ever to charge Boney's line. He'd reasoned with me, he'd flirted, he'd gently lectured, and he'd subtly challenged, all in aid of improving my spirits.

More than that, though, he'd *listened* to me. He'd taken quiet walks with me, first in my back garden, then around the fenced-off square my household shared with several others. He'd encouraged me to put off my weeds at the prescribed time and escorted me on quiet morning hacks and then to a few musicales and at homes that should have been no challenge for me at all.

And yet, I'd been terrified to set foot out of my coach without the protection of a widow's veil.

I'd lost my breakfast at the thought of having to make small talk with people I'd known for years.

Hugh had borne my fears calmly, as if every widow was entitled to strong hysterics at the thought of greeting her neighbors, and gradually, the demons of anxiety, isolation, and sadness had been banished from my house.

Now Hugh, who had become confidant, friend, and then lover, was lost to me. I had granted him permission to court me, a gesture of enormous trust, given the lamentable facts of my first marriage.

I knew Hugh had married in Spain, a union of expedience and gallantry occasioned when a young lady following the drum had lost her husband. Ann's choices had been to become a camp follower or to marry the handsome French doctor. I did not blame her for taking the latter option. Unless a woman was one of a few officers' wives enrolled with the regiment, she was very much cast on her own devices should her soldier perish.

By Hugh's accounting, the marriage had been inauspicious in all particulars, and yet, I had the sense he had done his best by his young wife, such as a man battling impossible medical challenges in the midst of war could. Ann had lasted less than a year before deserting him, and he'd been told she'd died at the hands of a French patrol.

She had *not* died, and she had borne St. Sevier a child, or so she'd claimed when she had most inconveniently turned up barely a month past, at a gathering at my family seat to which St. Sevier had escorted me.

Hugh and Ann might have gone their separate ways, quietly turning their backs on a wartime union that had served neither of them as intended.

But there was that child, a solemn little girl with Hugh's brows and her mother's flaming red hair. The Hugh St. Sevier I esteemed would never abandon that child and would never legally set aside her mother.

I had resented Freddie for playing the part of the gentleman. I resented Hugh for being a gentleman in truth—and I loved him for it too.

I also missed him. I missed him as the companion who'd made my travels over the past year both interesting and pleasant. I missed him as a wise friend was missed, and I missed him sorely as an affectionate and skilled lover was missed.

I missed him in that regard a *very* great deal. In the short time during which we'd been intimate, I'd learned much, about tenderness and joy, about how physical and emotional closeness could complement and reinforce each another. I had allowed Hugh into my bed, and he had allowed me into his heart.

Five years of marriage to Freddie hadn't encompassed one-tenth the wonder of a few months as Hugh St. Sevier's lover. If I lived to a biblical age, I would remain in St. Sevier's debt for confirming that my marriage had been a pathetic excuse for a relationship compared to what a relationship could be.

There was *nothing wrong with me*, in other words. I had needed Hugh St. Sevier's regard to show me that.

"You are brooding." Lucy Hewitt set down a tea tray, though I had not rung for tea, and a lady's maid did not typically step and fetch for the kitchen.

"I am thinking," I replied.

"About him. You're mourning." She checked the strength of the tea, then poured me a cup, adding a drizzle of honey and a dollop of cream. The soothing scent of jasmine wafted to my nose, and I realized I had missed luncheon.

"St. Sevier is not dead, Lucy." Though I felt all over again as if a part of me had died. A precious, fragile, joyous part. "If you intend to be so impertinent as to intrude on my solitude and accuse me of brooding, then you can say his name."

"He's worse than dead," Lucy said, adding a tea cake to my saucer. "He's married."

Lucy and I were overly familiar, and I thanked God nightly for her presumption. She was blond, a few years younger than I, sturdily built, and she did not suffer foolishness, most especially from her employer.

She'd opened the door to St. Sevier when I'd insisted I wasn't home to callers. She'd trimmed my second mourning clothes with white lace when I'd told her I wanted no adornments. She'd brought flowers into the house and seen me bathed and dressed when I had been brooding in truth.

In her way, Lucy was fierce and wise, and I owed her much. She was also impertinent, saucy, and honest, for which I owed her even more.

"St. Sevier is not only married," I said, "he has a daughter, and that is an end to the matter."

"Did he *know*?" She moved about my private parlor, rearranging pillows on the fainting couch, tidying up the writing implements on the escritoire. Lucy had the knack of making any space orderly and comfortable, though she lacked the gift of silence.

"He had no clue," I said. "He caught a glimpse of Ann in Perth, but Scotland is full of red-haired women, and he told himself his imagination was playing tricks." Imaginations did that. After Freddie's death, I'd thought I'd heard his voice, thought I'd seen him on the street. I'd caught a whiff of his pipe tobacco when his study had long since been aired.

Ghosts might not walk the earth, but they certainly stalked the mind.

"Why not send the lady back to Scotland or to France?" Lucy asked, giving the sofa cushion a hard swat.

"She is his wife, and he is a gentleman. They might well remove to France, but that is none of my business." Hugh had asked for permission to correspond with me, but I had not seen any point to such a connection. If he and Ann were to make a go of their marriage, then letters to me could not aid that cause.

And yet, I longed to know how he was managing, longed to know that he was well. Longed to know even where he bided.

"It's not right," Lucy said, swiping a finger down the length of the mantel. My lady's maid was, in fact, inspecting the work of the house-keeper and parlor maids, a job reserved for the lady of the house.

"It's not convenient," I replied. "But St. Sevier loves children, and it's to Ann's credit that she did not keep the child from him once she knew how to find him."

"Took her blessed time finding him, if you ask me. If she thought he was alive, why couldn't she simply send a letter to Horse Guards asking his whereabouts?"

That very question had occurred to me, but my brother Felix, who had also served in Spain, had had a damnably credible answer.

"Firstly, Horse Guards is besieged with such letters, and between poor spelling, bad penmanship, and a lack of proper documentation at headquarters, half of those letters go unanswered. Secondly, St. Sevier was a gentleman volunteer serving in a medical capacity, and Horse Guards did not keep such close track of those volunteers. They had their own chain of command, and documentation did not figure heavily in its priorities. Thirdly, I suspect Ann was ashamed to have left her husband, and a woman ashamed often makes regrettable choices."

I knew that eternal verity firsthand.

"Drink your tea, my lady, and have something to eat. If you start skipping meals, I will not answer for the consequences."

Meaning Lucy would notify my family, which now included two sisters-by-marriage. While my four brothers and my father might not know how to contend with a woman nigh jilted at the altar, the Deer-field womenfolk were made of sterner stuff.

"You are concerned for me," I said, dutifully picking up a sand-wich. "I appreciate that, but I have no intention of permitting myself a decline."

She sent me a baleful look over her shoulder as she rearranged books on the shelves behind the desk. "You permitted yourself the last one? Woke up one fine Tuesday and decided to stop eating, stop leaving the house, stop *talking*?"

Lucy's bluntness was like a tonic—unpleasant but fortifying. "I admit it was bad, but I know better now. St. Sevier taught me better, and that is a gift I get to keep, even as I must let other trea-sures go."

Those putridly gracious words brought a lump to my throat. Hugh had said tears could be healing, but I suspected the embrace of a true friend was the more effective balm.

"If you go all noble on me, my lady, I will give notice. The whole situation is rotten, and I wish you'd take a mind to return to Scotland. You were happy there. Had roses in your cheeks, and I even heard you laugh a time or two."

St. Sevier and I had become lovers in Scotland, and I did not think I could bear to return there for some time.

"I am contemplating travel, Lucy."

She left off rearranging my books. "To France?"

"Not to France, to someplace in the Home Counties where I can buy a small manor house. I have not been happy in London, and maintaining this address is expensive."

"Not Surrey?"

The family seat of the Earls of Derwent was in Surrey. My dear mama was buried there. My two nieces and infant nephew were in Surrey. My four brothers and—lest the obvious be overlooked—*my father* were in Surrey.

"I'll look elsewhere first."

Lucy stared past my shoulder, her mind clearly already taken up with packing and other preparations. "How long will we be gone, and when do we leave?"

If I intended to inspect several properties, I'd be away from London for several weeks, at least. My solicitors had given me a list, and while none of the prospective homes was ideal, they all conformed to my most pressing requirements: a commodious house in good repair within a short journey of Town.

Henry, my first footman, rapped his knuckles on the doorjamb. "Beg pardon, my lady, but you've had an express."

Express correspondence was seldom good news. Henry passed me the letter and hovered while I slit the seal. I did not recognize the hand, which was legible and without flourishes, nor did I recognize the specific direction in Kent. The message was brief—and as shocking for the signature as for the news it bore.

Henry and Lucy were both watching me, doubtless concerned that bad news now would send me tumbling back into melancholia or worse.

My days of passively enduring black moods were behind me, if I had anything to say to it, *and I did.*

"Henry, please tell John Coachman to ready the traveling coach. We will be journeying to Kent with all due haste. We leave as soon as Lucy can have me packed and ready to go."

~

"What can you hope to accomplish, my lady?" Lucy's question held the banked frustration of a woman resorting to reason when she'd rather shout.

"I hope to stop a hanging," I replied.

A relatively mild climate and proximity to London meant Kent as a county was heavily cultivated. Harvest was underway, and thus my coach was frequently stuck behind wagons full of produce or hauling laborers from one property to another. I caught the occasional snippet of song from the crews, but mostly I heard Lucy's fingers drumming on the leather of the opposite bench.

I read the note for the two dozenth time since receiving it that morning.

My lady,

Monsieur is being detained on suspicion of having committed murder. I did not know who else to ask for help. Please come posthaste.

Madame Ann St. Sevier

The dire implications had not changed, but that Ann would seek my help on her husband's behalf raised her in my esteem. Hugh St. Sevier himself would never trouble another to come to his aid, though he'd promised me to the contrary.

"How can you stop a hanging, ma'am?" Lucy asked. "Interfering with the king's man is a crime. Criticizing the crown is a crime."

"If a murder has taken place, then finding the killer is not a crime."

Lucy muttered something which I knew better than to hear clearly, but the words *rubbishing* and *stupid* might have been mentioned.

"He won't thank you for it," she said a few minutes later. "He'll be all charming and gallant and stoic."

"I do not seek thanks, Lucy. I seek the truth, and the truth is that Hugh St. Sevier would never take another's life." Except possibly in self-defense or by accident.

The coach hit a rut, the thousandth such rut in less than half a day's travel. I was put in mind of the countless miles I had journeyed with Hugh as my escort, the length and breadth of the realm. I had been devastated to think that he and I would never again grouse and cuddle our way across the countryside.

I had found it mortally unfair that I would never again share a morning cup of tea with him, and I had been outraged that another woman would share his bed while I kept company with only memories and regrets.

But I refused, utterly, to contemplate a world without Hugh St. Sevier in it, and woe to any rural magistrate who sought to thwart me.

"Mrs. Bonaventure might not have received your note yet."

"She will receive us, Lucy. Now is not the time to be contrary."

A mulish glower served as Lucy's reply, though her doubts were justified. I did not know Pamela Bonaventure well. She had been widowed several years earlier than I had, and we had some acquaintances in common. At a summer house party the previous year, she and I had struck up a wary association short of friendship, though our paths had seldom crossed since.

In addition to both grain and garden produce, Kent boasted a sizable crop of titles. Because my father was an earl, I knew many of those families, had come out with some of their daughters, and stood up with many of their sons.

I had avoided prevailing on those connections to host me for this journey for reasons having to do with my father's tangled web of alliances, and also because Mrs. Bonaventure had met St. Sevier. She might not stake her reputation on his innocence, but she would regret the death of a handsome, charming fellow on general principles. She was that sort of widow—pragmatic, tolerant, *discreet*.

I had not visited her home previously, but as my coach tooled up a long drive lined with ancient lime trees, I added another adjective to that list: Pamela Bonaventure was *wealthy*, or at least quite well provided for.

The Gauges, her country home, was a three-story temple to whitewashed brick serenely situated halfway up a gentle rise. I counted twenty windows—each one taxed, of course—across the façade. The double front doors and shutters were painted a cheery light blue, and potted red salvia lined the front terrace and steps.

The overall impression was gracious, pleasing, and pretty. The

Gauges was large enough to be stately, but small enough to feel inviting. Exactly the sort of country home I sought for myself, and I had a fanciful sense that the house was glad to have a visitor.

A groom rose from the mounting block as the coach came to a halt at the foot of the steps, and a liveried footman marched forth from the house to open the coach door. The groom was tidy, the footman's livery all in order. No hasty buttoning up of his jacket or slicking back his hair.

Pamela Bonaventure knew how to make a proper first impression, even in absentia.

"Welcome to The Gauges, Lady Violet," the footman said, offering his hand.

He was tall, blond, and handsome, as footmen were supposed to be, and he managed to exude cordiality without actually smiling. He handed me down, then performed the same courtesy for Lucy. All quite correct, and by the time he'd ushered me into the keeping of an equally cordial—and equally youngish—butler, my coach had drawn away from the front door.

A frisson of unease came over me as I realized I was far from home, preparing to prevail on the kindness of a near stranger in a matter with the potential for both scandal and tragedy. Then too, for the first time in my life when journeying someplace besides the Deerfield family seat, I'd traveled without a male escort.

I pushed the unease aside and replaced it with determination and a smidgeon of pride. Widows were permitted to travel unescorted, particularly for short excursions. Why not avail myself of that freedom?

"Mrs. Bonaventure will greet you herself shortly," the butler said, taking Lucy's traveling satchel from her. "She is unavoidably detained at a neighbor's, but we expect her home any moment. Mrs. Weaver will show you to your apartment. Please do ring if there's anything we can do to make your stay more comfortable."

He passed Lucy's satchel to another handsome devil of a footman and toddled off, doubtless to oversee the porters unloading my trunks.

"Lady Violet." The housekeeper curtseyed and came up smiling. "It's an honor to claim you among The Gauges's guests. Mrs. Bonaventure said we are to accord you every courtesy and convenience. She's put you in the garden suite, and we will have a tray up in no time."

The tray, through some miracle of domestic wizardry, was waiting on a low table when the housekeeper admitted me to my apartment. I could feel Lucy taking visual inventory of the house and in particular of the sitting room we found ourselves in.

The wallpaper was a soft, marine green, adorned with strutting, jewel-toned peacocks, intricately detailed pink and white camellias, and darker green foliage. The carpet and curtains echoed those colors, creating an impression of a quiet moment in some exotic forest.

The room was beautiful, though its appointments were modest.

"That door," Mrs. Weaver said, nodding at a panel nearly hidden by the pattern of the wallpaper, "opens onto the conservatory. Your balcony overlooks the garden, and you have a fine view of Belle Terre as well."

Lucy opened the French doors, and a gust of country-air-and-stable joined the lavender-sachet scent in the room.

"Belle Terre." Mrs. Weaver gestured to a magnificent edifice in peach-pale stone on a distant rise. "Who knows what's to become of it now, what with the owner behind bars and the squires up in arms? Beautiful house, though. My cousin is housekeeper there."

"Who owns Belle Terre?" An upwelling of foreboding accompanied my question.

"Monsieur Hugh St. Sevier. We never saw much of him—he preferred London or his other properties, but the day Belle Terre fell into the hands of a Frog was a bleak day indeed, my lady. He's a proper enough gentleman, according to my cousin, but we took the war very seriously here in Kent. We stare across the Channel at Calais and well knew who would be first to feel Boney's sword if the French invaded."

Oddly enough, Sussex, Suffolk, and a half-dozen other counties along the southern coast had known the same thing.

"Monsieur St. Sevier served with Wellington," I said. I had anticipated that bigotry would be among the challenges St. Sevier faced on the road to exoneration, but that a housekeeper would disparage a neighbor to a guest was alarming.

"You know him?" Mrs. Weaver asked.

"I do, and I would trust him with my life. He is a highly skilled physician and an exceptionally honorable gentleman." I *had* trusted Hugh with my life, come to that, but kept that fact to myself.

"But he did not *fight* under Wellington, did he?" Mrs. Weaver replied, opening the lid of the silver teapot and peering at the contents.

"Physicians serve in a different capacity," I retorted, "and Monsieur volunteered his services."

She closed the lid on the teapot. "Who better would know how to take a life than a physician, or so they're saying at the Boar's Tail. One must admit the point is valid, my lady."

A tap on the door heralded the porters arriving with my trunk. Lucy shooed them into the adjoining bedroom and disappeared to start the unpacking. I secured from Mrs. Weaver the services of a groom to carry a note to Belle Terre and got a cool visual assessment —or reassessment—in return.

The staff at the Gauges was gracious and attentive, but the housekeeper lacked the perfect decorum of her London counterparts. Mrs. Weaver hadn't exactly gossiped with me, but she'd made it very clear that St. Sevier was not well regarded in the neighborhood.

He owned an astonishingly impressive property, likely provided employment for dozens, and was admitted to be a "proper enough gentleman" who had volunteered to patch up Wellington's injured troops, and yet, nationality alone was sufficient to convict him of murder.

When Mrs. Weaver had withdrawn and taken the porters with

her, I poured Lucy a cup of tea and took it to her in the dressing closet off the bedroom.

"This has to be about the prettiest guest room I ever did see," Lucy said, closing the door to a tall cedar-lined wardrobe. "That tea had best not be for me, milady. I have standards, and you do not wait upon me."

"Drink it," I said. "Where do you suppose this wallpaper came from?" The peacock and camellia theme was repeated in the bedroom. The bed, swagged in green hangings and covered in a green, white, and pink quilt, felt like a leafy bower. Afternoon sun slanted through sparkling latticed French doors, and a privacy screen painted all over with peacocks and parrots stood in the corner.

The best touch was a vase of pink roses on the mantel. The flowers emitted a heady, spicy perfume.

Whoever had appointed this apartment had an eye for domestic beauty. I was itching to explore the rest of the house, but first I must send along a note informing Ann St. Sevier that I had arrived in the neighborhood.

Lucy took the cup and saucer from me and sipped. "Could be a little stronger, but plenty hot. You aren't having any?"

"Soon. The coach travel has given me indigestion." That, or the prospect of Hugh St. Sevier's demise at the end of a rope had upset my belly.

Lucy finished her tea and returned the cup and saucer to the tray in the sitting room. "Eat something, and your tummy will settle. I had no idea Monsieur owned a palace."

"It's merely a stately home, Lucy. He's not the king of France." Many an Englishman had found Louis deserving of his fate... until the violence had expanded to include his wife and small children and exploded into years of state-sanctioned savagery. The Corsican had stepped into the resulting chaos, and at the time, many an Englishman had been relieved that somebody had come along to make France settle down.

"Your friend is doomed," Lucy said. "Mrs. Weaver's cousin works for the man, and she's ready to string him up simply for being French."

I wanted to reprimand Lucy for speaking too plainly, but instead penned my note to Ann St. Sevier, informing her that I would call as soon as I had greeted my hostess, before supper if possible.

Lucy took the folded and sealed note from me, promising to see it into the hands of a groom, along with a coin to ensure its immediate delivery.

"You are good to come here," she said, pausing at the apartment door, "and you are good to try, my lady. You've had luck with tough puzzles in the past, but your handsome Frenchman is not long for this world."

She was trying to be kind—and failing. "He's not my handsome Frenchman, and he didn't murder anybody. Be off with you and learn what you can belowstairs, please."

She curtseyed with ironic politesse and silently withdrew.

I considered pouring myself a cup of tea, but still, my digestion refused to settle. Instead, I took myself off on reconnaissance, a point-less exercise that nonetheless appeased my curiosity and gave me an excuse to simply *move*. I needed to familiarize myself with my surroundings, and I needed to dispel the sense of anxiety that was doubtless giving me an upset tummy.

A footman—apparently, they were all gorgeous at The Gauges—directed me to the library, but before I'd gone more than a dozen yards down the indicated corridor, I heard raised voices from behind a closed door. Pamela Bonaventure had returned home, and she was most unhappy with a gentleman who was apparently also quite displeased with her.

CHAPTER TWO

Eavesdroppers never heard any good of themselves, which bothered me not at all, but I did want to get off on the right foot with my hostess. If Pamela Bonaventure was dressing down a tippling steward or taking her butler to task, she would not appreciate an audience.

I had retraced a half dozen of my steps when a door opened behind me.

"Giles, get back here!" Pamela called.

A young man emerged into the corridor, his tread agitated. He was nicely turned out in a country gentleman's riding attire. He carried a shiny black top hat, and his auburn hair was stylishly disarranged. I put his height at slightly less than six feet—a good height in a dancing partner—and his features were pleasing enough that he'd qualify for a footman's post in this household.

He stopped short when he saw me. "Pamela, you have a caller. Greetings, ma'am. Giles Bellamy, at your service." He executed a correct bow, though annoyance radiated from him.

Pamela joined us in the corridor. She was attired in a smart, royal blue riding habit, her toque trimmed with pheasant feathers. Though her blond hair was perfectly styled in looping side braids, her hems were dusty, and she clutched a pair of black gloves in her hand.

"Lady Violet." In a silent instant, she transformed herself from an excessively vexed woman into a gracious hostess. "You made good time."

She tended to the introductions, during which I endured a tacit perusal from Mr. Bellamy.

"Your papa is Earl of Derwent, isn't he?" Mr. Bellamy asked, his manner thawing. "I have a passing acquaintance with Mr. Hector Deerfield and Mr. Ajax Deerfield. Capital fellows, if I do say so."

My middle brothers were the family socializers, but then, they were also the unmarried sons of an earl, and thus they enjoyed a bachelor's entrée with the hostesses.

"Lord Derwent has the honor to be my father," I replied, manufacturing my best London drawing room smile. "Did you meet Hector and Ajax at university?"

"Perhaps we can pursue this topic over a pot of tea?" Pamela suggested. "And you can regale us with the Town news, my lady. Giles, you are welcome to stay."

The invitation to me was genuine. The invitation to Giles barely qualified as an invitation. He nonetheless smiled genially and offered me his arm.

"A spot of tea would be just the thing," he said, "and I am always interested in the latest news from London. What brings you to our corner of Kent, Lady Violet?"

Determination to save a former lover's life was not the socially acceptable answer. "I am searching for rural property to purchase, Mr. Bellamy, and there are several in the area that might serve my needs." This was true, if I included the estates at the very bottom of my solicitors' list. "Mrs. Bonaventure was gracious enough to heed my plea for temporary accommodations."

"You'd abandon London?" he asked as Pamela led us into a sunny parlor done up in lavender, blue, and green. The touches of gilt were

understated—on sconces, framing a pier glass, in the ceiling fresco—
but they amplified the brightness of the afternoon sun pouring
through the windows.

The parlor's wallpaper was painted with scenes of billowing
lavender borders, stately irises, rolling green vistas, and azure skies
reflected in a placid lake. The effect was marvelously restful, as if we
occupied not a room within the house, but a folly in the middle of a
vast and beautiful garden.

My digestion had settled enough that I managed not only tea and
cakes, but some sandwiches of buttered watercress. Mr. Bellamy
helped himself to more substantial fare—ham and cheddar—while
Pamela mostly held her cup and saucer and looked coolly gracious.

She was an attractive woman, willowy *and* well curved, and probably somewhat past thirty. The years looked good on her, though I
knew her marriage had been a love match, and she missed her
husband sorely. Pretty she might be, and wealthy, and quite self-
possessed, but I doubted she was happy.

A mutual friend had escorted Pamela from time to time during
the most recent London Season, and that good fellow had reported to
me that Pamela was not looking to remarry—ever.

I had recited for Mr. Bellamy some of my brothers' more recent
travels and garnished my narrative with a few bits of Town gossip.
When Mr. Bellamy had partaken of the last sandwich, I decided I'd
wasted enough time on country pleasantries.

"Mrs. Bonaventure," I said, "might I ask for the loan of a horse?
I'd like to take the measure of the neighborhood generally before I
look at any specific properties. The day is fine, and particularly after
spending hours shut up in my traveling coach, I'd like some fresh air."

Pamela stood. "We have several ladies' mounts you can choose
from. Shall I ride with you?" She asked, she did not insist, as a hostess
might have.

"Thank you, no. The services of a patient groom will suit me. I'll
be poking about at will, and I doubt my horsemanship will be up to
your standards."

Mr. Bellamy was on his feet as well. "Allow me to join you, my lady. I am born and bred in these surrounds and know all the local families. I'd be happy to trot 'round the shire with you."

I did not want Mr. Bellamy *trotting 'round the shire* with me. His smile had become considerably more friendly, and he'd laughed at all my stale London trivia. My objective was to pay a call at Belle Terre, the sooner the better.

Moreover, I had yet to explain to Pamela the true reason I'd come haring down from London, all but showing up on her doorstep unannounced. I wanted a quiet word with my hostess, and without Mr. Bellamy's smiling presence.

"Her ladyship must change into a habit," Pamela said. "You will not want to linger while she sees to her wardrobe, Giles. Perhaps your offer of a guided tour might be renewed later in the week?"

An excellent suggestion. "Even tomorrow would suit," I said. The history of the village church or the venerable Boar's Tail and the habits of the neighborhood's flora and fauna interested me not at all. Nonetheless, if Giles was a local man, he would know the magistrate and all the gossip relating to St. Sevier's situation.

By tomorrow, I would be up to subtly interrogating him. Today, I needed to hear Ann St. Sevier's version of events.

"Tomorrow, then," he said, bowing over my hand. "Will nine of the clock suit?"

"Of course."

He patted my hand and tapped his hat onto his head. "Mrs. Bonaventure, my lady, I stand before you a man anticipating a very pleasant morning. I'll see myself out." He bowed to Pamela and jaunted off, and some tension inside me departed with him.

"Bachelors," Pamela muttered, closing the door to the parlor. "They have their uses, but their company can be tedious. You are here to take up the cause for Hugh St. Sevier?"

How I adored plain speaking. "I am. His wife asked me to do what I could for him."

Pamela went to the sideboard and poured herself a drink from a decanter. "How loyal of her."

"Are you being ironic?"

"Care for a drink?"

I consulted my belly, which was reasonably content, a state I did not seek to aggravate. "No, thank you."

"I am not being ironic. That grand edifice on the hill would likely fall into Mrs. St. Sevier's hands should anything untoward occur to her husband—or into the hands of her small daughter. We were all quite agog to learn there *was* a Mrs. St. Sevier. I was particularly surprised because I knew you and the doctor were on such good terms."

I ignored the possible barb in Pamela's words, because St. Sevier and I had, in fact, been on excellent terms. "If St. Sevier is convicted of a felony, his goods are technically forfeit to the crown. Ann St. Sevier has nothing to gain by sending her husband to the gallows." Except freedom, but then, she'd had freedom of a sort for years and had chosen to track Hugh down and introduce him to his daughter.

Had she learned of his wealth? Realized he might well be building a future with me? There was much I did not know about Ann St. Sevier.

"Juries," Pamela said, taking a considering sip of her drink, "can usually be trusted to find that the condemned felon has no property of value. They strike back against a profligate monarch that way, and they've been doing it for decades. You believe St. Sevier's innocent?"

"You've met him. What do you think?" Even from halfway across the room, I could detect the subtle fragrance of good brandy.

"St. Sevier is a complicated man from a foreign culture. He's been to war, seen endless violence, and the French are not known for their self-restraint. The situation does not bode well for him."

A list of coincidences held together with bigotry. "St. Sevier was raised in England and educated in Scotland. His record under Wellington was spotless if not heroic. Stop baiting me."

Once upon a time, I had done Pamela a courtesy, preventing others from discovering her in an awkward situation. I presumed on that favor by rebuking my hostess.

Her retort was a faint smile. "I am trying to *warn* you, my lady. You are in the shires, and if the gentry are united in one cause, it is their absolute authority over all matters rural. The magistrate has detained St. Sevier, but he has not yet arrested him. One blundering inquiry on your part, and you could well seal St. Sevier's fate."

I seized on the only relevant fact in that recitation, for I had been raised in the shires and well knew how rural prejudice worked. "Why not arrest him?"

Pamela finished her drink. "Lack of a body. Well, there was a body, but then it disappeared. Some say that ought to add another charge against St. Sevier—interfering with a corpse, which physicians have been known to do. Others say that without a body, there can be no inquest, and thus no charges have been brought. St. Sevier needs a good solicitor, and instead, you turn up. You will cause talk, and that cannot aid his situation."

"No body?" And had Ann sent for a solicitor?

"There was a body," Pamela said, gaze on the lovely rolling countryside that fell away from the terrace beyond the parlor. "But somebody made off with it, or so we are to believe."

How very convenient for whoever was trying to put a noose around St. Sevier's neck. "Who found the supposed body?"

She brushed a glance over me, pitying, I suspected. "Giles Bellamy. You can ask him all about it when you ride out with him tomorrow. He will regale you with the tale at exhaustive length, but don't be fooled by his handsome-bumbler routine. He is shrewd in his way, and you underestimate him at your peril. You will want to change into your habit now."

I had the sense Pamela wasn't dismissing me so much as she had reached the end of some emotional tether. The shrewd Mr. Bellamy had vexed her, and now was not the time to inquire as to how.

"I hope to return before supper," I said.

She shook her head. "We keep country hours at The Gauges, my lady. Supper is served before dark here. Take your time with Mrs. St. Sevier, and if she doesn't feed you properly, Mrs. Weaver will have a supper tray sent up when you return."

"I need not ring for a tray?"

Another head shake, almost resigned. "Before you have walked up from the stable, Mrs. Weaver will know where you went, how long you stayed, what you did while making your call, and whether you walked, trotted, or cantered the distance home."

Another warning? "Fast work, even for a housekeeper whose cousin is employed at Belle Terre."

I liked being able to fire off proof that I could do some fast work of my own.

Pamela collected her little hat from the low table and opened the parlor door. "I am begging you to proceed with utmost caution, Lady Violet. St. Sevier will not want you poking your nose into accusations of murder, not even to clear his name. I saw how he looked at you, and he would rather die than involve you in scandal. Your family has little influence here, and you don't know these people. They will turn on you in an instant, and you will be the next person charged with a crime you did not commit."

Lucy's words, about interfering with the lawful duties of the king's man, came to mind. "I will be careful. Would you prefer I find somewhere else to stay?"

She hesitated before speaking. "You have a knack for solving puzzles, and St. Sevier has no other allies. Just be discreet."

Unless I prevailed on Hugh's wife, I *had* nowhere else to stay. "I will be careful and discreet."

"Then I will see you at breakfast, and you may ask me any questions you please then, though I doubt I'll have any answers."

She parted from me at the foot of the steps that led to my apartment. As Lucy helped me into my riding habit, I wrestled with lingering unease.

Pamela had guessed exactly why I was in the neighborhood, and yet, she had welcomed me. I was nonetheless convinced that she would not be forthcoming at breakfast. She had answers, and I would be hard-pressed to get them out of her.

~

"Lady Violet." Ann St. Sevier offered me a proper curtsey.

I returned the gesture. For a woman whose husband had been accused of murder, Madame St. Sevier was looking well. I resented her for that. I resented her for having gorgeous red hair and a beautiful complexion, and I resented her for breathing. She was probably none too keen on my existence either.

"Thank you for coming," she said, closing the parlor door behind her. "Shall we walk on the terrace?" That suggestion all but announced that my hostess did not trust her staff to protect her privacy.

"I would enjoy that. How is your daughter?"

"Bearing up, thank you for asking."

The child, Fiona by name, was perhaps seven years old—I was not good at judging such things—and she had Hugh's luminous brown eyes. More than her mother had, that child had cost me a future with Hugh, but I, who had suffered two disappointments while married to Freddie, could not resent an innocent child.

"How are you?" I asked.

Ann gestured to the door and escorted me through a series of parlors. The approach to Belle Terre was such that the visitor was given a nearly 360-degree view of the property, which had clearly been designed to embroider on the theme of the Parthenon.

From a distance, the effect of all those massive columns and friezes was majestic, but up close, the house more nearly resembled a single, monolithic block of yellow stone. No ivy softened that impression. No flowers adorned the steps and terraces. No fountain provided the cheerful sound of splashing water.

Not so much as a strutting pigeon dared intrude on Belle Terre's architectural consequence.

The interior held up to the promise of the façade, both in terms of grandeur—ceilings of at least twelve feet complete with swirling celestial frescoes—and coldness. The house was literally chilly, and also gloomy. On an overcast winter day, St. Sevier's palace would be beyond oppressive.

Ann must have noticed my perusal of the gods and nymphs cavorting on the ceilings. "A St. Sevier lady from days gone by married an Englishman," she said, "and she used her settlements to turn this place into her personal Versailles." Ann crossed the corridor with me and led me into a smaller, less ornate parlor. "A hundred years later, the English line died out, and the property reverted to the French side of the family, to the horror of all, including St. Sevier."

"Belle Terre is... magnificent." Also entirely wrong for Monsieur.

"Hugh wants to sell it." Ann pushed open a French door and led me out onto a terrace. The afternoon sunshine in contrast to the house's shadows was nearly blinding. "He brought me here only because he felt it would be a good place for a fresh start. He's never lived at Belle Terre, only visited occasionally to consult with stewards and such. The other properties..."

She turned away from me, and I beheld the vista before us.

The roof of The Gauges peeked from above what was probably the home wood, but between the terrace and the trees, somebody had fashioned a French formal garden. A miniature canal stretched from east to west, and statues of Ariadne and Acis, exact copies of their counterparts at the French palace, graced the corners of the terrace. The grass-and-walkway patterns of the parterres echoed the curving fancies of Louis's Orangerie, right down to potted citrus trees ringing the perimeter.

"Quite... French," I said.

"Quite expensive," Ann retorted, "and the locals hate it. They take Hugh's coin to work here, but delight in grumbling about the place. Belle Terre is just a drafty old house, but French money built it, a French mind designed it, and a French woman left her mark here."

The English commoner had been given a choice by those in charge of the realm: John Bull could continue to rail against a profligate monarch and a greedy peerage, or he could instead hate the French people for making war on their neighbors and trying to destroy a social order supposedly ordained by God.

That France's neighbors—the Austrians—had started the hostilities was somehow not relevant. That warfare between England and France was practically a tradition between their respective monarchies was of no moment.

That the French people had suffered terribly before, during, and after their revolution mattered not at all. That hatred of the French was merely a convenient tool for managing the taxpaying English citizenry escaped the notice of that citizenry, even as bread prices remained exorbitant, and wages were pitiful, the better to line the pockets of the squires and lords.

Those subtleties of history and politics were known to me only because my late husband had been keenly interested in the workings of government and the marketplace, and astutely—and discreetly—critical of the peerage. St. Sevier himself had added to my political understanding on our long coach journeys, and even my father—a somewhat enlightened Tory—could be prompted to discourse knowledgeably about Parliament's machinations.

Rather than lament entrenched prejudice, I asked the most pertinent question. "Is Hugh guilty?"

Ann sent me an unreadable look. "You call him Hugh."

I'd hoped to call him husband. "When Monsieur no longer has a noose dangling over his head, we can hiss and swipe at each other like a pair of stable cats, if you insist, though I honestly wish you well. For now, I'd rather focus on clearing his name."

Ann took a seat on a stone bench, the afternoon sun striking her full in the face. She was, blast and perdition, a lovely woman. She'd followed the drum at sixteen and been widowed at seventeen or eighteen. I realized with some consternation that she and I were likely of an age. Her red hair would not be considered fashionable, but her complexion was flawless and her features delicate.

No wonder the officers and gentlemen of the regiment had been dicing to see which of them would have the privilege of raping her upon the loss of her first spouse, the louts.

"I got hold of the casualty reports," she said, "once I was back with a Scottish regiment. A Hugh St. Sevier was listed among the dead. That was a mistake. My husband had suffered a minor injury, apparently, or a different Hugh St. Sevier died. Nobody corrected the error. I did not mean to upend my husband's pretty life, but we have a daughter..."

She did not owe me that explanation either, but I was grateful for it. I settled beside her, and the bench at least had been warmed by the sun.

"And there he was," I said, "walking down a street in Perth one day, and abruptly, you and he had no good options. Neither of you could marry another, because years hence, somebody could declare those subsequent marriages invalid. As a mother, you could not deprive your daughter of the security her father could afford her, and St. Sevier would never turn his back on a child."

While part of me wanted to cover this old ground later, another part of me needed to understand why the idyll I'd enjoyed with Hugh had been shattered and must remain so.

"I want—I need—to hate you," Ann said tiredly. "I can't seem to manage even that."

"Likewise, I'm sure." But I loved Hugh, and part of me always would. "Might we move on to more pressing matters?"

"He was happy with you," Ann said. "He was never happy with me. I knew that. Even as a grieving girl, I knew he and I could not suit. And now..."

Now he never would be happy with her? Much to my surprise, I did not want endless misery for Hugh or for Ann—and certainly not for myself.

"Now we must clear his name. Tell me what you know."

"Precious little. Hugh is in the habit of riding out early on fine days, primarily to meet with his tenants. Sometimes the steward accompanies him, but mostly he's on his own. He was trying to become better acquainted with the property, trying to take it in hand instead of simply keeping it from sliding into debt."

"So he was frequently alone on horseback for long stretches of time?" Not good, but then, most conscientious rural landowners were in the habit of hacking out over their acres.

"Alone on horseback for hours. Because St. Sevier is not entirely familiar with the surrounds, he usually travels by the lanes, and that takes longer. The locals know the shortcuts and game trails, know where to hop a stile or ford a stream. Hugh meanders about, and he's too stubborn to simply take a groom to show him the way."

Too stubborn, or too much in need of solitude? "St. Sevier was off on one of these reconnaissance missions when the crime took place?"

"Apparently so. We knew nothing about it until we sat down to a late breakfast this morning, and our meal was disturbed by the magistrate and four constables—if you can call them that—who insisted Hugh accompany them to the magistrate's house for questioning. About the crime itself, I know only what my maid has been able to glean from the staff, and that's not much."

As Ann spoke, her speech became more heavily accented with the sound of her native Perthshire.

"Tell me what you've learned," I said. "And leave nothing out, no matter how insignificant you believe it to be."

"The deceased is—was—Miss Holly Faraday, daughter of a squire whose land joins Belle Terre to the west. She was well liked and comported herself as if she were an heiress of some sort by local standards. I think we met her once or twice in the churchyard. A nod and greeting, not introductions and you-must-come-to-call. Nobody pays calls on Belle Terre, and I didn't feel... That is..."

"They are English, and you are Scottish, and you and St. Sevier do not intend to dwell here permanently."

"Aye. Before those men took him away, Hugh was allowed a parting embrace with his wife. He told me to get back to Scotland, and the solicitors would look after me and Fiona. I am to put as much distance between myself and *this farce* as possible."

And Hugh, being Hugh, would likely have conveyed that warning in French and thus created even more suspicion about his character.

"And yet, you are not only still here, you have also sent for the most expedient of reinforcements." For which I admired her. English justice was often violent and wrongheaded, and it was also notoriously swift. "Has anybody fabricated a motive for St. Sevier's supposed murder of this young woman?"

Ann's smile was bitter. "Physicians are always on the lookout for a handy dead body—that explains not only his guilt, but also why the body disappeared. My very own housekeeper came up with that logic, according to my maid. Giles Bellamy happened upon Miss Faraday's remains on Belle Terre land and went back to the village to seek aid. When he returned with the magistrate, the body was gone. Miss Faraday has not been seen since yesterday morning."

"Does the magistrate claim that because the body was reportedly on Belle Terre property, Hugh is the only suspect?"

"I do not know what the magistrate is claiming, my lady, though I'm sure my housekeeper does."

I did not care very much for this housekeeper. "St. Sevier has not, apparently, been arrested. My hostess told me that much. He's only been detained. That little business of there being no corpse on hand has likely confused the proceedings, but if a charge of murder is unavailable, somebody will eventually get around to suggesting Miss Faraday was abducted. Who benefits from attacking St. Sevier's character?"

Ann looked at me as if I'd sprouted snakes for hair. "How can you do this? How can you make your mind work? I cannot think. I don't know what to tell my daughter. I don't want to eat, but I know I must. I feel as if, all over again, I am eighteen years old and being told that my choices are to whore for the regiment or to marry the big, silent Frenchman who always smells of bloodshed and death."

I did not want to like, pity, or sympathize with this woman, but she spoke as a widow would speak, of the unrelenting pull that a time of sorrow and pain exerted over the rest of one's life.

"I had to learn to think," I said slowly. "I went straight from the schoolroom, where I sought the approval of teachers and governesses, to a fussy little come out, where I sought the approval of the insular *beau monde* nincompoops whom I believed were my entire world. From there, I married, hoping to gain my father's approval at long last and to secure my husband's as well. I was to contemplate nothing besides keeping others around me happy. Thinking of anything else— myself, for example—was a habit trained out of me from infancy."

"You've acquired the knack," Ann said.

"In defense of my wits, but first I nearly lost those wits. We can discuss that sad chapter some other time. Who benefits from ruining St. Sevier?"

Ann was quiet for a moment, then she sat up a little straighter. "I did wonder about that as I was pacing in the garden. It's known that we want to sell this place. If somebody wants to buy it, then seeing Hugh hanged would likely result in a bargain price."

"Who wants to buy it?"

"The house? Nobody in particular, but half the shire would love to see the acreage broken up. Hugh owns everything from mature timber to good fishing to fenced pasture and cultivated fields. The house is a mausoleum, but the land is among the best in Kent."

And all that stood between a mob of greedy neighbors and ownership of the land was one inconveniently healthy Frenchman.

"Tell me of the magistrate. Is he fair?"

Ann laughed, a bitter sound. "My husband is French and

wealthy, I'm Scottish. The magistrate is an English squire. How fair do you think he'll be?"

I wished I could offer a stout reply in defense of English justice, but Pamela Bonaventure had been right. Things were not looking good for Hugh St. Sevier.

CHAPTER THREE

I made my way back to The Gauges as the sun sank to the western horizon. My groom, a youngish, lanky, freckled fellow named Biddle, took me on a shortcut through the woods in deference to the waning light.

"Was it in these woods that Mr. Bellamy discovered Miss Faraday's body?" I asked.

If Biddle thought it odd that a lady would raise such a topic, he gave no sign of his dismay. "So he says, my lady. Mr. Bellamy has lived in these parts, man and boy. He knows the surrounds as well as anybody."

Meaning Giles knew the woods better than the landowner himself knew them. "Do you believe Monsieur St. Sevier is guilty of murder, Biddle?"

Biddle stretched up in his stirrups and adjusted the kerchief about his neck. His mount was a handsome dappled gray, and Biddle rode with the natural ease of the born horseman.

"Not my place to say, my lady."

The correct answer. I hadn't really expected an honest reply. "Who has a reason to wish Monsieur dead?"

Fleeting impatience crossed Biddle's freckled visage. "The man's French. Most everybody would rather him gone from these parts, but he pays well, and there's plenty of work at Belle Terre. Mr. St. Sevier hasn't enclosed his part of the common, and he won't allow his game-keeper or land steward to set out mantraps. I'm not saying he'll be missed, but he weren't the worst of the lot."

Biddle had just listed three more reasons why St. Sevier's neighbors would wish him ill: First, Hugh had left a portion of the common land available to the villagers for their own use. The local families could keep a cow or a few pigs on those acres, run geese, or even raise some garden crops. The surrounding landowners, by enclosing land formerly regarded as common acreage, had taken all that security and independence from their village neighbors, many of whom had been cast into urban poverty as a result.

In return for the expense of enclosing the land, he who financed the building of the walls and cozening of Parliament could put the acreage under cultivation or turn it to pasture for his exclusive use. The landowner grew richer, while claiming to increase agricultural yield for patriotic purposes, and the common folk either perished or moved into the cities to work for a pittance, because all of *their* agricultural industry prior to the enclosure apparently counted for nothing.

Rule, Britannia.

That St. Sevier would guard a few acres from the rapine of the landed class was a dire offense against those landowners.

Second, St. Sevier also did not take harsh measures against poachers—no mantraps that could kill or maim any passerby—and third, he paid good wages. That last transgression was probably the worst offense, but how else was a French absentee owner to ensure his staff remained at their posts?

The mare I was riding moved a little more quickly as her home stable came into sight. "If I asked you to show me where the body was found, Biddle, could you do that?" Not '*would* you do that?' For such a request placed the decision on Biddle's muscular shoulders.

"We're losing the light, my lady."

And in the morning, I had scheduled my outing with Giles Bellamy. "So we are. If you could describe the location, perhaps I could find it myself tomorrow."

"Best not, my lady. St. Sevier didn't hold with mantraps, but others around here do, and they aren't always particular about where the property lines go. The woods aren't safe for strangers."

His tone was properly deferential, but his warning was clear. *Don't meddle. Don't intrude. Don't presume to interfere.*

In my past adventures with house-party thefts and such, I had always had Hugh's counsel and support, as well as that of another friend, a man I'd known since my childhood. Sebastian MacHeath, Marquess of Dunkeld, had been raised on an estate adjoining Derwent Hall, and while he was not the warmest of individuals, Sebastian was shrewd, fierce, and protective of those he cared for.

He was also supposed to be on his way back to Scotland, from whence he was unlikely to return until next spring, if then.

I had never attempted to solve a murder before, and I did not feel equal to the task now. St. Sevier faced the closed ranks of a rural English village, and Wellington's infantry squares would not have been a more daunting or deadly prospect.

As I handed off my horse and made my way up the path to The Gauges's back terrace, I considered contacting my father, whose estate lay about twenty miles to the west, in Surrey. Papa would tell me to go back to London, to let the king's man do his job.

But the magistrate would think twice before binding St. Sevier over for the assizes if a belted earl was seen to take an interest in the case. I mentally consigned enlisting Papa's aid to the last-resort category—the very last resort.

When I returned to my apartment, intent on changing directly from my riding habit into my nightclothes, I found a covered tray had already been delivered to my room and that Lucy was waiting for me. The signal flags between estates were clearly in good working order.

"They knew you were back, belowstairs," Lucy said, taking my hat from me. "Knew even before I saw you and the groom emerge from the trees."

I started on the buttons of my jacket. "You were watching for me?"

"I was. You will be interested to know that two riders departed the premises immediately after you rode out, both of them at a gallop."

"Messengers?"

"They weren't toddling down to the Boar's Tail for a pint, my lady, and they were dressed for stable work. One of them had a sizable bundle tied behind the saddle—and no, that bundle was not big enough to be a body. About half that size, I'd say. How is Mrs. St. Sevier?"

"Admirably well, considering. She was sitting down to a meal with her husband one moment and watching him led away under threat of arrest the next. Her staff is not loyal to her, and St. Sevier's parting words to her were to go back to Scotland posthaste." I undid the stock at my throat, which I had tied loosely in deference to the summer weather. "I am abruptly so weary I dare not close my eyes for fear I will topple into a swoon."

"Whereas I," Lucy said, taking my jacket, "had sense enough to steal a nap on the cot in the dressing closet. Sit, my lady, and let's have your boots off."

I was soon swaddled in my nightgown, robe, and slippers, and ensconced on a vanity stool while Lucy brushed out my hair. The weariness I'd alluded to intensified, reminding me of childhood. Back then, I would play hard, climbing trees, tearing about the garden or the home farm, pestering all in my ambit, only to fall asleep in the conservatory the moment I sat down.

More than one general alarm had been sounded because I'd dozed off in an unlikely location, a habit I'd outgrown after my mother died.

The next thing I knew, Lucy was jostling my shoulder. "You should eat something, my lady. The kitchen sent up a cold collation in addition to a tea tray. You have had a long day, and good food shouldn't go to waste."

Good food did not go to waste. Good food might be sent back to the kitchen, but it never went to waste in a well-run household.

"No meat," I said, catching sight of myself in the vanity mirror. Lucy had put my hair into a single braid over my right shoulder. My eyes were tired. I looked a trifle pale, not that I had Ann St. Sevier's perfect complexion, and I also looked... worried.

For good reason.

I managed a sandwich of butter and brie and half an orange— Lucy would dispatch the other half—and then I was climbing into bed, barely an hour after sunset. I remained awake long enough to say a prayer for St. Sevier's safety and another for the wellbeing of his wife and child, but then I was sleeping the sleep of the dead and dreaming of grooms sent galloping into hell.

～

Were I not investigating a murder, I would have found Giles Bellamy to be a knowledgeable, if loquacious, escort. For a garrulous man, however, he said little that served my purposes. I wanted to see where the body was found, I sought to know more of the local magistrate, and I needed to determine, as nearly as I could, when the murder had taken place.

Given that half the shire aspired to see St. Sevier dead or in disgrace, it became imperative that I establish a sequence of events. If I could fix the time of death, I could begin eliminating suspects. Eliminating an entire village would take time, and thus Giles Bellamy's maunderings tried my patience.

"The church tower was originally a watchtower," Mr. Bellamy said as we turned our horses along yet another leafy bridle path. "The Vikings passed through here a thousand years ago or so, and some claim they built that tower. They liked to winter their armies hereabouts, and I suppose a wintering army might get up to building a tower. They did a decent job of it, if that was the case."

He launched into a recounting of the construction of the church itself, an edifice I had noted in passing as my coach had sped through the village. St. Ivo's had struck me as just another village house of worship. Gray granite façade, moss and lichens encroaching, as they tended to do, a thatched lych-gate leading to a grassy, walled graveyard.

That humble establishment's history fueled Mr. Bellamy's oratory for the next quarter hour as the horses meandered through the vast wood separating Belle Terre from The Gauges.

"And has your family always hailed from these parts?" I asked as a squirrel scolded us from above.

"My father's family, yes. My mother claims a connection with some knight serving the Conqueror." Mr. Bellamy drew his horse to a halt as we approached a fork in the path. "Would you like to see the garden at Belle Terre? A Versailles in miniature, according to those who've visited Louis's palace."

"Would that not be trespassing, Mr. Bellamy?"

"Might be, but the local magistrate is a clever sort and a good neighbor." Mr. Bellamy guided his horse onto the leftward path, and my mare toddled along in that direction as well. "Thaddeus Freeman takes an enlightened view of the law. Ancient byways predate private ownership of the land, and thus the public has a continuing right to use them, according to Freeman. He said that argument carried the day when King Charles had Richmond enclosed."

I added Mr. Freeman to the list of people I was prepared to dislike at sight. "I would not want to intrude on Belle Terre grounds when the family is in the midst of difficulties."

Bellamy's cheerful expression faltered. "You would hear about that. Pamela's footmen are mostly down from London, but the senior servants are local. They will talk."

And I would—finally—ask a few productive questions. "You found the body?"

"I am almost certain I did." Mr. Bellamy pretended to inspect the path, which he probably knew blindfolded.

The trees looked to me like ancient growth, an increasingly rare find in the English countryside. The Royal Navy had requisitioned most mature standing hardwood specimens. Those they did not cut down outright, they claimed a right to harvest should the tree ever fall.

In this little corner of Kent, we were surrounded by the forest primeval. The canopy stretched high overhead, the trees a mix of oak, beech, and lesser specimens—rowan, chestnut, ash. I saw evidence of an occasional coppicing, which resulted in patches of sunlight and denser undergrowth.

Wildlife would love these woods, and St. Sevier had doubtless enjoyed them too.

Poachers would adore so vast and lush a forest. "How is one 'almost certain' one has come across a corpse, Mr. Bellamy?"

"Pamela said you were forthright. She likes boldness in women."

Mr. Bellamy's enthusiasm for bold females was less evident. What a pity. "Has the magistrate secured a statement from you yet?"

His next glance included veiled annoyance.

"Mr. Bellamy, my father has served many a time as the king's man. I know how these things are handled, and a statement from witnesses and interested parties at the earliest opportunity prevents memories from fading and malefactors from intimidating witnesses. I can think of no crime more serious than murder, and thus the utmost care should be taken investigating the situation."

I sounded like that vexed squirrel chattering from above.

"If you must know, once I'd established that Miss Faraday was beyond aid, I rode like Harry Hotspur to fetch Mr. Freeman. I explained to him precisely what was afoot. When we returned to where I'd found Miss Faraday, she wasn't there anymore. I know what I saw, and I know she was deceased."

He sounded genuinely upset at this recitation. "You could not have mistaken the location?"

He shook his head. "I grew up playing in these woods, my lady. I've ridden and tromped every path through them and stolen raspberries without limit from the hedges and stream banks. Miss Faraday had, too, in as much as country girls are permitted such activities. I did not mistake the location."

The woods stretched over hundreds of acres—Mr. Ballemy could not know every corner of them, unless he'd apprenticed himself to the gamekeeper—but I was putting my guide out of charity with me, so I made my questions count.

"Did you notice any signs that the body had been moved?"

He shifted his reins to one hand, took off his hat, swiped his forearm across his brow, and replaced his hat. "We aren't exactly awash in jack-booted thugs hereabouts, my lady."

"Was Miss Faraday a woman of sizable proportions?"

He sighed, which I hoped meant he was resigned to my interrogation. The clever Mr. Freeman should have put these questions to him, and many others besides.

"She is—was—a sturdy young lady. I've known her for ages. She came to about my shoulder. A grown man in good health could have moved that body. A strong woman could have as well."

"You are certain she was dead?"

"She did not move, Lady Violet, but I did not grasp her wrist and feel for a pulse, if that's what you're asking."

"How did you ascertain that she was dead?" And why in God's name hadn't the magistrate covered this ground?

"She looked dead. She was inert. I called her name loudly, repeatedly, and she remained still. She was not asleep, I promise you that. I surmised that a tragedy had occurred and galloped for Freeman's house."

He'd panicked. Drawn the worst conclusions and created the biggest possible fuss, and now he looked a fool.

"Dead bodies don't move themselves," he muttered. "Clearly, somebody overpowered Miss Faraday, and I frightened them off.

When I left the scene, that same somebody removed the evidence. Freeman saw that much straightaway."

"And immediately arrested St. Sevier?" Without taking a proper statement from Mr. Bellamy, without investigating the crime scene, without questioning Miss Faraday's family?

"Monsieur is not under arrest. The murder occurred on St. Sevier's land, and Freeman merely has a few questions for him. Enough about all that, if you please. We're approaching Belle Terre. You can see the gardens through those trees." He gestured to the right with his riding crop, and my mare took exception to having a whip brandished in her face.

"Sorry," Mr. Bellamy muttered, lowering his crop. "You can see the water feature from here, the little canal, and all the formal parterres. It's pretty, if you like the Frenchified look."

Everyone had liked the Frenchified look back in the day of William and Mary. Windsor Castle still boasted French formal gardens, as did many stately homes. Others had gone in for the reclaimed landscapes of Capability Brown, and still other landowners—my father, for one—struck a balance between tidy, ordered gardens and a natural park beyond.

I halted my horse and regarded the view through the trees. The garden fell away from Belle Terre in a series of descending terraces, culminating in the water feature. From there, the land rose again, climbing to the wooded hillside from which we viewed the house. The stable was in plain view, too, as was the carriage house, springhouse, and summer kitchen, all situated below the main house and thus out of sight from the primary approach.

And all of it in plain view of this hiding place. "Lovely grounds," I said. "Impressive edifice."

"When the fountain is turned on, it's even more spectacular. Frolicking in that fountain was one of the dares passed around among the local boys, not that we ever managed it. We made use of the swimming hole in the woods, though."

Mr. Bellamy was trying to revert to the guise of local tour guide. I could not, alas, indulge him. "How was Miss Faraday attired?"

This sigh was more of a huff. "Riding habit. Boots, a hat, gloves."

I nudged my mare back the direction we'd come, having no wish to spy on Ann St. Sevier's household. "What color was her habit?"

"Dark green. She is—was—blond and green-eyed, and that color flattered her. She was an accomplished rider. Most of the young ladies hereabouts are."

My mount was more than willing to move in the direction of home. "Could she have fallen from her horse?"

"There wasn't any perishing horse at the scene, my lady. I must insist we change the subject. I did not invite you to hack out so you could appease an unseemly curiosity about a local tragedy. If you persist with these ghoulish questions, I will escort you back to The Gauges without further ado."

He did the "affronted gentleman" quite well. For St. Sevier's sake —and for the sake of Miss Faraday's memory—I could not humor Mr. Bellamy's histrionics.

A lady did not mistake her riding habit for a walking dress. There *had been* a horse, which Mr. Bellamy likely knew.

"If you would like to return me to The Gauges," I said, "I will certainly understand, but I must ask that you take me by the place where you discovered the body."

"In the name of all that is decent, why?"

Either Bellamy wasn't very bright, or he was quite certain the magistrate would never conduct a proper investigation.

"Because, Mr. Bellamy, if *you* killed Miss Faraday, what better way to cover your guilt than to sound the alarm and then stand by while a neighbor is bound over for your crime? And if you did *not* kill her, then your most prudent course of action is to help me ascertain who did. I can assure you, Mr. Freeman's efforts thus far fail to impress, if the objective is uncovering the truth."

Mr. Bellamy's expression confirmed that his bumbling-bachelor persona was not the true sum of his parts. He knew enough to be angry with me—truly angry.

"I did not kill Holly Faraday. You insult me by suggesting I could."

"Then you regard a simple application of logic as an insult. Hugh St. Sevier did not kill Miss Faraday. When his innocence becomes apparent, where do you think suspicion will fall next?"

"Nowhere." Mr. Bellamy urged his horse into the trot. "Death by misadventure or mischief by person or persons unknown. Freeman has doubtless detained the Frenchman in an abundance of caution and for St. Sevier's own safety."

An interesting claim. "You will show me where you found the body, Mr. Bellamy."

Had he galloped off into the woods, I could have found my way back to The Gauges simply by giving my mare her head. I was none-theless uneasy at the thought of being left alone in a forest where a young woman had come to grief. Giles Bellamy did not strike me as a murderer—not that I was an expert in identifying murderers at sight —though more to the point, as far as I knew he had no motive for ending Miss Faraday's life.

"And if I simply escort you back to The Gauges?" he asked.

Peevishness in a gentleman was so unbecoming. "I will notify my father, the Earl of Derwent, that I am very concerned that the king's justice in these surrounds has been thwarted by incompetence, or worse. I will suggest he convene a parliamentary commission to inves-tigate the actions of Kent's rural magistrates. I will *cry*, Mr. Bellamy, in St. Ivo's churchyard over the fate of that poor young woman, into whose death nobody has conducted a proper inquiry."

"You should go back to London," Mr. Bellamy said, all preten-sions to gentlemanly manners cast into the ditch. "You meddle here at your peril, no matter who your father is. This is not your patch, and these are not your people."

"Every person with a claim to honor ought to consider justice his patch." I did not add that St. Sevier was very much my people—and always would be. "Show me where you found the body, Mr. Bellamy, for the sake of all concerned."

He slowed his horse to the walk. "A lady would never ask such a thing."

A weak volley, that, or perhaps I had become incorrigible.

What a fortifying thought. "When ladies are no longer murdered in the English countryside, I will refrain from making such bold requests. Lead on, Mr. Bellamy."

He led me to a clearing by a stream, a lovely place encircled by ferns and mossy rocks. A handy boulder thrust up out of the water in a perfect location for dangling bare feet in the shallows or jumping into the deeper currents.

"Is this where you went wading as a boy?"

He sat atop his horse, gaze on the bank. "We all did. It's also a trysting spot and a swimming hole. Boys come here to try to smoke their papa's cheroots. Girls might as well, for all I know."

A popular location, in other words, particularly in the summer months when lounging away an afternoon by the cool water would have appealed strongly. Why commit murder here?

"We can return to The Gauges now," I said, steering my horse back toward the path a few yards away.

"You won't sniff the ground, kick over rocks, or look for a cudgel submerged in the water?"

Not with Mr. Bellamy watching my every move, I wouldn't. "I can detect no sign of a struggle, sir, which is the primary reason I wanted to see this place." I'd come back later and do a thorough examination of the scene, because signs of a struggle would be subtle.

Snapped twigs, the scrape of a bootheel against the mud of the stream bank, a divot gouged from the grass... Evidence easily obscured by the murderer, or by Mr. Bellamy and the magistrate blundering around.

How I wished St. Sevier, with his physician's eye and subtle grasp of natural science, were with me.

"Then I conclude our outing is at an end." Mr. Bellamy took a side path, little more than a game trail, and I followed. We splashed across shallow rapids—a perfect spot to stop and enjoy some wading, had the occasion been different—and within minutes, we were trotting through The Gauges's deer park. I made a special note of where our trail had emerged from the trees, because I intended to return at the first opportunity.

"Pamela has company," Mr. Bellamy observed as we approached the stable. "If I'm not mistaken, that gray is Freeman's favorite morning horse. I don't recognize the bay, though."

I studied the lathered, dusty bay, a substantial beast standing at least seventeen hands. "I recognize him." The gelding's name was Hannibal, a former warhorse who'd adapted to peacetime pursuits.

I could only pray Sebastian MacHeath, Marquess of Dunkeld, hadn't come to Kent in hopes of hauling me back to London.

CHAPTER FOUR

"My lord!" I dismounted without aid, affixed my most cheerful smile to my face, and called a greeting to Sebastian, who was making his way up the path to the manor house.

He turned slowly. "My lady." A bow followed. An answering smile did not.

Sebastian's hat, coat, and boots were dusty, his eyes tired and watchful, and yet, I rejoiced to see him. We would very likely argue—we'd been arguing since childhood—and he'd doubtless come to "talk sense" to me, another futile undertaking of longstanding with us.

But he was dear, familiar, and prodigiously shrewd. St. Sevier excelled at seeing evidence I overlooked, while Sebastian's particular gift lay in peeling away layers of motivation to reveal human truths. He understood men, and people in general, in a way I did not. Perhaps this was the legacy of a quiet Scottish boy banished among English tutors and neighbors, or perhaps Sebastian was simply canny by nature.

Sebastian turned his perceptiveness on me from time to time, but I had never enjoyed a comparable ability to lift the covers on his thoughts or actions. He was very much his own man and always had been. His presence nonetheless explained at least one of the messengers sent hotfoot from The Gauges the previous evening.

Sebastian offered another bow to Mr. Bellamy, who'd handed his horse off to a groom. "Sir, you have the advantage of me."

How I loved that Scottish burr all dressed up in proper manners.

I launched into the introductions, Mr. Bellamy's demeanor undergoing a predictable transformation when he learned that a *marquess* graced The Gauges's stable yard. To me, Mr. Bellamy had tried to present himself as a genial young Squire Jollychops. To Sebastian, he was the hounds-and-horses man, full of rural vigor and masculine bonhomie, bedrock of the nation and all that.

Bellamy's performances were facile and convincing, at least initially. What other roles did he play, and why?

I took Sebastian's arm as we wandered up to the house, in part because I wanted Bellamy—who had invited himself along—to see that the marquess and I were on familiar terms. I also simply longed to touch my friend. Had Bellamy not been present, I would have hugged Sebastian in greeting.

Mrs. Bonaventure greeted Sebastian effusively, deftly gliding past the whole question of what had prompted a Scottish marquess to admire the rural splendors in her particular corner of Kent when he doubtless had a thousand pressing matters to see to. Sebastian and Pamela knew each other socially, and he'd been her London escort on occasion.

He had assured me he harbored only a cordial regard for Mrs. Bonaventure, but I had not asked the lady about her feelings toward the marquess—nor would I.

"You have arrived in time for luncheon, my lord," Mrs. Bonaventure said as we gained the terrace steps. "I've arranged for a meal al fresco, but first I'll show you to your room so you can freshen up. Lady Violet, Mr. Bellamy, I'll be only a moment. Mr. Bellamy, would you like to stay for lunch? Mr. Freeman has graciously agreed to be my guest and awaits us in the library."

Though her smile was pleasant, the invitation was equivocal. Not *please stay*, or *won't you join us?* But a simple yes-or-no question.

"Thank you, no," Mr. Bellamy said. "I will take my leave of you, and thank Lady Violet for her company on the bridle paths."

Some unspoken sentiment passed between Pamela and Mr. Bellamy, one I could not fathom. Not romantic, not threatening, not easily deciphered.

"I'll see you at divine services, then," Pamela said, curtseying.

I did likewise, pleased to be free of Mr. Bellamy's company. He was not what he appeared to be, and his recitations about Miss Faraday's murder had been as porous as a bridal veil. Perhaps he was avoiding being in the same room with me and the magistrate, given that the magistrate had yet to properly interrogate him.

"Do I have time to change out of my habit?" I asked as Pamela led us into the house.

"Of course. We will await you on the side terrace. I'm sure Lord Dunkeld and Mr. Freeman will need at least a quarter hour to discuss crops, politics, and the weather."

We climbed the steps together, though at some point I had slipped free of Sebastian, and Mrs. Bonaventure had taken the place at his side. His room was two doors up from my apartment, so I left my hostess and her titled guest to chat about bell-pulls and dinner gongs, while I considered my morning's work.

Lucy had laid out an afternoon dress on the bed, but of my maid, there was no sign. She was a friendly soul, and the house was full of handsome footmen. I did not begrudge her some socializing, but getting out of my riding habit wasn't easily done without assistance.

I had removed my boots and jacket when a knock sounded on my sitting room door. Lucy, no doubt, though her knock was usually louder. Sebastian slipped into my sitting room as soon as I cracked the door.

"What do I need to know before I break bread with the local magistrate?" Sebastian asked.

"Good day to you too," I retorted. "Did Mrs. Bonaventure send for you?"

His dark hair was damp-combed, and he smelled of lavender soap and horse, a good combination.

"Of course she did. She did not feel she could turn you away, and she is concerned for you. She thinks you might need an escort back to London on short notice. I believe her worry for you is genuine."

I marched into the bedroom, intent on removing the feathered toque from my hair. "I'm sure she is worried, but not for me. St. Sevier is suspected of killing a young woman, though the body mysteriously got up and left the scene of the crime. When I asked to see that crime scene, Mr. Bellamy—who found the deceased—took me to the most popular socializing spot in the woods. One which the magistrate has apparently not inspected with any thoroughness."

I did not care for the shawl Lucy had laid out, so I took myself to the dressing closet to find another.

"When Miss Faraday was killed," I went on, "*if* she was killed, she was wearing a riding habit, and yet, nobody thought to look for signs that she'd taken a bad fall from her horse. Is her horse missing? Was she riding about in the woods on her own, and if so, why trespass on Belle Terre land? A riding habit is not a walking dress, Dunkeld, and the woods are densely overgrown in places. A young lady not only *would not* easily tromp about in her riding habit, she *could* not, unless she remained on the bridle paths."

I emerged from the dressing closet with a blue merino shawl that did nice things for my eyes, and I ran smack into a broad male chest.

Sebastian hugged me. "I've missed you," he said. Growled, more like. "You haven't been here twenty-four hours, and already you are crusading on St. Sevier's behalf. How are you, Violet?"

The temptation to remain cuddled against him was nearly overwhelming. He smelled good—like my dear Sebastian—and he was somebody before whom I'd never had to dissemble. He knew the whole of my situation with St. Sevier and had even known Hugh in Spain.

"I am wobbly," I said, stepping back. "I had turned my mind to moving on, to wishing a good, dear man and his lawfully wedded wife well, while I... found myself a rural estate."

"You wanted a place to grieve."

Did I? I had not married Hugh. I had not even been intimate with him for all that long, but I had hoped...

"To sort myself out," I said. "I grieved for my husband in London. It did not go well, if such things can go well. I prefer the countryside, now that I'm given a choice about where I dwell. Undo my buttons please." I gave him my back and soon felt deft fingers working my buttons free. Unbuttoning my shirtwaist would afford Sebastian no opportunities to peek—I also wore a chemise and stays—and I was anxious to make Mr. Freeman's acquaintance.

"Thank you," I said, wrapping the shawl over my shoulders and taking a seat at my vanity. "What I've learned so far is that St. Sevier's home is easily spied on from the woods. He owns those woods, but I gather they are crisscrossed with all manner of old bridle paths, which are regarded as common thoroughfares."

I unpinned my hat and took down my braid while Sebastian prowled the room, looking out of every window before taking a seat on the cedar chest at the foot of the bed.

"You're saying anybody could have come upon the victim with malice aforethought, but only St. Sevier has been detained?"

"It's worse than that, my lord. Belle Terre is apparently quite the wealthy estate, from timber to fishing to arable land and various bodies of water. The squirarchy would love to see it broken up at bargain prices—it's not entailed—and if a Frenchman is sent to the gallows along the way, that can only speed matters in a helpful direction."

I undid my braid and took a brush to the unbound length of my hair. "From what I can see," I went on, "there is no body, there has been no proper investigation, and there will be no attempt to see justice done if Miss Faraday has indeed come to harm. And yet, as you say, St. Sevier alone has been detained for questioning."

In the folding mirror, I could see Sebastian perched on the cedar chest at the foot of the bed. To have him in my bedroom should have been awkward, except that he and I had shared many a picnic blanket, tree house, and sunny stream bank in my girlhood. To my four brothers, I'd been a pest, but to Sebastian—far from home, only a few years my senior—I had become an unlikely ally.

As he was to me.

We'd gone through a long rough patch, occasioned by misunderstandings and distance, but for the most part, that was behind us.

"You assume the motive at work here is simply discrediting St. Sevier," Sebastian said.

"Or removing him from the scene entirely. He's French, an absentee landlord who refuses to enclose the last of the area's common land, and he pays good wages."

"A country squire's worst nightmare, but perhaps you're missing the point." Sebastian rose and plucked the brush from my hand. "Perhaps you ought instead to be looking at who wished Miss Faraday ill. If she's not dead, where is she? Why was she out on horseback without a groom?"

Sebastian had the knack of brushing a lady's hair. He knew to be patient with the occasional tangle and to work his way up from the bottom. His touch was different from Lucy's. Not as brisk. He had soon restored my braid to order and left the pinning of it to me while he once again patrolled the windows.

"You won't consider simply returning to London and leaving it to me to sort this out?" he asked.

He'd surprised me with that exceedingly kind offer. "Ann St. Sevier has no allies, Sebastian. She's in at least three awkward positions at once, with a small daughter to think of. Then too, I sense that Pamela Bonaventure knows much more than she's saying, and yet, when I offered to stay elsewhere, she did not wish me farewell. I suspect she wants me where she can keep an eye on me."

Sebastian merely regarded me, his expression unreadable.

"Two heads are better than one," I said, though resorting to platitudes was cowardly.

"You don't trust me to look after St. Sevier," Sebastian said. "Given that I am Scottish and hold no land in the neighborhood, perhaps that's prudent, but—"

"It's not that." I shoved the last pin into my braid, fixing my plait into a coronet, and rose from my vanity stool. "Something untoward is afoot here, Sebastian. The groom warned me not to interfere, Giles Bellamy warned me not to interfere, as did Pamela herself, in so many words. I suspect Mr. Freeman will do likewise for good measure."

"Thus you are honor-bound to interfere?"

"St. Sevier's life is at stake."

Sebastian scrubbed a hand over his face. "I know. He might kill a man in self-defense, but a woman? I can't see it. The lengths he went to in Spain to save British lives earned him the resentment of his English medical colleagues and the adoration of the rank and file. For him, the preservation of life is a calling."

"He'd kill to protect the innocent," I said slowly, not liking the idea at all. "We need to have a thorough look at the clearing in the woods, Sebastian."

If that was even the crime scene. *If* there had even been a crime...

"Violet, please let me deal with this. I won't be arrested for interfering with the king's man, while you..."

"I am a woman." Also a commoner.

"You love St. Sevier." Sebastian spoke gently, which made me want to smack him. "You won't be objective."

"I love a lot of people. If you were accused of murder, I'd be just as determined to clear your name. Besides..."

We were arguing. I should not have taken joy from that, but as a girl, scrapping with Sebastian put me to rights in a way nothing else could. Apparently, I could still derive some comfort from a good skirmish.

"Besides?" Sebastian prodded.

I scooped up the dress from the bed and headed for the dressing closet. "If I left you on your own to poke about in the undergrowth, I'd worry about you. St. Sevier could end up on the gallows because somebody wants to irrigate a pasture and another somebody wants to fell a stand of oak. If they will see him hanged for their enrichment, then they could well aim a poacher's bullet at you."

Dark brows rose. "You seek to *protect* me?"

I whisked past him into the dressing closet. "Of course I seek to protect you. I'll see you on the terrace." I closed the door firmly, but it was a moment or two before I heard Sebastian's footsteps retreating from my bedroom.

~

I was prepared to take my midday meal in the company of a bluff, hearty country squire, one who studiously avoided any mention of his first investigation of a major crime. But then, in Merry Olde England, hanging or transportation could await a boy who poached a hare for his mama's empty stewpot or a girl accused of stealing a spoon.

If Freeman had spent any length of time as magistrate, he'd sent a neighbor off to the assizes before, and very likely to the gallows too.

As had, I realized, my own father, and yet, Papa seldom spoke about his duties as magistrate.

I joined the company on the terrace, ready to do justice to the meal, regardless of the situation. My morning had been active, and I had partaken sparingly of breakfast.

Pamela occupied a seat at a wrought-iron grouping, the chairs and table painted white and situated in shade. Sebastian was seated to her right and a blond fellow to her left. Both gentlemen rose as I emerged from the house.

"Lady Violet Belmaine," Pamela said, "may I make known to you my neighbor, Mr. Thaddeus Freeman."

Because the occasion was a meal, nobody wore gloves. Mr. Freeman took my proffered hand in a secure, warm grip and bowed. I curtseyed, though this man's appearances would turn any sighted female's knees a bit unreliable.

If Pamela's footmen were gorgeous, Thaddeus Freeman was Saxon male perfection. He was tall, blond, blue-eyed, lean, and slightly weathered. The effect of the sun on his complexion was to make his eyes an even more startling blue and to add a touch of gravitas to his features.

And those features could have graced a bust of some Roman general. Aquiline nose, deep-set eyes, noble brow, defined jaw, his hair worn tied back in an old-fashioned queue... His mouth was neither thin nor full, but exactly proportioned to balance the rest of his features.

I did not hate him at sight—he wasn't to blame for having the looks of a rural male paragon—but neither would I make the mistake of assuming that a beautiful man was also a good man. He'd detained St. Sevier, failed to interview Giles Bellamy, and done little enough to examine the crime scene, after all.

"My lady, a pleasure." He bowed, his smile neither presuming nor obsequious. "Tell me how your brother Felix goes on. He and I served together briefly, and I understand he's married now."

Former military, then, doubtless a former officer. Did that signify an arrogant confidence in his own infallibility, or presage a thoroughness that would result in the truth being revealed?

"Felix and Katie are the proud parents of one very small, very loud boy," I replied, my smile equally polite. "My brother has turned his hand to raising horses over in Surrey. Are you acquainted with my lord Dunkeld, then?"

A look passed between Sebastian and Mr. Freeman. "I have had the honor," Mr. Freeman said. "Dunkeld and I were never under the same commanding officer, but my lord rode dispatch and was thus a generally known—and respected—figure."

I took my seat with Sebastian's assistance, and it wasn't until the food was served—hot soup, cold sandwiches—that I realized that Mr.

Freeman never used his left hand. Not to drape his table napkin across his lap, not to lift his wineglass.

I waited until the fruit and cheese were brought out and the footman dismissed before launching my first broadside.

"Tell me, Mr. Freeman, did you know Hugh St. Sevier in Spain?"

He patted his lips with his table napkin. "I knew of him. A Frenchman patching up British soldiers was something of a novelty. He was good at it, and tireless, so his efforts were appreciated, even if he was held at arm's length in other regards. We like to think that all the French lined up on one side and all the British on the other, but between desertion, anti-Bonapartist sentiment among the French and anti-royalist sentiment in our own fair isles and among the Spanish... Nationality was not dispositive of loyalty."

Dispositive. This man was either university educated, or he'd had very thorough tutoring at home.

"Felix has made the same observation about nationality and loyalty," I replied, offering Mr. Freeman a bowl of blueberries. "So how much longer will you detain Monsieur?"

Mr. Freeman scooped up a handful of fruit and popped a berry into his mouth. "Are you attempting to interfere with my investigation, my lady?" He managed to edge the question with both threat and humor.

"Certainly not. I am attempting to ascertain on what basis you detain my friend and your neighbor. St. Sevier has no motive for harming a young lady who was all but a stranger to him—if she has come to harm. He has no history of criminal behavior, but rather, served as honorably as you and the marquess. St. Sevier, most significantly, has no allies to hold you to account if you take a convenient, rather than a conscientious, view of your duties. I am here to rectify that last state of affairs."

Sebastian studied his wineglass, while Pamela winced. My tone had been polite, but then, the best insults were always rendered politely.

Mr. Freeman calmly munched his fruit. "Your loyalty to Mr. St. Sevier is commendable, my lady, and I can assure you I am most conscientious in the prosecution of my duties. My next task will be to thoroughly inspect the place where Giles claims to have found the body. Then I will question Miss Faraday's family about her movements yesterday, though I'm told they are nigh insensate with grief and shock. Following those efforts, I will speak to the gamekeepers in the area, and I've already sent a note to Mrs. St. Sevier asking for a moment of her time."

He finished his fruit. "Monsieur is not languishing in some dank oubliette, my lady. He enjoys the hospitality of my own home and has the freedom of the premises. He has been a polite, if not quite willing, houseguest."

Freeman held out the bowl of berries to me, and I felt compelled to take a few.

"I can further tell you," he went on, "that St. Sevier has no alibi. He was known to be in the vicinity before Giles discovered the body, and while St. Sevier may not be a criminal, he has behaved less than cordially toward some of his neighbors."

I could not imagine Hugh ever being less than cordial. "You will explain yourself. Monsieur is at all times a gentleman." And more significantly, how was St. Sevier known to be "in the area," meaning riding through his own woods at dawn?

"St. Sevier is a *French* gentleman, and his views of England's devotion to agricultural progress are those of the minority. He will not petition to enclose the last of the common acreage, and this occasioned words in the churchyard not two weeks past."

My meal sat uneasily, for all I'd been hungry. "You leap from a man debating politics in the churchyard to accusing him of murder?" Though any sort of debate in a churchyard was ill-mannered, at least. Hugh must have been quite out of patience. "Who was the other party to the argument?"

Pamela answered me. "Mr. Anthony Bellamy, Giles's father. Half the congregation heard them go at each other. Bellamy's land marches with the Belle Terre portion of the common, and he is adamant that the acreage be enclosed. Given the price of grain, you'd think St. Sevier would see the wisdom in Bellamy's demand."

For reasons nobody quite understood, the population of Britain was growing by leaps and bounds, while her ability to grow grain, while far greater than in previous eras, had not kept pace. The result was pressure to import grain, especially cheap Baltic wheat, a pressure the government countered with tariffs to the delight and enrichment of the landed class.

English producers of wheat were highly motivated to keep their acres productive, which was regarded as a common good, though the benefit of high grain prices went almost exclusively to the landed class, and the burden of exorbitant bread prices fell on the shopkeepers, and the increasing masses of urban poor.

"St. Sevier is a physician," I said. "He is incapable of ignoring human suffering. By enclosing the last of the common land, he might indeed earn himself more coin—which he does not need—but he would also deprive village families of their cows, pigs, sheep, and vegetable plots. He would no more allow greed to justify such behavior than he'd take the life of an innocent young woman."

I was becoming upset, but to sit on this pretty terrace, eating off Pamela's pretty porcelain plates, struck me as obscene when Hugh was clearly being pilloried for the sake of his neighbors' avarice. Then too, Pamela's disclosure, that Mr. Bellamy senior coveted Hugh's land, only made Giles's "discovery" all the more suspect.

Freeman regarded me with unnerving calm. "You are sure St. Sevier has no need of coin?"

"If he needed money, he'd simply sell Belle Terre, wouldn't he?" I retorted. "He could coppice or harvest that monstrosity of a wood. He could let out the house. Rent out more acreage. You will have to work very hard to find anything approaching financial necessity where Monsieur is concerned, Mr. Freeman, and surely you can see that Mr. Bellamy has every reason to cast St. Sevier into disrepute?"

"Bellamy only said what most in the surrounds are thinking, my lady."

Sebastian had watched this exchange dispassionately. I could not tell if he was allowing me to do the terrier work on purpose, or wroth that I was antagonizing the magistrate. Possibly, he was angry with Freeman, though when it came to Sebastian's inmost sentiments, he rivaled the sphinx for inscrutability.

"St. Sevier has wealth," Sebastian said. "Substantial wealth in England, and some of his family's lands in France have been restored to him as well. He has the means to enclose that acreage, but as her ladyship has said, he would not deprive his neighbors of sustenance for the sake of his own gain."

Mr. Freeman took a leisurely sip of his wine. "And how do you know St. Sevier's financial particulars, my lord?"

"I had occasion to investigate Monsieur's situation in preparation for some business dealings that never came to fruition. I'm sure he's also had a look at my situation, as one does."

As far as I knew, Sebastian and St. Sevier had never contemplated any such business dealings. Sebastian was either fibbing, or he'd nosed around Hugh's finances on my account. My reaction to that conjecture was a cross between how-dare-he and surprise.

Pleased surprise.

"Then I thank you for the information, my lord." Mr. Freeman set down his wineglass. "This conversation has been most stimulating and the meal delightful. Mrs. Bonaventure, thank you for your hospitality. I'm off to have a ramble in the woods, if the company will excuse me."

He rose and bowed, but I wasn't about to let him off so easily. "I'll accompany you," I said, "if you'll give me a moment to fetch a hat."

Freeman looked down at me, his expression losing any pretensions to geniality. "My lady, I am examining the scene of a violent crime, and that is a tedious and exacting undertaking. I must decline your generous offer of company."

I was done with his cool manners and subtle innuendo. "You propose to examine that scene a full day after a body was supposedly found there," I retorted. "You posted no guard to secure the surrounds, you allowed an interested party in the person of Giles Bellamy to return there with you yesterday and again today with me. Who stopped him from returning yet again yesterday afternoon to plant evidence or remove it? Certainly not the king's man."

I had progressed from insult to outrage in the course of a few sentences, but somebody most assuredly ought to be outraged. Hugh St. Sevier could end his life on a scaffold because Mr. Freeman wanted to appease his greedy neighbors.

Oddly enough, my tirade provoked Freeman into offering me the first genuine smile I'd seen from him.

"Very well," he said. "Come along, but if I tell you to remain standing beneath a rowan tree, you will bide beneath the indicated tree without comment."

I hated, hated, that he was genially demanding *obedience* from me, but I realized as well that I'd gained a significant victory.

"Give me one moment," I said, rising smartly. "I will fetch my hat and..." I sank back into my chair as my vision dimmed, and my ears began to roar. "Damnation." I did not know if I'd cursed aloud, because sounds were fading as my vision had.

"Violet," Sebastian said at my side, "just breathe. You stood up too quickly on a full stomach. Give your head a moment to clear."

"The wine and the heat," Pamela said. "I must be careful of that combination myself. Then too, coach travel always knocks me sideways for a day or two, and her ladyship was up quite early this morning."

Lucy was sent for, and as my fit of the vapors passed, it was decided that Sebastian would accompany Freeman into the woods, while I would be tucked up in my bed for a nap.

I wanted to argue and rail and protest, but when Lucy came for me, I instead followed her meekly—*and slowly*—up the steps to my bedroom, where I did, indeed, take a substantial nap.

CHAPTER FIVE

I perched on the ladies' mounting block in the stable yard, prepared to wait until Domesday for Sebastian and Mr. Freeman. They came riding across the park not five minutes after I'd opened my book of poetry, and to all appearances, they were chatting amiably.

"My lady." Freeman nodded from the saddle. "I hope you're feeling more the thing?"

"I am much revived by some rest, thank you for asking."

"Glad to hear it. Dunkeld, a pleasure to renew old acquaintances, but I must be getting on lest Lady Violet chide me for slacking." He leavened that comment with a slight smile. "I will take my leave of you both."

Not so perishing fast. "I'd like to visit Monsieur St. Sevier, sir. If he is not under arrest, you can surely extend him that courtesy."

Freeman glanced heavenward, as if importuning the Almighty for patience, and I steeled myself to prevail in a verbal donnybrook. For a person suspected of a crime to be housed at the magistrate's domicile while awaiting the quarter sessions was an accepted practice, particularly if the suspect was of genteel birth. If the arrangement lasted any length of time, the magistrate was compensated for the expense of housing his "guest."

Sebastian swung down off his horse. "I'd like to look in on St. Sevier as well," he said, "and I expect Mrs. St. Sevier will make the same request of you."

Ah, the benefits of having a marquess stick his oar in. Freeman and I would not have our donnybrook today.

Freeman gathered up his reins in his right hand. "As soon as I've had a chance to put a few questions to Mrs. St. Sevier, you are all free to call upon my guest."

"Why not release him?" I asked. "He has no motive. He was on his own land at the time the supposed murder took place, though how you know Monsieur's exact whereabouts at the dawn hour in the middle of hundreds of acres of private property remains a mystery. You have no body and, as far as I can see, no case against him."

Sebastian was looking at me in some puzzlement. He'd apparently not thought to wonder exactly how Freeman had placed St. Sevier at the scene of the crime, and Freeman certainly hadn't volunteered the information.

Freeman's horse, a rangy gray, executed a neat walk pirouette. "Many in this neighborhood enjoy hacking the bridle paths early on a summer's day, my lady, and St. Sevier himself has confirmed that he was among that number yesterday morning. I'll bid you good day and send word when I can allow you to visit your friend."

Send word? Send word, would he? And *many in this neighborhood* might have been trotting about on the woods yesterday morning?

"I will join you when you question Mrs. St. Sevier," I retorted. "She will want another lady present, if your inquiries range beyond the general."

I was doubtless the last person Ann would want underfoot if awkward topics had to be raised, but like her husband, she was without allies, and she had sent for me, after all.

"I don't believe that will be necessary, my lady. I'll wish you good—"

By the simple expedient of wrapping my hand around his reins at the horse's bit, I stopped the magistrate from making a grand exit.

"Ann St. Sevier is far from home. She has a bewildered and upset child to deal with. She has no friends in this blighted shire, and her staff is spying on her for the likes of you and the Bellamy family. Since she has arrived at Belle Terre, nobody has called on her and her husband, not out of curiosity and certainly not out of kindness. Instead, the good folk of the neighborhood have picked fights with St. Sevier in the churchyard and spied on him from his own land. You will not question her unless somebody she can trust to take her part is also on hand."

Freeman looked to Sebastian, who had taken the place at my right side. If the magistrate expected his lordship to gainsay me, or to *deal with me*, he was to be sadly disappointed.

"My lady has the right of it," Sebastian said, petting the gray's neck. "Madame St. Sevier is due every courtesy, and she will likely be more cooperative if she is shown some consideration. Scottish women are like their English cousins—they take poorly to disrespect."

He had not raised his voice. He had not raised so much as a dark eyebrow, but he'd made his point. How I envied him that ability.

"Very well," Freeman said. "When Mrs. St. Sevier agrees to receive me, you will accompany me on the call. If my lady would kindly unhand my horse, I will be about my duties."

He gave the word *kindly* a little fillip of irony, and I turned loose of the reins. "Thank you, sir. We are at your disposal on short notice."

"Tomorrow morning will suit, but it appears I must await the pleasure of the ladies. Good day."

From the halt, the horse lifted into a flowing canter. Freeman did not direct his steed down the drive, but rather, back across the park.

"He's going over the damned gate," Sebastian muttered as the gray pounded up to a wooden gate at least four feet tall. The jump was foot perfect, right in rhythm with the horse's stride, and Freeman's form was exquisite.

"Was he cavalry?" I asked.

"Nominally, but his real job was to build and break codes, and he was legendarily good at it. He had a team of similarly inclined individuals, and they were not like any other group of soldiers you will ever meet. He did not care if a man hailed from the gutter or was in line for a title, if that man could decipher and devise codes. Freeman employed at least two women that I know of and would brook no disrespect toward them."

This was not good news. "He's a war hero, then? A quietly acknowledged war hero?"

"A war hero, and those of us who served know of him, but he would accept no commendations, and Wellington could not mention him in the dispatches. The French put a price on his head before I'd even arrived in Spain. That price went up year by year."

Worse and worse. "You are saying I must respect him."

Sebastian winged his arm and escorted me from the stable yard. "The situation is even more dire than that."

"What could be worse than a brilliant magistrate intent on blaming an innocent Frenchman for a crime that might not have taken place?" Though why would a man such as Freeman get up to such tricks?

Sebastian leaned near and lowered his voice. "You might bear a grudging liking for such a magistrate and come to realize that if he arrests St. Sevier, he'll have reasons for doing so."

I unlaced my arm from Sebastian's. "St. Sevier is not guilty, Dunkeld. You know that."

Sebastian gazed past my shoulder to the woods, which on this summer afternoon should have been a tangle of sylvan verdure instead of a forbidding wall of green.

"We found blood on the rocks, Violet, or what we believed to be blood, right near the water. St. Sevier could tell us for certain, ironically, but Freeman and I have both seen enough battlefields to know blood when we see it. Somebody or something did a copious amount of bleeding beside that stream."

"That proves nothing," I snapped, moving off in the direction of the back terrace. "St. Sevier is known to decry mantraps, and any village boy might have gutted a rabbit beside the stream and tossed the entrails into the water."

"If you were a village boy, and you knew Freeman was charged with bringing poachers to justice, would you leave that much evidence of your crime?"

"If I were a murderer, I'd be even more careful." Unless, of course, I'd taken a life in the heat of temper...

Sebastian ambled along beside me, and I was abruptly assailed by the temptation to cry. Crying would solve nothing, but I was unable to protect a man dear to me, and I was very much afraid the forces ranged against me would overwhelm my best efforts.

"Come here," Sebastian said, taking my hand. "You are working yourself into a state when, as you say, there is no body. Even Freeman shouldn't be able to do much with a murder charge in the absence of a corpse."

Sebastian led me down a shady path, between borders of blooming rhododendrons. The house and stables were lost from view, and we emerged into a clearing where some considerate soul had placed a wooden bench.

"I left my book at the stable," I said, the first thing that popped into my head because this was a spot meant for lingering with a book or a sketch pad and a picnic hamper.

"You weren't reading. You were lying in wait. Sit with me." Sebastian drew me down onto the bench that the slanting afternoon sun had warmed. "We are friends, are we not?"

That sounded serious. "Of course."

He'd kept my hand in his, and I braced myself to be gently lectured about the necessity of returning to Town, allowing Freeman to do his job, or some other well-intended tripe. Sebastian was very dear, and very persuasive, but his exhortations were doomed to fail. Ann St. Sevier had asked for my aid, and by God, she would have it.

"Violet, are you well?"

What the devil? My impulse was to retort that of a certainty I was

well. I was always well, except that would be untrue. I had become
very ill in spirit as my mourning had progressed, my first experience
with any sort of serious bad health. Then too, Sebastian had put the
question to me privately and quietly, and his concern was apparent in
the very simplicity of the inquiry.

"I am adjusting," I said. "I had plans for Hugh St. Sevier, and
those plans have been dashed, but, Sebastian, it's as if some part of
me knew that would happen. If something is too good to be true, then
it's too good to last. I can't say I was expecting Hugh to be whisked
from my life, but..."

"But you were?"

"But he has been, and I'm forlorn and resentful, though there's
nobody to blame, and I cannot regret a moment of the time I spent
with that man. Hugh saved my sanity and my life, and it would be
churlish to wish him anything but great good fortune and a comfortable old age." Wishing him a large and happy family was beyond me,
though, for now.

Sebastian wrapped an arm around my shoulders, and I let myself
rest against him. "Be churlish, Violet. When your heart's desire has
been ripped away, you are entitled to some churlishness. I would ask
you to consider aiming that sentiment someplace besides the magistrate detaining your former intended."

"Valid point." Valid point, gently made, damn him. I wasn't by
nature rude, but my dealings with Freeman had done me no credit. "I
do not trust English justice, Dunkeld, and now that monster has St.
Sevier in its lethal and ruthless grasp. Have I thanked you for not
insisting I return to London?"

"Are you thanking me now?"

Why did Sebastian always smell good? All cedary and woodsy, of
a piece with this quiet glade.

"Yes. Thank you for not lecturing me, not telling me what to do,
not interrupting me when the magistrate is in need of guidance.
Why can't Freeman go make codes for the Americans or
something?"

"Because he loves his homeland. You've seen all the pretty wall paintings at The Gauges? The irises and peacocks and whatnot?"

"I have. They are unusual and lovely." As was this quiet conversation with Sebastian. We had been affectionate as adolescents. Sebastian had taken my hand, hugged me, or put an arm around my shoulders in many an odd moment, and I'd treasured him for it.

I had grown up in the household of a bereaved father much concerned with parliamentary matters and shared my home with four older brothers much concerned with their own infinitely important affairs. I had struggled equally with a sense of being invisible and a sense of being different, the odd *man* out who wasn't even a man.

Sebastian had preserved me from the worst of that loneliness and bewilderment, treating me as simply his friend and expecting the same casual, precious familiarity from me. We'd argued, we'd discussed. We'd spent quiet hours fishing and reading away an afternoon or pretending to search for butterflies while mostly pilfering raspberries or orchard fruit.

We'd pelted neck or nothing across my father's land on our trusty steeds, and as often as not, my mare had bested Sebastian's gelding. My brothers would never have risked that ignominy, while Sebastian had never refused my challenges or—worse—allowed me to win.

"Why do you mention the wall paintings?" I asked as the urge to sleep rose up like a wave approaching the shore.

"Freeman did them. He was quite the artist before he bought his colors. The French put a bullet through his hand—he was apparently left-handed—and that was the end of his art. He took to breaking codes and was even more skilled at that than he was at painting posies."

I opened my eyes and sat up. "Then he has a motive to hate the French, doesn't he? A very personal motive."

"Freeman himself said nationality was no proof of where a man's loyalties lie. You are being churlish again."

I let my head fall back to Sebastian's shoulder. He made a wonderful pillow, despite all appearances to the contrary.

"A Scottish philosopher gave me permission to be churlish. There is no greater authority on the subject than he."

Sebastian chuckled, the sound a little sad.

Be churlish, Violet. When your heart's desire has been ripped away, you are entitled to some churlishness. Had my Scottish philosopher spoken from experience? I let myself slip into another nap, rather than attempt to answer that question.

∼

After supper, on the pretext of needing to stretch my legs, I made my way to the stable and sent a note to Ann St. Sevier through the good offices of Biddle the groom.

I warned her that Freeman intended to question her in the morning and that the magistrate had agreed that Sebastian and I would be present on that occasion. My missive was couched in general terms on the assumption that Biddle was literate, and I was in enemy territory.

"You will go through the wood?" I asked him as he led out a piebald cob.

"Aye, milady. There's enough light, and I know where I'm going. Jester's a good lad, and we'll keep to the paths."

He swung up, touched a finger to his cap, and trotted off across the park. He disappeared into the wood using the same trail Giles Bellamy and I had traveled on our morning hack.

Biddle apparently had no fear of poachers *or murderers* as he traveled the darkening woods. Was that significant?

I was tempted to wander back to the clearing among the rhododendrons on foot, because at this time of year, the light took its time fading from the sky, and I had much to ponder.

As I strolled away from the stable, a second groom led out another horse, this one with a sizable bundle tied behind the saddle. He acknowledged me with a nod, but did not stop to offer pleasantries. He climbed into the saddle using the ladies' mounting block—the bundle lashed behind the saddle made the business awkward—and then he trotted down the drive.

Lucy's description of another parcel, also about half the size of a human body, came to mind.

The groom could have been on any one of a thousand errands—lending spare linen to a neighbor entertaining a house full of guests. Taking horse blankets or harness off to the livery for mending before winter returned. Delivering a sack of potatoes to a tenant family whose garden was faring poorly.

The hour was odd for any of those undertakings, but then, The Gauges household routine was upset by the presence of guests, to say nothing of hanging felonies occurring in the adjoining woods. Then too, in the summer months, any sort of travel was more comfortable when the sun did not lend its heat to the journey.

I decided against tarrying on the secluded bench, though I was in need of solitude. My earlier conversation with Sebastian had stayed with me, particularly the bit about half expecting to lose Hugh St. Sevier in some fashion sooner or later.

Perhaps that was a lesson widows learned—to hold anything precious loosely, because life itself was temporary. If so, soldiers doubtless learned the same lesson many times over, as did far too many parents.

On that sobering thought, I returned to the house. Lucy had lectured me within an inch of my wits after lunch. I was to take better care of myself, to realize that a shock to the heart could manifest in many ways. If I did not make more of an effort to eat properly, tend to my rest, and leave fretting to others, she would despair of me.

When Lucy was truly wroth with me, she threatened to give notice. I had no wish to inspire that degree of upset, so I approached the terrace with every intention of going straight up to my room and settling in with a book.

Lucy's voice, drifting through the shadows from the side terrace, stopped me.

"This is how it started, my lord. Milady went off her feed, then got her days and nights mixed up. She was up at the crack of doom, then slept half the day away, then wandered the house into the wee hours. I felt as if I was watching a dropped stitch unravel a whole shawl."

My lord had to be Sebastian, but when he replied, I heard only a baritone rumble.

"She were sore smitten with the Frenchman, my lord," Lucy said, "and he with her. I won't bear tales, but I doubt her own husband ever wooed her like that."

He hadn't. Freddie had gone down on bended knee readily enough, secured my assent, and then popped to his feet to flash a ring at me. *Will it do, old thing? Will I do?*

Old thing. I'd been seventeen.

Again, Sebastian replied to Lucy in soothing tones, while I debated the folly of eavesdropping. Lucy was worried about me, and she'd taken that worry to the one person likely to understand her concern and share it. I could not fault her for that, but still...

I had merely stood up too fast after a meal taken in the heat. This had happened to me before, and to Lucy herself, I was sure. I wasn't pining away, which both surprised and pleased me. I'd spent a good fortnight silently railing against an unjust God, tearing up every hapless weed attempting to sprout in my London garden. I was sad to lose the dream of a life with St. Sevier, but not bitter. I expected I would be sad where Hugh St. Sevier was concerned for quite some time.

I had not only loved him, I had permitted myself a careful, deliberate version of being *in love* with him, or very nearly. I loved him still, but as I'd told Sebastian, I loved many people, in many different ways.

And I was much better now at being angry than I'd been as a wife or a new widow. I'd excused myself from divine services for the nonce, begun a regular correspondence with both of my sisters-in-law, and done a thorough, long-overdue cleaning of my late husband's office.

I was intent on finding myself a country abode, and that exercise would distract me handily—for a time at least—from a future that did not include Hugh St. Sevier.

I left it to Sebastian to allay Lucy's fears. I was fine, though the heat and travel had made my digestion a bit tentative. I'd taken all of one nap—well, two, if dozing on Sebastian's shoulder counted—and passing fatigue was no moment.

None whatsoever when we had a killer to catch.

~

"Do you normally take breakfast with your husband after he rides?" Thaddeus Freeman had declined Ann's offer of a tea tray and got right down to the king's business. His demeanor was that of a particularly detached physician inquiring of a patient's symptoms.

I could not tell if he found the interrogation distasteful, or if he believed a slight officiousness would gain him more useful answers.

Useful and *truthful* being very different articles.

"We do break our fasts together," Ann replied, "if Monsieur rides out. When the weather is disobliging or his schedule otherwise requires him to remain at home, we have our meal earlier. Otherwise, he will hack out, stop by the nursery upon his return, then join me for at least a snack to tide him over until noon."

Ann had chosen the formal parlor for this ordeal, and I approved of her decision. The soaring ceiling, classical art, severe symmetry of the arrangements, and even the tall windows all lent a sense of dignity and substance to the lady of the house.

She occupied a wing chair, her manner as regal as a queen's, while I sat on the sofa with Mr. Freeman. Sebastian, predictably, was on his feet by the windows, his back half turned to us in what I supposed was a bid to respect Ann's privacy.

"And was there anything unusual about your husband's movements two mornings ago?" Freeman asked.

"No. Hugh rose as it began to get light, donned his riding attire, left our apartment, and I soon heard hoof beats from the direction of the stable. Our room is on that side of the house, and we keep the windows open when the weather is mild."

I hoped that to all appearances I was as composed as Ann sounded. Her reply had informed me, though, that she and Hugh *shared a bed*. That she *had watched him dress*. That they had discussed details such as whether to leave the window open through the night.

They had been separated for years, but they had resumed at least some particulars of domestic life readily enough. I had not thought Hugh and Ann would eschew the pleasures of marital congress indefinitely, but Hugh had not exactly dawdled on the road to reacquaintance with his wife.

As I stared at the carpet, and Mr. Freeman droned on about who in the stable usually saddled Hugh's horse, I counted up weeks and realized that Hugh and Ann had had nearly half the summer to effect their rapprochement. Weeks during which I had reeled, silently ranted, gathered my composure, and taken it into my head to leave London.

We were, all three of us, moving on, and in separate directions. I did not like knowing that Hugh and his wife were intimate, but Ann very likely hated knowing that Hugh and I had been lovers. He would have told her that, and he, being Hugh, and quite sophisticated, would be managing the whole business with the sort of philosophical humor that had alternately exasperated and delighted me.

The ache of missing him had already faded to a dull and intermittent weight on my heart. Someday, that weight might dissipate altogether, but today was not that day.

"And why does your husband refuse to uphold the laws against poaching?" Freeman asked.

Ann leveled a stare at him. "He does not violate those laws. Would you expect a physician to advocate measures that maim and mangle a man who is simply trying to feed his family off the fat of the land? Is the life of a few trout worth more than a child's wellbeing under English law?"

"If he's that concerned for the poor of the parish," Freeman retorted, "he can have his gamekeeper gift his tenants with game, or he can simply donate to the parish coffers."

That was not a question, nor was the comment offered in the clipped, dry tones of a patient interrogator.

When Ann regarded Freeman this time, her gaze held the glacial contempt of generations of Scots cleared from their Highland farms by greedy landlords eager to overrun the hills with sheep. The cleared families were left with two choices—starve or emigrate—and that was considered the price of "progress."

"Hugh gives generously to the local parish," Ann said, "well in excess of his tithes, but the Williams children have rickets anyway, don't they? As do the Grant girls, and I don't hold out much hope for any of the wee Donohues. Mrs. Donohue lost the last child at birth, perhaps because she could not afford for the midwife to attend her."

Ann rose and paced before the hearth. "Granny Underwood cannot afford spectacles," she went on, "and so she sits all day with nothing to do but knit, except she cannot afford yarn and thus has nothing to sell. You value the right to blast game from the hedges more highly than you do your elders or your neighbors' children, Mr. Freeman. If Hugh came upon a poacher—and as far as I know, he never has—I'm sure he would alert you to the situation, but you cannot force him to sprinkle his property with lethal devices for the sake of your stupid conceits. Besides..."

She subsided into her chair, abruptly looking tired and bewildered. "The real issue is the enclosure, isn't it? Hugh won't toss the peasants off the land in the grand old tradition, and for that, a good man who has saved many an English life must hang."

"Mama, no!" A small child scampered into the room and lashed her arms around Ann's neck. "Papa must not hang. Papa is coming home. You promised." She'd scrambled into her mother's lap, though she was beyond the lap-child years.

"Hush, Fiona," Ann said, closing her arms around the child. "We have guests."

Freeman's features had gone carefully blank, as if he'd forgotten that Hugh had a daughter, one only newly introduced to a father who loved children dearly.

Sebastian said something quietly in his native tongue, and both the girl and her mother looked over at him sharply. The child answered Sebastian, also in Gaelic. She sent a fulminating look at Freeman that translated easily enough.

"Mr. Freeman has only a few more questions for your mother," Sebastian said, holding out a hand. "Come with me, child, and I will introduce you to my horse."

Ann whispered something in her daughter's ear, and she hopped off her mother's lap. Sebastian was led from the room, though the child paused at the door and stuck her tongue out at Freeman. Clearly, Miss St. Sevier had her father's instincts regarding human nature.

"What about the enclosure situation do you find problematic?" Freeman asked, as if the proceedings had not been interrupted. I had the odd and cheering thought that the child had frightened Freeman, and not only in the manner that assertive females have been frightening powerful males from time immemorial.

"Nothing in particular is problematic about enclosing the last of the common land," Ann said, "except that there's no work in London, and those in the village with only labor to sell need those acres to survive. Enclosure allows for greater agricultural production, or so the gentry claim, but they never account for the agricultural production *lost* when that land is walled off for the use of one already-wealthy family."

Freeman looked pained. "Madame, are you a radical?"

"If finding excessive greed distasteful makes me a radical, then yes, sir, I am a radical. Why don't you detain me for questioning, and then I will at least know how my husband fares? I'm sure Lady Violet will see my daughter cared for, and you can send two innocent people to the gallows instead of one." She smiled brightly. "I'm not French, but I am Scottish, which will do in a pinch to prove criminal tendencies, won't it?"

Ye gods, she was magnificent, also entirely wrongheaded to be antagonizing Freeman, but then, I'd antagonized him as well, hadn't I?

Though not with nearly the skill and acumen Ann St. Sevier brought to the task. I was reminded that Ann had followed the drum across Spain, buried one husband before she'd been legally of age, married a virtual stranger to avoid utter ruin, and then taken her chances across open country in the midst of war.

She was brave. Reckless, too, perhaps, but brimming with courage, and I—who was not brave—admired her for it.

"I have taxed your patience," Mr. Freeman said in a monument to understatement that nonetheless appeared to be sincere. "I apologize for that, but a young lady is missing, if not dead, and I am tasked with holding the malefactor accountable. I will confer with our vicar regarding the families you mentioned."

"Hugh already has," Ann said, rising. "He got a polite lecture about the unkindness of fostering false hopes of ease and advancement in the less fortunate and the shiftless."

Freeman stood as well. "When I approach the vicar, I will not be subjected to the same lecture, I can assure you. I know those families, but I hadn't realized... That is to say, I will do what I can."

I was reluctantly impressed with Freeman for showing some simple decency. He bowed over Ann's hand, then she was showing us to the door.

"You will find Dunkeld still in the stable," she said. "That child loves horses. Hugh saw to getting her a pony, and now he can do no wrong in his daughter's eyes."

She spoke wistfully, and I caught a glimpse of the terrible burden of worry she had to be carrying. She cared for her daughter *and for her husband*. That realization comforted me in a way I had not foreseen.

"If your husband is innocent," Freeman said, "he will go free. I promise you that, Madame." More sincerity, though why wasn't Hugh free now?

"When can Madame see her husband?" I asked as Ann passed me my bonnet and parasol. "Dunkeld and I are available to escort her at your earliest convenience."

"Come by after supper," Freeman said, tapping his hat onto his head.

Ann passed him his walking stick. "Don't you mean after dark, when the neighbors won't see that you've permitted your prisoner to meet with visitors?"

Freeman looked to me, as if I'd provoked Ann into sharing that insight. "He's not my prisoner," he said with banked impatience. "He's a detainee."

"Next time you come by," Ann replied, opening the door, "you can explain to the daughter who has known her papa less than two months why that distinction should reassure her. Good day, Mr. Freeman. Please give my husband my most tender regards."

CHAPTER SIX

Freeman did not exactly scamper through the door, but he certainly moved briskly, and I followed in his wake. He held his peace as we traversed the terrace running the length of the house's northern façade, and I wondered if the interview had served any investigative purpose at all.

"Was that difficult for you, my lady?" he asked. "To hear that your former fiancé has already settled back into married life?"

Oh, delightful. We were to enjoy a bout of polite sniping. I mentally nocked my arrow and let fly.

"So you are capable of competent investigation when it suits your purposes. How very encouraging. I assume Pamela filled your ear with all the delectable details?"

"She is concerned for you," Freeman replied mildly. "You were apparently summoned by St. Sevier's wife, the very woman whose untimely resurrection ruined your own aspirations for the handsome doctor. This is the stuff of farces and French satires, and yet, nobody is amused, are they?"

"No," I replied. "I am concerned that a good and decent man is embroiled in some sort of Kentish border war, and you are cast in the role of high sheriff. If you send him off to the assizes, you will commit a grave injustice, and if you fail to determine what befell Miss Faraday and at whose hands she came to harm, you are a failure as a magistrate and a man."

"You put the situation quite succinctly. I can either prove St. Sevier guilty, or I can find another villain, but find a villain I must." He sounded resigned rather than resolute.

"Why? For all we know, Miss Faraday has decamped for a repairing lease in Cornwall, and she will return after the New Year with a baby she claims to be a cousin's orphaned offspring."

Freeman gestured to one of the benches overlooking the garden, and it occurred to me that I would like to know—to honestly know—how his investigation progressed and that he might genuinely appreciate some assistance with it.

I took a seat and was presented with the orderly and imposing garden vista. I was struck by the effort that had gone into subduing nature for man's enjoyment. The dense expanse of trees beyond the garden struck me as nature's reply. Patient, powerful, willing to wait centuries for a chance to reclaim land indentured to man's vanity.

"I've spoken with Miss Faraday's family," Freeman said, coming down beside me. "Her horse returned to the stable by the time her parents were breaking their fast. They at first assumed she'd taken a tumble. She was an enthusiastic horsewoman, and the occasional fall will happen. Then Giles claimed to have found her body... and I am left with a significant puzzle."

"Many crimes go unsolved."

He took off his hat and ran his hand through golden hair. "This is more than a crime, my lady. We sent every farmer's son and chandler's apprentice off to war and taught him how to use firearms of all types, at the same time we learned how to make those firearms more and more accurate. Then we brought our soldiers home by the thousands, home to a land deeply in debt, one that expected those fellows would have military employment indefinitely."

I'd heard my father, among others, repeat this same litany.

"Now an abundance of workers means wages are low," I said, "and the price of bread is exorbitant. Steam power promises to put even more people out of work, and our esteemed monarch wants to burden the exchequer with fetes and architectural follies. Taxes have been unrelenting, particularly on the shopkeepers and middling sorts, and those taxes are enacted by a Parliament answerable to no one. Did we defeat the French only to find ourselves in the midst of our own bloody revolution?"

"Precisely. St. Sevier does not want to see another lad lose a foot to a mantrap. I understand that better than he thinks. We have no physician dwelling in this neighborhood, not even a competent surgeon, and tangling with a mantrap is a death sentence.

"But those lads aren't landowners," he went on, "and without the landowners, nobody has anything to eat, and England has nothing to export. Turn a blind eye to whatever villainy has happened in St. Sevier's woods, and the next thing we know, we have sedition in the pubs, machine breaking, and agitation on every hand. St. Sevier can gift anybody he pleases with all the game he can shoot. He can and clearly has been providing medical services to the local poor. He can donate to charities. He doesn't have to storm Parliament to bring about the changes he seeks."

And the local squires did not need every last acre stripped from the control of the village families—even my father would have agreed with me on that, and he was a staunch Tory. Rather than make that point, I returned to the matter at hand.

"Did you learn anything useful from Miss Faraday's family?"

Freeman pinched the bridge of his nose, a gesture I resorted to when I had a megrim. "She apparently had a beau."

My theory about a repairing lease in Cornwall became more plausible. "Do her parents know who had taken her fancy?"

"They do not, or they would not say, but she'd been riding out more, refusing to take a groom. Claiming she was off to call on a neighbor, and then the neighbor would show up to pass along a jar of honey and report that Miss Faraday never paid any such call."

"Typical behavior among young people intent on romance." Though I'd never engaged in such behavior. But then, an earl's daughter wasn't permitted that degree of foolishness. "Can you find out who the beau was?"

We were discussing Miss Faraday in the past tense, and that bothered me. Blood on the rocks bothered me. St. Sevier's daughter worrying that her papa might hang bothered me most of all.

"How do I do that, my lady?"

"You talk to her sisters, and you talk to the local girls who aren't as pretty or charming as Miss Faraday. The wallflowers at any gathering hear everything."

He rose and offered me his hand, which I took as I got to my feet. "How could you know such a thing?"

"I was one of those not-quite-attractive girls, and if you wanted to learn precisely what my brothers got up to, or which scullery maid was sweet on which underfootman, I could easily have told you." He offered his arm as we started down the hill toward the stables. "You don't think St. Sevier is guilty, do you?" I asked.

"I learned in the army that leaping to conclusions is the behavior of a fool. An open mind, a lot of questions, and luck are often how the toughest puzzles are solved."

To the extent that I had solved a few puzzles myself, I agreed with him. "When do you have to make a decision about the assizes?"

"Next week. If I don't bind St. Sevier over by then, he'll miss the next quarter sessions, and the judges don't reliably sit every quarter when they have more pressing business elsewhere, which means another six months before the case can be heard. Nobody will tolerate a delay of that magnitude, and St. Sevier should be not be denied a fair hearing in any case. I can offer him the hospitality of my home in the short term, but once I've laid charges, he'll be subjected to His Majesty's accommodations."

Meaning jail, where diseases killed far more unfortunates than did the noose.

Days, then. I had mere days to sort through intrigues, politics, squabbles, and trysts if I was to exonerate a man who wanted only to alleviate suffering and heal the sick and wounded.

"Dunkeld has made a conquest," Freeman noted as we approached the stable yard.

"Hannibal has made a conquest." Sebastian had put Fiona up on his gelding, and she was clearly delighted to sit astride such a mighty steed.

"You are on first-name terms with Dunkeld's horse, my lady?"

I was on first-name terms with the marquess. Perhaps Freeman needed to know that. "Sebastian and I have been friends since childhood. Hannibal was his last cavalry mount and has adjusted well to civilian life."

"The same cannot be said for many of us," Freeman replied, pausing at the edge of the stable yard. "Lady Violet, do I have your word that if you come across information material to my investigation that you'll share it with me?"

I was unwillingly flattered to know that my word held weight with the king's man. I was also curious. "What makes you think I will be more effective than you at unearthing such information?"

"That bit about the not-quite-attractive girls. Miss Faraday has two sisters, and they are understandably overshadowed by a lively sibling. I did not think to question them. Now I must make another visit, which will raise eyebrows, and every eyebrow in the shire is already raised because we have a killer loose in our woods."

St. Sevier's woods, when it was convenient to regard them as such.

"Or you have a kidnapper, or a young lady has gone to great lengths to make somebody look like a killer, or Mr. Anthony Bellamy has done Miss Faraday an injury in hopes of ridding the shire of the obstreperous Frenchman and his radical wife. You did say an open mind was conducive to a successful investigation."

"What a prodigious memory you have, and an equally prodigious imagination. The evidence of my own eyes suggests you are not infallible, though."

Of course I wasn't infallible.

Sebastian eased the child from the saddle, perching her on his hip. They made a lovely picture, smiling at each other and chatting in their native language. I was reminded that Sebastian also had a daughter, perhaps a year or two younger than Fiona. I, by contrast, had had two miscarriages, a sorrow I tried not to dwell on.

In a wife, the inability to fill her husband's nursery was a significant instance of fallibility.

"I am persistent," I said, "and devoted to those dear to me, but far from perfect. St. Sevier is not guilty."

"Somebody is guilty of something, and it's for me to puzzle out what. You are wrong, though, about being not quite attractive. In the spirit of the honesty I hope to foster between us, I must tell you that vapid prettiness and true attractiveness have little in common, though young men can seldom distinguish between the two. You might not have been the typical English rose, but I have no doubt you were as attractive earlier in life as you are now."

We pretended to watch Sebastian and the child taking a mock-formal leave of each other. Fiona curtseyed to the marquess and to his horse, then turned and saw Freeman standing beside me. Her smile dimmed, her brows knit. She sent Sebastian a wary glance and then ran hotfoot back toward the house.

I knew precisely how she felt, for if I grasped the intent of Freeman's words, he had just paid me a very personal compliment.

"I appear to have given offense," Freeman said, tapping his hat back onto his head. "I suppose that's part of the job."

"You surprised her," I replied. "She has been through much, and somebody she cares for and is powerless to protect is in peril thanks to you."

"True enough." Freeman bowed over my hand, took his leave of the marquess, and strode into the barn, calling for a groom.

"Was he flirting with you?" Sebastian asked.

"Trying to gain my trust, I believe. He has conceded that I might be useful in getting to the bottom of the murder, if a murder there has been."

Sebastian stroked his hand along Hannibal's glossy shoulder. "If somebody gutted a hare on those rocks, Violet, the wee beast parted with every drop of its lifeblood in the process."

And that fact had preyed on my mind. "I made a passing inspection of the same scene, Sebastian, and I don't recall seeing *any* blood. Either I missed the most obvious evidence of a violent crime, or somebody added that blood between when Giles and I left the wood and you and the magistrate returned to the scene."

"Not a long window of time."

"Two hours at least. Was the blood fresh?"

A groom led out my mare, and Sebastian waited until we were riding side by side along the wooded bridle path to answer my question.

"I do not know if the blood was fresh, though again, St. Sevier, could have told us. We can have another look on the way back to The Gauges, if you're up to it."

"Why wouldn't I be?"

"No reason."

We toddled along the fern-bordered path, and I was torn between amusement and consternation. Sebastian MacHeath had just dodged a verbal altercation with me, and I had allowed it. We moved no faster than the walk on our progress through the woods, and for some reason, I allowed that too.

~

Sebastian parted from me at the foot of The Gauges's main staircase. His traveling coach had arrived in our absence, bringing his valet, trunks, a pile of correspondence, and business requiring his attention.

A marquessate did not manage itself.

I climbed the stairs and realized I was slightly sore for spending so much time in the saddle. Sore in a way that suggested I was reclaiming some of the fitness I'd enjoyed as a younger woman.

"Was it awful?" Lucy asked as she tugged off my riding boots. "I don't mind telling you, the staff is none too keen on the king's man."

"How have you been able to determine that?"

"It's in what they don't say, mostly. Freeman's name comes up, and the servants' hall gets quiet, or a footman sneers something into his pint of ale. Nobody corrects him for the disrespect. Upjohn noticed the same thing."

"Fast work, Lucy." Upjohn was Dunkeld's valet-cum-batman and a particular favorite of Lucy's.

"He noticed that the footmen are uncommon lovely in this household too," Lucy said, grinning as she helped me out of my jacket. "Put him on his best behavior with me."

"You've missed him."

"Aye, but has the missing been mutual?" She went silent for a moment while she extricated me from my skirts. "The dratted man would never admit he's pined for me, because he's too loyal to his marquess." She stepped back, the voluminous fabric of my habit draped over her arm. "I've ordered you a bath, and we might as well wash your hair because it will take all day to dry. Did Mrs. St. Sevier give the magistrate what for?"

"She did, though I doubt that was wise." I wore only my chemise, which felt lovely. The heat of the day was building, and a bath sounded like just the thing. "Have I told you lately that you are the best lady's maid in all of Britain?"

I timed that question for when Lucy had ducked into the dressing closet, because Lucy was also one of the least sentimental lady's maids in all of Britain—or so she'd have me believe.

"You have not," Lucy said, emerging into the bedroom with a lacy dressing gown in her hands, the perfect choice for an increasingly warm morning. "Feel free to trumpet my genius to Upjohn anytime you please. I gather Mrs. St. Sevier didn't confess to coshing Miss Faraday on the noggin?"

Lucy's question brought to mind the crime scene and a new source of puzzlement. "Somebody coshed somebody, apparently. I vow that when Giles Bellamy took me to that clearing by the stream yesterday, I saw no blood, but then, he and I sat on our horses a dozen yards downstream from the bloody rocks."

Lucy held up the dressing gown, and I slipped into it. "Bloody rocks sound bad."

"Very bad, but why didn't I notice the bloody rocks when I first visited the scene? Was I too far downstream? Did Giles purposely fail to direct me to the proper spot? Was the blood not there? Was I in too much of a hurry to divest myself of Giles's company? Was Giles confused about where exactly he'd found the body? And speaking of the body, where is it?"

Sebastian and Freeman had seen no evidence that Miss Faraday's remains had been dragged into the undergrowth. No trail of snapped twigs, disturbed bracken, or crushed ferns. If the young lady was still alive, was she wounded, and if so, who was caring for her?

"In this heat," Lucy said, "a dead body would be hard to hide for long."

Valid point. "And removing a body without dragging it would take considerable strength." A coach or cart could not have come near the stream, meaning somebody—or several somebodies—had physically wrestled the corpse at least as far as the bridle path. But in the soft earth of the stream bank and its surrounds, a burden of eight or ten stone would have meant deeper footprints, or at least depressions in the earth indicative of a bootheel.

Sebastian had pointed that out to me, and we'd found no such evidence.

"I want to go back to the supposed crime scene," I said as a procession of maids trooped in, bearing buckets of water.

Lucy awaited the footmen in the sitting room while I took down my hair. She pushed the wheeled tub into the bedroom herself, doubtless having dismissed the footmen rather than let them get a peek at me in deshabille. I was decently covered, but Lucy was protective of my privacy, for which I treasured her.

She commenced dumping buckets into the tub. "So how does Mr. Freeman expect to bring any charges if he has no body?" she asked. "Has he even held an inquest?"

"He can hold an inquest even without a body, apparently." Sebastian had explained that to me as well. When a body was washed out to sea, mangled beyond recognition, lost in a conflagration, or was otherwise unavailable for inspection, an inquest could yet be held.

"What if she's not dead?" Lucy said, taking my dressing gown and chemise from me. "What if she's lost her memory, like all those women in all those novels, and she's locked away in a pirate's castle, trying to recall if she married the blackguard claiming to be her husband?"

I sank into the water, which was barely tepid and thus a little taste of bliss. "Don't let me fall asleep. This is too wonderful to nap through, and you are too fanciful for words."

Lucy passed me a bar of hard-milled French soap, a lavender-scented extravagance I took with me on all my travels.

"They have a swimming hole," she said, laying out an afternoon dress along with stockings, shawl, and embroidered house slippers. "One of the footmen told me that even the young ladies have been known to use that swimming hole after sunset. I must say, Kent is not at all like London. I could grow to like it here."

"The neighbors leave something to be desired." I was tempted to close my eyes and just soak, but luncheon approached, and drying my hair enough to make me presentable would take some time. I scrubbed myself from nose to toes, Lucy helped me wash my hair, and I was soon rinsed off and feeling much refreshed.

Lucy toweled and brushed my hair to damp-dry and arranged it in a loose braid and chignon. "What will you do with yourself this afternoon, milady?"

"I will ask for my father's guidance." I also wanted to re-examine the crime scene in greater detail. I had the sense I was missing something important, and if I was missing it, Freeman was as well.

Lucy went to the window. "No flying pigs, but it's early in the day. On what subject would you accept the earl's direction?"

"Not direction, guidance." I wiggled into a summer-length chemise of finest lawn. "Papa knows the law as a magistrate is expected to know it. He knows rural customs. He knows many of the judges who ride the rural circuits. I will ask him what he'd do with the facts we've unearthed so far."

By seeking Papa's opinion, I was also preparing for the day when I needed him to actively intervene. He might not be able to prevent St. Sevier from being arrested and found guilty, but he could see a death sentence commuted to transportation—I hoped.

Though, would Hugh thank me for meddling to that degree? Ann would, and so would Fiona, and thus as I dressed, I mentally began composing my letter. Lucy passed me the shawl, which was more of a silky suggestion than an article of functional attire. I had asked her not to lace me as snugly as she usually did, and between the looser stays, a softer coiffure, and the summer-weight attire, I was more comfortable than I had been in ages.

"Now, who would that be?" Lucy was again by the window, though rather than studying the sky, she was intent on the path that led from the stables to the back terrace. "He's a man intent on his business, that's a certainty."

I joined her to see a lean older fellow striding along, swishing his riding crop at the occasional fern or hollyhock. He was in a country gentleman's riding attire, his boots a trifle dusty, his pace brisk. Something about him struck me as familiar, which wasn't possible given that I knew almost nobody in the neighborhood.

"Whoever he is, he's timed his arrival to earn him an invitation to lunch. Perhaps he's a friend of Mrs. Bonaventure."

"With footmen like hers, she needs no gentlemen friends, especially not a gent likely to smell of horse and hayfields."

"We're in the country, Lucy. Horses and hayfields are what pass for fresh air here." And I liked both scents.

Lucy took the shawl from me, arranged it loosely around my shoulders, and used an amethyst pin to secure her artistry. The result was to bring out my eyes—a usually nondescript blue—and affect a sort of relaxed, graceful informality in my appearance.

I was reminded of Freeman's earlier comment, about attractiveness and prettiness. Trying to flatter me into trusting him, perhaps, but he should know that was a doomed strategy.

The lunch gong sounded, and unlike dinner—which was usually a matter of three gongs—lunch merited a single summons. I went down the main staircase, prepared to pass the time over sandwiches with a local squire. We'd hear about his crop of foals and his prognostication regarding the harvest. If he was a genial sort, he'd tell a humorous tale involving my hostess.

After an enjoyable meal, I would write to Papa, then slip away for another examination of the stream in the woods and its surrounds. After supper, I'd join Ann and Dunkeld for a visit to the prisoner and glean from St. Sevier his wisdom regarding further avenues of investigation.

My day thus planned to my satisfaction, I made my way to the side terrace. Pamela introduced me to her guest, Mr. Anthony Bellamy, and within five minutes of making that fellow's acquaintance, I bore him an enmity I usually reserved for mice, vermin, and mildew.

CHAPTER SEVEN

"Ask the marquess," Mr. Anthony Bellamy said, gesturing with his fork. "He'll agree with me. Scotland got rid of its slackers. The lot of 'em took the king's shilling or were put on ships bound for Newfoundland. The land prospers now, and in the colonies, the lazy bastards don't have time to sit about bemoaning the housecleaning Cumberland did for us in the last century."

He speared another bite of steak. In the past half hour, the squire had proven himself equal to demolishing both a meal and any pretensions to social subtlety. The Duke of Cumberland's sobriquet in Scotland was Butcher Cumberland.

For reasons.

"Farming a Highland croft is not exactly an easy life," I said, for Sebastian had gone silent two rants ago. Mr. Bellamy had allowed as how the temperance societies had got it all wrong. The lazy ne'er-do-wells cluttering up London's streets should be allowed to drink themselves to death, the sooner the better. Drinking was one of two activities at which they excelled, and he was too much of a gentleman—in his own faultless opinion—to mention the other.

His first tirade upon sitting down had been aimed at the crown, which, according to Mr. Bellamy, had never been in less competent hands. Fat George was apparently much like his poorest subjects in that his greatest skills were excessive consumption of food and drink and "misbehaving with the ladies."

The London poor whom the squire held in such contempt would have been arrested for maligning the sovereign thus. The squire, by contrast, was offered another glass of wine by one of Pamela's handsome footmen.

"How fare your crops?" I asked as Mr. Bellamy was doing justice to the vintage. "My father hopes for a good harvest this year."

"Don't we all?" Bellamy replied, lifting his wineglass a few inches in my direction. "I've put every acre I can into corn and to blazes with the sheep. The wool market has turned fickle, but folk will always need to eat."

"Did the wool market turn fickle," I asked, "or did the military cut back its wool purchases?" The military had become the mainstay of the British economy, forcing innovations and mass production of everything from firearms to canvas to boots.

Bellamy smiled at me, exhibiting a surprising degree of charm. "Brains in a female are a most confounding quality, my lady, though you have the right of it. Even with the Corsican cutting us off from Continental markets, the army bought enough of everything to make up the difference. Not that I have anything good to say about that bloodthirsty scalawag or the wars he caused."

Pamela signaled the footmen, who began removing plates. "How is Nigel, Anthony?"

"He bears up. What else is there to do?"

"You are Nigel Bellamy's father?" Sebastian asked.

"I have that honor. You know my boy?"

"I know *of* him. When an officer escaped his French captors, everybody heard of him. You must be very proud of your son."

Bellamy hunched forward, and a bluff if bigoted countryman in his prime became, with that slight shift, a father weighed down by the years.

"Nigel endures. I should never have let him go to war, and thank God my Giles was too young. His mother would not hear of sending both boys, and I wasn't keen on buying a second commission. The prayers that woman sent heavenward, begging the Almighty to return her son to her..."

Pamela was our hostess, and as such, it was her responsibility to steer the conversation out of this morass of sadness and serial excoriations. She appeared either unequal to the task or unwilling to take it on.

"I gather your son gave more than most to the defense of the realm?" I asked.

"Gave half his damned mind, my lady. He's a shadow of himself, takes odd flights, spends all his time doing puzzles and reading. I would despair of him, but his mother says I must not. Damned female cannot stop hoping and praying. His sisters are just as bad, always trying to drag poor Nige out of doors. My girls are hoydens, I don't mind telling you. We've a murderer for a neighbor, and the girls yet hare all over the shire at odd hours, doing exactly as they please. Thick as thieves with the Faraday chit, and she was as obstreperous as they are, not to speak ill of the dead."

He finished his wine at one go, which, given the inferiority of the vintage, bespoke a strong constitution.

"My girls say I can take 'em up to Town for a Season if I don't like 'em enjoying the fresh country air. Their mother was never like that. Back in my day, we knew how to comport ourselves, but then, back in my day, the infernal French weren't killing or maiming every other bachelor a young lady might fancy."

Mr. Bellamy had provoked me in any number of ways, but I could not remain angry at him. His family had slipped the leash, and to a man like Anthony Bellamy, the role of respected paterfamilias would matter greatly.

His firstborn had returned from the wars much the worse for his gallantry. His daughters, by Bellamy's own admission, took full advantage of the freedoms available to them in their home shire, and his wife had apparently turned unrelentingly pious.

Of course he tried to control every possible acre. Of course he feared for his ability to bring in a good harvest. And of course, Giles, overshadowed by siblings both heroic and headstrong, had learned not to have a single substantial thought in his handsome head.

To appearances.

"Might we call upon your son?" Sebastian asked. "I'd like to look in on a fellow soldier, and I'm sure Lady Violet would like to make his acquaintance too."

Bellamy turned an appraising gaze on the marquess. "He might receive you. I can never tell with Nigel. He and Freeman seem to get on well enough, though as far as I can see, all they do is sit in the library and swill brandy. My Delia says they don't even talk, and she's the best spy of the lot. They simply sit about like a pair of handsome lumps, staring at the fire."

The squire had spoken honestly when he'd referred to his daughters as hoydens if they eavesdropped on such moments. I would probably prefer the company of the Bellamy ladies to that of their menfolk.

"We'll come by tomorrow morning," I said. "And perhaps you might give us the benefit of your thinking regarding Miss Faraday's disappearance."

"She didn't disappear," Mr. Bellamy said, rising. "The damned Frenchie killed her. I heard them arguing as plain as day. No man should address a lady like that, though it were half in French, and I couldn't make it out. Miss Faraday was quite out of charity with Monsieur."

I rose as well, my insides in riot, though I kept calm. "Where was this?"

"I take my morning horse out three days a week when the weather's fair to keep him in condition and inspect my acres. Like everybody else, I use the shortcuts through the woods when it suits, and on this occasion, I saw the two of 'em. They were both mounted, and

Miss Faraday was giving as good as she got. No girl from this shire will meekly take a scolding from some Louis-come-lately just because he thinks he can show her that discourtesy."

"Miss Faraday was without a groom?" I asked.

"We aren't like you lot in London," the squire said. "Our girls are raised half in the saddle, and many of them ride to hounds. Not in the first flight, mind, but they give a good account of themselves, and our boys respect them for it. Miss Faraday hadn't any brothers to attend her, and grooms have work to do."

Protecting a female from various perils could not, apparently, be allowed to interfere with mucking stalls or polishing harnesses. Even my brothers tended not to hack out alone if they expected to do any hard riding.

"Have you told Mr. Freeman about this altercation?" I asked as the four of us moved away from the table.

"Of course I have. Freeman's no fool. He'll see the Frenchman held accountable."

"And if the Frenchman is not responsible?" I countered, as pleasantly as I could. "What then?"

"He is responsible, but even if he ain't, he's a Frenchman. They get up to no good often enough that eventually they should be held accountable for something. I'll wish you good day, my lady. Mrs. Bonaventure, my lord, a pleasant day to you too. My thanks for a good meal, and I will tell my missus to expect callers tomorrow morning. We aren't fancy, but she'll get out the silver teapot for you."

He bowed stiffly to me and to Pamela and marched off down the path to the stables.

"They aren't all like that," Pamela said. "Most of my neighbors are quite congenial, but Anthony has had a rough go of it. He took too long to give up the sheep, and he does have three daughters to launch."

Sebastian watched the squire disappear around a bend in the path. "Did his call have a purpose?"

Pamela smiled faintly. "Other than to offend everybody in his ambit with his blunt brilliance? Yes. He was asking me for the loan of my London house in the event that Giles is willing to escort his mother and sisters up to Town for some shopping. Summer is the cheapest time to shop in London—Bellamy has figured out that much—and Giles enjoys doing the pretty in the clubs and gaming hells."

"Giles is a bit of dandy, isn't he?" My sympathy for Giles had grown in the past hour, though I was not looking forward to tomorrow's call.

"He's chafing at the bit to leave this bucolic paradise behind," Pamela said. "Ironic, isn't it? Once the Season ends, polite society can't abandon London fast enough. We're all for the rural house parties, the grouse moors, the hunt field. We tolerate a few months of London's smoke and silliness in spring, but it's the countryside we crave."

"While the squire's children," Sebastian said, "long for the blandishments of the capital. Violet, you are frowning."

"Considering the vagaries of human nature. I must change my shoes, and then I will enjoy some of The Gauges's abundant fresh air. Pamela, thank you for an interesting meal."

My escape was thwarted by Sebastian's announcement that he would walk with me, the blighter.

"What schemes are you hatching, Violet Marie?" he asked.

I'd donned a floppy-brimmed sun hat, changed into half boots, and retrieved my parasol. Sebastian had accosted me at the foot of the main stairs, but I wasn't to be deterred from my errand. "I'm off to have a wander in the woods."

"Again?"

"A dead body doesn't just disappear, Sebastian. A live body might. Everybody is too busy declaring Miss Faraday murdered to bother looking for her. If she's injured, that is precious time wasted."

Sebastian ambled along at my side as I made for the back terrace. The air had grown uncomfortably close, but when we reached the out of doors, I saw no thunderclouds promising relief anytime soon.

"A live body might get up and walk away, I agree, but that's not a new development. What has you in such a taking?"

"The king's man."

Sebastian stopped at the top of the terrace steps. Pamela's garden was more typically English than Belle Terre's, a charming arrangement of walks bordered by flowers, with a folly to one side and a fountain on the other. What my mother had called a reading-and-strolling garden, rather than a formal garden.

"Freeman has earned your renewed ire?"

"He tried to cozen me, asking me to promise him full disclosure of all we discovered, while withholding from me the fact that St. Sevier and Miss Faraday were seen arguing."

"That bothers you."

"Vexes me exceedingly. St. Sevier would never raise his voice to a young lady unless his patience was tried to the utmost." My patience was tried to the utmost by Bellamy's notion that St. Sevier should swing because all Frenchmen eventually commit crimes.

Sebastian might have remonstrated with me, or worse, tried to reason with me. Instead, he kissed my cheek.

"Mind the heat, Violet, and we can ask St. Sevier about his various public debates when we see him this evening."

I nodded, more appreciative of Sebastian's forbearance than he knew. "I cannot lose him, Sebastian. He's not mine, I know that, but I cannot watch him give up his very life to English stupidity. His only daughter has just met him, and..."

Sebastian wrapped me in a hug, and I was tempted to cling. "I know, *mo chridhe*. I know. Go thrash about in the woods, mutter profanities, and let your mind run free. Scream loudly if a rabbit so much as looks at you askance, and if you are not back in one hour, I will come find you. St. Sevier has doubtless been pondering the situation as well, and he is nobody's fool. I'm not inclined to let him swing either, and I don't get the sense Freeman is all that convinced by a few arguments and coincidences."

That was as much reassurance as I was likely to get, and for the present, it was enough and much appreciated. I set a leisurely pace across the park, letting my mind run free, as Sebastian had suggested. By the time I reached the clearing by the stream, I had more questions than answers.

Why hadn't Miss Faraday screamed? The grooms at The Gauges would have heard her.

Why wasn't Anthony Bellamy a suspect, when he too had been abroad in the woods at the requisite hour?

How did Giles Bellamy afford London entertainments, even if he had free lodgings while in Town?

I examined the bloody rocks and the undergrowth on all sides. I trod the distance from the stream to the bridle path, moving in slow, small steps and examining all the flora up to a height of six feet. I had stared at the area for the better part of an hour when it occurred to me that nobody had apparently thought to search *across the stream* from where Miss Faraday had supposedly fallen.

I moved down the bank at a fast scramble and splashed back across the shallows, determined to undertake that search myself.

~

Freeman ushered all three of us into his sitting room. St. Sevier stood by the window with a book and had apparently not been warned that he was to have callers. He all but tossed the book onto a nearby escritoire and took three swift steps to join Ann in the middle of the room, for she had dashed toward him as well.

Their embrace was silent, fierce, and entirely genuine. While I watched the reunion of husband and wife, Freeman watched me.

Being raised as an earl's daughter meant I had acquired a few useful skills. I could keep a pleasant smile on my face while imagining somebody's immediate social ruin. I could graciously accept condolences despite enduring a pounding headache and roiling nausea.

I could also, with a perfectly bland expression, watch my erstwhile lover prove, beyond any doubt, that he and his wife cared deeply for each other. St. Sevier might not be in love with his Ann, nor she with him, but they clearly shared mutual esteem.

Hugh St. Sevier was, above all, an honorable man. He would make his marriage the best it could be, and in that regard, Ann apparently intended to give the union her best efforts as well. St. Sevier had found a way to inspire not only her fidelity, but her loyalty and respect.

I hated him a little for that, and while I understood my hatred to be foolish and immature, I also grasped that it was healthy and, in its way, hopeful. Hugh was a good man, a dear and lovely man, but not a saint, and though he'd been my salvation, our marriage would have had its rough moments too.

"He's not feeding you," Ann said, stepping back and appraising her husband with a critical eye. "Mr. Freeman, a man does not drop weight in a few short days if he's getting adequate rations."

"Mr. Freeman feeds me," St. Sevier said, amusement and patience lacing his tone. "Allow me to greet her ladyship and his lordship, and perhaps Mr. Freeman will permit us some privacy while we enjoy a civil visit."

I had always loved Hugh's voice, the slight accent, the subtleties of humor and ire that gilded the edges and swirled in the undercurrents. To hear him speak was still a pleasure.

St. Sevier did look a bit peaky, though. He was an attractive *and* handsome man, having substantial height, lovely brown eyes, and wavy chestnut hair. More than that, he had attractive ways—the graceful hand gesture, an understated elegance to his attire. He was to initial appearances a well-turned-out English gentleman, but details—a dash of lace, nacre buttons, a touch of embroidery on his cuffs—imbued his habiliment with a Continental flair.

He eased from his wife's embrace, took my hand, and bowed correctly. "I apologize for involving you in my troubles, my lady. Please feel free to be about your business, as I'm sure this passing unpleasantness will soon resolve itself."

Nothing, not the look in his eyes, not an innuendo in his words, suggested that he and I had recently contemplated marriage after having sampled joys a lady traditionally reserved for the connubial sphere.

"Madame St. Sevier invited me to take a hand in matters," I replied. "I regret to inform you, Monsieur, that your wishes don't signify when your wife has made her own plain. Who wants to see you dead?"

Sebastian muttered something, but St. Sevier smiled, maybe even a trifle wistfully.

"Very well, my lady. You are here. Your talent with puzzles is formidable. As far as I know, the whole shire would rejoice to see me disgraced, if not dead. My neighbors lust after my home wood, resent my unenclosed common acres, and hold me accountable for every death caused at the Corsican's hands. I have achieved the status of a public enemy, all the while simply riding my acres or lamenting the weather to my wife, in standard English fashion."

"They will kill you," Sebastian said, his tone flat. "They will dress it up with solicitors, judges, and formal proceedings. They will take weeks or even months to end your life, St. Sevier, and they might well trust to the foul diseases rampant in the jails to do what is properly the job of a noose, but they will kill you. The jury might not even do you the courtesy of pretending you are a pauper, so they will kill you and steal everything you own from your wife and daughter. If you are exhausted, then blow retreat, but at least allow your reinforcements a clear shot at the enemy." He took a step closer to St. Sevier. "Think of wee Fiona. She needs her father."

Hugh scrubbed a hand over his face. "Unfair, Dunkeld."

Brilliant, Dunkeld, and Sebastian had delivered that scold while the magistrate lingered silently by the door.

"Mr. Freeman," I said, "perhaps you'd be so good as to see about some refreshment for Monsieur's guests." I delighted to address the magistrate as if he were little more than a footman. When he'd bowed and departed, Sebastian spoke again.

"Answer her ladyship's question, St. Sevier. Who has done this to
you?"

"Freeman has asked me much the same question. Who wishes
me ill? Who has threatened me? Anthony Bellamy, of course, has
been the most vocal about my stubborn Frenchie backwardness, but
he does not strike me as capable of harming a female."

That observation meshed with my own estimation of the squire.
Bellamy could not even scold his own daughters into submission,
much less raise a lethal hand against one of their friends.

"Shall we sit?" I suggested. "Freeman won't allow us much
opportunity to speak freely, and we have a great deal to discuss."

Hugh and Ann took a love seat, and—I'm sure this was not intentional on her part—Ann held her husband's hand. I waited for resentment to well—I had frequently held that same hand—but it did not.
She and I both feared for St. Sevier's life, and I could not begrudge
her so simple a comfort.

Sebastian took one wing chair, and I took the other. The parlor
put me in mind of The Gauges, for Freeman's artistic talent was on
display here too. We sat as if in the midst of an English cottage
garden, surrounded by borders of yellow lilies with their abundant
greenery, towering hollyhocks in myriad pastels, and purple and pink
foxgloves.

At each corner of the room, Freeman had painted a maple tree,
and the branches extended onto the ceiling in a lifelike replication of
beautiful nature. Songbirds perched amid the leaves, and a majestic
hawk soared in what appeared to be the distant sky.

What sort of mind created this ingenious variety of beauty, then
calmly arrested an innocent man for murder? What did it do to
Freeman to see on every hand evidence of the talent a French bullet
had taken from him?

"You were observed arguing with Miss Faraday," I began. "What
can you tell us about that?"

Hugh waved an impatient hand. "The young women in this shire
are incorrigible. They have few bachelors to torment, save for the

young Mr. Bellamy and several others of his ilk, who long only for a life of idleness in London. The ladies make free with a bathing pool in my woods, venturing there at sunset and after moonrise."

Hugh was no prude, but clearly, he had become a papa. "You came upon them venturing?" I asked.

"Cavorting like sirens, a half dozen of them. I did not make my presence known, but when I encountered Miss Faraday on the bridle path a few days later, I asked that she and her friends desist from such activities."

"According to Anthony Bellamy, you did more than ask," Sebastian said.

"Miss Faraday argued with me most emphatically. She declared that using the pool was akin to using the common rights-of-way—which point of law I beg leave to doubt where bathing naked is concerned—and that were young men going for the occasional swim after a hot day, I would not begrudge the fellows that pleasure."

Oh dear. I might have liked Miss Faraday, had I known her. I asked the first question that popped into my mind. "What were you doing in the woods after sunset, St. Sevier?"

"I find evening a peaceful time to enjoy nature," Hugh said, with a perfectly pleasant expression.

I had known St. Sevier for several years. He had never once, in my experience, gone riding or even walking in the evening hours.

Ann sat up a little straighter. "Monsieur and I have occasional differences of opinion, about Fiona, about where to make our home, about... many things. Hugh rides out to give me time to reconsider any harsh words and to marshal his own patience."

"Has anybody other than Bellamy confronted you about enclosing your commons?" Sebastian asked.

They sorted through various names. Some men had muttered a word or two in the blacksmith's yard. Ann had "overheard" a pair of ladies discussing *the value of responsible land use* when she'd taken Fiona for a bun at the bakery. Murmurings and innuendo, such as I had been subjected to during my brief penance as an unmarried young lady in Mayfair.

I let the talk wash over me as I considered what I knew of the whole situation. Hugh was innocent. I would stake my life on that, but he was also, in some part of his mind, already preparing to be found guilty. He had been to war, had overcome all the challenges facing a young émigré, had thought Ann lost to him under terrible circumstances...

He was brave and tough and resilient, but Sebastian had the right of it: Hugh was not in top fighting form, not among English gentry and their agricultural arrogance.

"What do we know of Miss Faraday?" I said slowly. "Whose beau did she steal? Whose advances did she spurn? Hugh has been detained to suit somebody's whim, but the young lady was either inspired to stage an elaborate ruse, or she's dead. She must have enemies."

"Giles Bellamy is the beau of the whole churchyard," Sebastian replied.

"I rode with him the day after he found Miss Faraday's body," I replied. "He did not appear to be a suitor broken by grief." He had desperately wanted to avoid the crime scene and had, in fact, led me not to the actual site, but a dozen yards downstream. Why?

I was reminded that Giles was the only person who claimed to have seen the body. His father wanted St. Sevier's land enclosed, and Giles himself aspired to a more expensive life in Town. If Anthony Bellamy hadn't taken Miss Faraday's life, perhaps Giles had, but then, why hide the body?

Unless Miss Faraday's body held clues to who had ended her life?

Had *St. Sevier* hidden the body in hopes of avoiding the very fate that had befallen him? Moved the body to another's land? Was that why Hugh seemed like a man defeated? He was guilty of tampering with evidence of a crime, failing to report a crime, interfering with the king's man...

Drat and blast.

"Did Miss Faraday have a dowry?" Ann asked. "Even among the English gentry, matches are often pragmatic. I get the sense Bellamy *père* is much preoccupied with a lack of coin."

So did I, as was Bellamy *fils*. "You think Holly Faraday and Giles were being forced into a union neither wanted?" The notion intrigued me and felt intuitively right. "He did not want to settle down, and she... I gather she was enjoying life as an unmarried lady." Cavorting unclad beneath the full moon, like the Druidesses of old.

"Did some other young woman set her cap for Giles?" Sebastian said. "Or did a group of young women decide that Holly should not have him, and a spat became something much worse?"

The notion of women doing violence to one another repelled me, though women were regularly violent. Their weapons in my experience were more likely to be words, silences, quiet laughter, rumor, and unkind glances.

"Did Miss Faraday refuse another suitable parti?" I rose to pace. "Did she toy with some fellow's affections?" The idea that the whole puzzle revolved around Miss Faraday rather than Hugh St. Sevier was provoking all manner of uncomfortable questions. "Did she make a promise to some man and then break it?" I went on. "Did she conceive his child, perhaps, and decide she could not marry him?"

"If we had a body," Sebastian said, "we could answer at least the question of whether or not she was with child."

"But we have no body," Ann said softly, "and thus I believe it's time my husband came home."

CHAPTER EIGHT

We came up with any number of unanswered questions regarding who might wish Miss Holly Faraday ill. When Freeman eventually returned with a footman carrying a tray, he entertained them all as if we debated a particularly interesting chess game.

During that exchange, St. Sevier remained silent, simply holding Ann's hand.

"Miss Faraday," Freeman said, "as far as I know, had no enemies. I specifically asked her parents that question. She was something of a ringleader among the local young ladies and quite thick with Mrs. Bonaventure. The cynical explanation for that friendship is that Miss Faraday sought Town connections, but I believe the parties genuinely enjoyed one another's company. More tea?"

I had had enough of tea and chess games for one evening. Pamela herself had not mentioned a particularly close association with the deceased, meaning the magistrate might be prevaricating, or Pamela might have misled me by omission.

"Did you inquire of Miss Faraday's sisters about her enemies, Mr. Freeman? Did you question any of the young ladies who were never invited to go bathing beneath the waxing moon in what is apparently a shocking local tradition? Have you put the whole situation to the vicar's wife, or asked Mrs. Bellamy what she thinks?"

My tone had taken on an edge, because a woman was dead or missing, and Freeman's investigation, as far as I could see, had been lax at best.

"We are less than seventy-two hours from the time of the crime, my lady," Freeman answered evenly. "I will certainly add those tasks to my responsibilities, but I've also been occupied with examining the crime scene, interviewing the bereaved family, and assembling a jury for the inquest."

Despite the French doors being open, the air in the parlor was still thick with the day's heat. I'd brought my fan and wanted to poke the magistrate with it.

"And did you plan to tell your prisoner of this inquest?" I snapped.

"As you know, we have no physician in this neighborhood. I had to send over to Haughton for a physician, and I just received word that Dr. Horace Deever is available the day after tomorrow to participate in the proceedings."

"Why wait on a physician when you have no body?" Ann asked. As if heaven itself wanted an answer to that question, thunder rumbled in the distance.

Sebastian rose. "Freeman waits on a physician because the greater the effort to appease appearances with procedural niceties, the less anybody will object to the lack of a factual case when St. Sevier is eventually arrested. Then too, the longer Freeman detains St. Sevier, the more guilty St. Sevier appears."

Freeman rose as well, signaling that the visit had come to an end. St. Sevier assisted his wife to her feet, and I, of course, rose on my own.

"I am doing everything in my power," Freeman said, "to get to the bottom of Miss Faraday's disappearance. Innuendo and slander solve nothing. Has it occurred to any of you that Monsieur is safer under my roof than he'd be anywhere else?"

"Yes, it has," I retorted, "and I dismissed the notion out of hand. If your neighbors are afflicted with such ungovernable tempers that they can contemplate murdering an innocent man with impunity, then your authority is insufficient for your post and you have many more potential felons to interview."

Freeman's brows rose, and a humid gust of air suggested the storm was moving closer. "What else would you have me do, my lady? You have enumerated tasks enough, and I will see to them. Is there more you'd have me take on?"

He was not angry. He was curious.

"Yes," I said. "When you and Dunkeld examined the crime scene, you did not search the opposite side of the stream. I found depressions in the soft earth of the bank that appear to have been made by bootheels, and some broken underbrush could signal either a woman traveling off the paths or somebody else's passing."

"You will show me these discoveries tomorrow after breakfast."

"I will be happy to, and you will release Monsieur at once."

St. Sevier studied the distant raptor soaring across the painted firmament.

Freeman shook his head. "I have confirmed that my guest made a habit out of riding the woods both early in the day and in the evening, if not at night. That habit in itself might not be damning, but he withheld the fact of his evening sorties from me. I cannot release a man who fails to cooperate with my efforts to exonerate him."

"That I have differences of opinion with my wife is nobody's business." St. Sevier had spoken in French, and as angrily as I'd ever heard him in any language. "Her situation is not easy," he went on in English, "and privacy is one gift I can give her."

"You eavesdropped," I said, marching over to Freeman. "You listened at the keyhole to our discussion."

"I did not."

Sebastian eyed Freeman with disgust. "Fiona told me her papa rides out after supper, but is always home in time to read her a story before bed. She spoke to me in the Erse, and Freeman understood her."

Freeman had the grace to look embarrassed. "Just so. The girl was chatting freely, and I cannot help what I overheard."

"This changes nothing," I said. "You also heard Fiona say her papa was home more or less by dark, and you very likely did not *ask* him if he rode out at sunset. He has answered what questions you did put to him honestly. Let St. Sevier go home to his wife and child."

"I cannot."

Ann leaned against her husband, her posture stricken. St. Sevier murmured something low to her in French, while I struggled with the impulse to do Freeman an injury. Ann and St. Sevier held a whispered conversation, while I wanted to scream.

"St. Sevier is innocent, and you are grasping at straws," I said. "I will see you after breakfast, and by that time, I hope you have come to your senses."

Freeman merely nodded. Because the French doors opened onto a terrace that sat on the same side of the house as the stable, we took our leave by way of the terrace. While Ann and Sebastian discussed details of the inquest with our host, I found myself standing next to St. Sevier.

"How are you, Violet?"

What was he asking? "'Bearing up' is the phrase, I believe. You?"

"Likewise. Please keep bearing up, for everybody's sake."

He meant for *his* sake, but his honor would not allow him to ask even that much of me. "I have no regrets, Hugh. I could never regret that Fiona will know a father any girl would be proud to claim."

"And the rest of it?" he asked quietly, gaze on the last of the light limning the western horizon. "Regrets, my lady?"

"No. Had you not come along... I owe you much. I will always owe you much and always value your friendship." This was the truth. A part of me wanted to throw my arms around him and drag him away from the magistrate's comfortable rural abode, but that instinct was protective, not possessive.

"I should say," Hugh replied, "that I have no regrets either, but I will not say that, because a gentleman is both kind and honest. I will say thank you for heeding Ann's request, but do not risk involving yourself in scandal on my account. Look after Ann and Fiona, to the extent Ann allows anybody that honor, and distance yourself from the situation in every other regard."

"Request noted."

We smiled at each other, a little sadly, a lot fondly, and then it was time to leave. The rain started just as Sebastian's coach pulled into The Gauges's drive, and the heavens opened with such a vengeance that I doubted my discoveries at the crime scene would survive the storm.

~

"I will light you to your room," Sebastian said, taking my cloak from my shoulders, "and then you will curl up with a lurid novel and forget the frustrations of this day."

"Will I?" The advice was sound, but I doubted even Mrs. Radcliffe at her Gothic finest could chase away the day's frustration. I removed my bonnet, which was the worse for the rain, and stripped off my gloves.

"Shall I order you a pot of chocolate?" Sebastian asked, taking off his hat and settling it on a hook near the night porter's nook. "Have a posset sent up?"

"No, thank you." The thought of a posset was distinctly unappealing, and Sebastian was showing an alarming degree of solicitude. "I'm in the mood for fresh raspberries in cream with a dash of honey." I'd first encountered this treat in the nursery and hadn't had it for years.

"At this hour?" He lit a carrying candle from the sconce near the door.

"The day has been vexing, Dunkeld, from daybreak right up to the present moment." I headed for the stairs, glad that Pamela had claimed the need for an early night. To recount for her over a pot of gunpowder exactly how trying my day had been was even less appealing than the prospect of a posset.

A magistrate more devious than competent.

A prime suspect in Anthony Bellamy who could no more harm a young lady than he could predict a plummeting wool market.

Another possible suspect in Bellamy's son, but one apparently without a motive to harm the victim.

A victim whose life raised more questions than anybody was inspired to answer.

And a crime scene being washed clean of evidence by a pounding rain.

Not to mention Freeman's tenacity when it came to keeping Hugh a virtual prisoner.

Sebastian gestured for me to precede him up the stairs. "St. Sevier is withholding something from us. Something he suspects Freeman knows, or something he has already admitted to Freeman."

"And Freeman is withholding something from us too. Did Fiona offer you any more damning confidences while she chattered away in Gaelic?"

"I don't believe so, but I am reminded that Freeman knows any number of languages. He might not be able to speak them fluently, but to him, a language is a code. Once he grasps the rules, he seems to pick up vocabulary easily. Nothing St. Sevier mutters in French will get past him, but St. Sevier knows that."

What else did St. Sevier know? He'd kept secrets from me before, but only because a physician honored a patient's confidences, and I had quickly deduced that rule at work. I paused on the landing, because I was that weary. The darkness above was typical of a country house at an hour when a London dinner party would still be gaining momentum.

"I am not despairing," I said, resuming the trudge up the steps, "but an inquest for appearances' sake, a detainee prohibited from going home when questioning is over, and a magistrate who has to be reminded to talk to young women when a young lady is presumed dead... I am discouraged."

We reached my sitting room, and once again, Lucy was not in evidence. Renewing her acquaintance with Rhys Upjohn, no doubt. Gather ye rosebuds and all that.

Sebastian lit the candles in my parlor, then did the same in the bedroom. "Shall I undo your hooks?"

"Yes, please." I wanted out of my corset in the worst way, and I wanted—desperately—that bowl of raspberries and cream. Perhaps in the morning...

I gave Sebastian my back, vaguely wondering when he'd become so expert at undressing ladies, but then, he was attractive, titled, wealthy, and in roaring good health. He had a daughter. He knew where babies came from.

His touch was as efficient and impersonal as Lucy's. When enough of my hooks had been undone, Sebastian took a shawl down from a hook on the privacy screen and draped the soft wool around my shoulders.

"Did you tell him, Violet?"

I closed my eyes, the better to savor a small comfort. "Tell who what?"

"Tell St. Sevier that you are carrying his child."

❦

I whirled, which had the effect of making me slightly vertiginous. "What in blazes are you talking about?"

Sebastian merely cocked his head. He'd had the same mannerism as a youth. We'd argued heatedly and often, though mostly I had debated with him for the sheer deviltry of it. Sebastian would humor me for a time, but when my oratory had reached ridiculous exaggerations and outlandish hypotheticals, he would go silent and give me that slight tilt of his head, usually accompanied with a faint, smug smile.

He was not smiling now. His gaze held, if anything, compassion.

"I cannot be carrying *anybody's* child," I said, though what should have been a brisk retort had come out sounding bewildered.

"Yes, you can." Sebastian led me by the hand to the vanity stool, turned it away from the vanity, and sat me upon it. He took up a perch on the cedar chest a few feet away. "You and St. Sevier were all but engaged, Violet, and unless you and he claim an enormous store of foolish virtue, that meant intimacies."

Of course it had. Glorious, soul-boggling, delightful intimacies such as I'd never known with my husband.

"But Hugh was careful, and I can't... That is to say, I haven't..." I could *conceive*, but I had never carried a child to term. I'd somehow leaped to a view of myself as barren, but my perception was not quite accurate. "I'm not carrying anybody's child."

But I could be.

"Lucy says your appetite is unreliable. You are napping at odd moments. You nearly fainted at luncheon. You are wearing your stays more loosely laced."

Lucy had said a great deal, or Sebastian noticed more than he ought. "I am adjusting to country air." Even as I said it, I mentally added to Sebastian's list of symptoms, one last bit of evidence: My courses had deserted me over the summer. I attributed that development to the shock of losing St. Sevier and to a general unpredictability where my lunation was concerned.

Sebastian studied me. "You are honestly surprised."

"Stop looking at me." I wanted to pull my shawl over my head and hide. I wanted to tear off my clothes and study my body. I wanted to devour a bowl of raspberries and cream.

And I wanted in some corner of my heart to rejoice. *If* I was expecting and *if* the child did somehow miraculously survive beyond birth, I would have Hugh's son or daughter to love for the rest of my days. I would also have many an awkward explanation to make, and the whole business with Hugh and Ann would reach new horizons of peculiarity, but...

A child. A child of mine and St. Sevier's... I wanted to laugh for joy and weep for the irony.

Sebastian went to the hearth, where a cheery fire had dispelled the chill of the rainy night. He filled the warmer with coals, tossed back the covers, and ran the pan over my sheets and pillows.

I watched him performing that mundane domestic chore while my mind lost all sense of forward direction.

A baby. The grandmother of all celestial pranks, both a miracle and a considerable puzzlement. I would worry about the puzzlement later. I began counting weeks, since St. Sevier and I had been first been intimate during our sojourn to Scotland. When had I last seen my courses?

I needed a calendar, and I needed to buy a property in the country as soon as may be.

"Say something, Dunkeld."

Sebastian dumped the coals back onto the fire and set the warmer aside. "Promise me you will mind your health. Get adequate rest. Eat well, and take extra care on staircases. Avoid strong spirits in any quantity, exercise the greatest of good sense in the saddle, if you must continue riding."

"You aren't telling me to go back to London."

"I already tried that. I cannot tell you what to do, but I can ask emphatically that you tell St. Sevier your news."

I could detect in Sebastian no censure, no newfound distaste for me, but he was quite firm on this last point.

"And if we cannot see him exonerated," I said, bending to remove my half boots, "would you send him to the assizes with not one but two children weighting his conscience?"

"Yes. I would send him off with eighteen children weighting his conscience if that would inspire him to defend himself."

"He maintains his innocence." I set aside my boots, wondering if I'd see the day when bending to remove them grew awkward. My son had been stillborn at six months, and until the pangs began, I would have said I was in the best health of my life. My condition had been apparent to the casual observer by then, but I'd withdrawn from Society, and thus my misfortune had not been widely known.

The first miscarriage had been earlier, and please, Almighty God, could there not be a third.

"Hugh maintains his innocence," Sebastian said, "and he maintains his reticence. Ann and Fiona managed without him for all of the child's life thus far, and they have family in Scotland. They will manage without him again if necessary, and St. Sevier knows that. We must give him more of a reason to fight."

"Or one more regret when a noose is placed about his neck." I rose, turned the vanity stool, and resumed my seat. "This is why you drew Ann into conversation with Freeman? So I could spring upon St. Sevier news that will not aid his situation one bit?"

Sebastian added half a scoop of coal to the flames. "I will insist that Freeman give you a few minutes of privacy with St. Sevier at the earliest opportunity. If Freeman wants to observe from a distance to ensure you aren't passing the prisoner a firearm or a folding knife, so be it, but St. Sevier deserves honesty from you."

I should not have been surprised that Sebastian took the part of truth. His stance pleased me. Many others in his position—titled, wealthy, et cetera—would have advocated a long repairing lease in Italy and a convenient upbringing for the child with a kindly couple unable to have children of their own. I might play the role of godmother or family friend, but my name would remain unsullied by scandal, and the truth need never trouble me.

These little fictions were enacted all the time, usually draped in some taradiddle about a cousin dying in childbed and a father unable to cope with his grief, or having six other children to support.

"I want my baby, Sebastian."

He replaced the hearth screen before the fire and stared into the flames as they caught on fresh fuel and blazed more brightly.

"Think very carefully, Violet, about what is best for the child and what is best for you. Your family will try to meddle, from your aunties, to Derwent, to your sisters-by-marriage. Ponder all considerations and set your course now, before they can try to sway you or provoke you into stubborn declarations."

I began fishing the pins from my hair, feeling both excited and weary. I had much to absorb and more reason than ever to see Hugh freed from the snare of English justice... If I was carrying.

"My family has no say in the matter." How fortunate that my late husband had left me *quite* well provided for.

"You have lady cousins," Sebastian said gently. "They have yet to marry. Derwent's standing with his peers will be affected by your situation. You are godmother to Felix and Katie's son. You have two nieces who will make their come outs within the decade. Society's memory is at least that long. If you have a son, he can take up a profession or live on the Continent, but a daughter will not have an easy time of it, Violet."

My braid slipped down over my shoulder. "You have been brooding about this."

"You will brood about it as well, once the shock wears off, and you will want this child to have every advantage."

He was right, blast him. I hated when Sebastian was right, but I loved how steadfast and sensible he was.

I undid my braid while Sebastian settled again on the cedar chest. I could see him in the folding mirror, his expression unreadable. Even as a youth, he'd had the ability to withdraw into inscrutable silence. As a man, he'd developed self-containment into a high art.

"I have had two miscarriages, Sebastian. I do not assume this child will ever draw breath." The words were hard to say, so fiercely did I already want for my baby to be well and happy. In the past few minutes, everything had changed, though here I was, unbraiding my hair as I had on countless other nights.

"All the more reason for you to consult St. Sevier. He's the only physician on hand, and he has taken a particular medical interest in children and childbirth."

Lord, it felt wonderful to undo my hair. "The decision of whether to tell him and when is mine, Sebastian. You will not gainsay me on this."

"Duplicity is not in your nature, and lies have a way of complicating the lives of all concerned."

Sebastian had known me in my girlhood—he well knew my *nature*—but when I'd left the schoolroom, he'd taken an officer's commission. Unbeknownst to me, he had asked my father for permission to court me and been summarily dismissed to the battlefields of Spain. Sebastian had been informed that I would never entertain the suit of a penniless Scot, however much his company had diverted me from the boredom of summers at the family seat.

My father—who had bought Sebastian's colors—had presented me with an engagement to Frederick Belmaine as a fait accompli, and only fairly recently had I learned why Sebastian had distanced himself from me. The years apart had created gaps in my familiarity with him—I knew nothing about the daughter he'd brought home from Spain, for example—but he was clearly still my friend.

In the coming months and years, I would need my friends very much.

"If I'm not to engage in deceptions, then do you suggest I simply go about my business, no explanations for the baby in my arms? I refuse to hand this child over to strangers, Sebastian. If God has seen fit to bless me with motherhood, I will not fling that miracle back in the Almighty's face for the benefit of a family with enough consequence to weather nearly any scandal."

"So fierce," he murmured, watching as I took up my hairbrush. "But St. Sevier might wish better than bastardy on his son or daughter."

"We took precautions," I said, my face heating. "Hugh warned me precautions fail, but we were in contemplation of marriage." And we had been in love. I'd certainly not been in love with my husband, and I'd blamed myself for that failing. I'd thought myself somehow lacking, thought I'd had no capacity for romance. I had wanted to be awash in tender regard for my spouse, had tried to be, and had even talked myself into believing I was.

Then I'd come across the jeweler's bill, paid in full, for a set of emeralds I'd never seen, much less worn. My coloring was not flattered by emeralds, and when I confronted my husband, he had apologized.

Freddie showed no remorse for heaping lavish gifts upon his mistress, but rather, he was nominally sorry for having left the evidence where I would find it.

"Perhaps you should be in contemplation of marriage again," Sebastian said. "The right sort of arrangement could solve myriad problems."

"My father found the right sort of arrangement for me when I seventeen. I want no more sensible unions that turn out to be a purgatory of powerlessness for me. I realize illegitimacy is to be avoided, but I am not ready to consign the rest of my life into the keeping of some impecunious baron who graciously agrees to raise a Frenchman's bastard. That will solve one problem only to create others, for me and for the child."

"Already you are protective of your offspring."

My hair was in riot as a result of the humid weather, and my reflection in the folding mirror revealed fatigue and some pallor. And yet, I fancied that my eyes held a battle light.

"No baby of mine," I went on, "will be the shameful burden tolerated by a husband all too happy to get his hands on my money while he sits in judgment of me and my child. St. Sevier will love this child, should he ever learn I'm carrying, and it's better to have the love of a father who cannot claim his baby than the sneering judgment of one who gives the child only a name."

"Those are not your only options," Sebastian said, rising. "You could marry me, and I vow to you, Violet, that any child of yours will be raised with all the love, loyalty, and protection I afford my own daughter. I know that you would be as much a mother to my wee Annis as you already are to the child of your body."

I had taken up the hairbrush, intent on taming my hair back into a plait. I set the brush down slowly and rose.

"You are proposing marriage? To me?"

Sebastian stepped closer. "Aye."

He meant this magnificent generosity with all sincerity. The rain had softened to a dull patter against the windows, and the fire crackled softly on the hearth. My hair was a fright, and I wasn't even wearing shoes, which for some reason registered in my awareness as I stood facing one of the most decent men I knew.

"Thank you. I don't know what else to say."

"Thank you is not a yes, Violet."

Ever the canny Scot. I considered what I knew of Society's memory for scandal and what I knew of the man so calmly offering marriage to me, despite my situation.

"Thank you is not a no either."

CHAPTER NINE

I broke my fast with buttered toast and tea. A special request to the kitchen had seen a bowl of raspberries in cream with a dash of honey added to my tray.

"You were naughty, Lucy," I said as I took the last, succulent bite of my treat.

"Sorry, ma'am. What with the rain, I did not hear the carriage coming up the drive last night, and nobody thought to tell me either. The staff here is something less than friendly."

She'd very likely fallen asleep in Rhys Upjohn's tender embrace. Upjohn had the slightly weathered features of the veteran soldier, and his antecedents were humble. He was shrewd, honest, loyal to his employer, and keen on Lucy's company.

"I do not refer to an evening at liberty, Lucy. I am capable of seeing myself off to bed." Provided some obliging marquess undid my hooks. "I refer to reposing confidences in Lord Dunkeld, confidences that reflected poorly on me."

She gave my pillows an indignant swat. "His lordship *tattled?*"

"He would never betray your trust, Lucy. I overheard you

speaking with him in the side garden. I will ask in future that if you are concerned for me, you address those worries to me directly."

Lucy fluffed the pillows and arranged them on the bed just so. She had a knack for making domestic spaces comfortable that suggested a former tenure as a chambermaid.

"I *have* addressed my concerns to you, and you ignore me. Begging your pardon, my lady, but you are more headstrong than a bullock heading for his oats. The last thing you ought to be doing is involving yourself with murder amongst a lot of strangers who want only for you to take yourself off, and yet, here you are."

"St. Sevier's life hangs in the balance." I spoke gently, because Lucy—my stoic, pragmatic rock—was upset.

"Monsieur's life hangs in the balance, and so does the life of his child." As soon as the words were out, she put the back of her hand to her mouth, her eyes wide. "I'm sorry. Please don't sack me. I ought not to have spoken so, but you will not listen. I could say nothing to you, lest you turn me off, and I never told his lordship anything other than that your appetite is indifferent, you started napping, and you are overly quiet."

"You didn't imply that I'm not lacing up as tightly?"

Lucy's mortification turned to indignation. "I would never. No lady with any sense laces up in summer as snugly as she would in cooler weather."

Then Sebastian had noticed that much on his own. I poured myself half a cup of China black and added a drizzle of honey and a dollop of milk.

"I would never sack you when your intentions were so kindly, and I appreciate your concern. I did not understand that I had cause to take extra care with my health, but I know that now."

She muttered something about the Quality being daft as she smoothed out a wrinkle on the quilt. "I thought maybe you were ignoring the situation. Hoping it would go away."

"That is the last thing I would ever hope." Lucy had been with me through both miscarriages. I need not say more. "If you would like to seek another post, I will write you a character sufficient to qualify you for any household in Mayfair. I would miss you sorely, Lucy, and I owe you a very great deal, but I know not how matters will unfold. My situation poses a very great risk of scandal."

Lucy opened a window. The storm had passed, and the day promised to be the sort of sunny, breezy marvel that made summer the subject of so many poems.

She drew back the second set of draperies and opened the next window. "Scandal is just talk among folk who haven't anything better to do. Both of my sisters were mothers within six months of speaking their vows. Nobody thinks anything of it."

"I am an earl's widowed daughter. I will be next Season's inaugural outcast." Unless I lost the child.

Or married Sebastian.

"I'll learn French, ma'am. If you want to take a house in Provence. Upjohn knows French, and he's been teaching me a few words. It's not that hard, if you don't try to spell it."

My first thought was that the child, being half French, should certainly know his or her father's native language and homeland. But then, the child should also know the father himself, and unless the inquest went very well indeed, such an eventuality was becoming unlikely.

St. Sevier might be spared death if he were found guilty. Transportation for fourteen years or for life was the likely alternative.

I had slept soundly and resolved precisely nothing. "I might well never become a mother, Lucy. I have some time to consider options, as do you."

She sent me a glower. "I would do it again, milady. His lordship holds you very dear, and if anybody can argue you into seeing reason, he can."

"Not Monsieur?"

"He were too besotted, more's the pity. He had other ways of convincing you to see his side of things."

True enough, and I did not for one moment regret letting him convince me. I considered another triangle of buttered toast and rejected the notion. Breakfast was sitting well, and I wanted to keep it that way.

"I'm to inspect the wood with the magistrate after breakfast. A coach dress will do." Though coach dresses, usually made of sturdy fabric, would be hot.

"A walking dress will do better. Upjohn says the bridle paths are mostly wide enough for a gig or a pony cart."

I resigned myself to months of this well-intended mulishness. "My riding habit, please. Dunkeld and Freeman expect me to accompany them on horseback. I have promised Dunkeld I will take no unnecessary chances. I will eat regularly, rest amply, and avoid the near occasions of danger. I make the same promises to you, but I will not be lectured or bullied."

I was soon attired in my riding habit, which was, now that I took the time to notice, a trifle snug about the waist. How far along was I, and was there any way to know for certain when my cycle was irregular? I could not imagine asking St. Sevier those questions—though he'd know the answers if anybody would—and I could not imagine putting my queries to a midwife who was a stranger to me either.

As I came down the main staircase, my hostess greeted me. "You are off to once again play in the woods?"

Pamela looked tired, especially for a lady who'd had an early night. Her house was commodious enough that a guest could have come and gone after dark without my notice even had I been on the premises.

Perhaps she was plagued with insomnia. Perhaps Giles Bellamy had disturbed her rest. For all I knew, she might have spent the night cavorting with her footmen. I was nobody to judge, was I?

"Another examination of the scene is likely futile," I replied, "when the rain has doubtless obliterated any relevant evidence that trespassers and game haven't already compromised."

"Then why bother? The local folk will not thank you, Violet, and

I doubt St. Sevier would either. If he simply announces that he intends to sell the property, I'm sure Freeman could be induced to let the matter drop. Holly will likely come swanning back from Town, some fellow's ring on her finger, and we will all look quite foolish for overreacting to a riding accident—if Giles wasn't having us on as part of the joke."

I wanted to get to the stable, where I was to meet Sebastian and Freeman, but I was also curious as to Pamela's theory.

"You think Miss Faraday was tossed from the saddle and bumped her head? Giles came along and misread the situation entirely—or was inspired to make a hanging felony into a joke—then Holly met up with some swain who eloped with her to Town, where they were married by special license? Are any swains missing from the area?"

Pamela waved a pale hand. "It's house-party season. Swains pop up in all manner of unlikely locations until the grouse moors open."

"Grouse season is just around the corner."

"For those fortunate enough to go shooting. The lesser sort of man doesn't always receive the invitations to the shooting parties, and Holly is an unconventional lady. She would delight in putting one over on her sisters."

I did not know Holly Faraday, but I knew young women generally. Putting one over on the family and neighbors by appearing murdered was no sort of practical joke. Far more likely that Miss Faraday would have secured a proposal from her suitor and then inflicted the sight of his devotion to her on all and sundry for weeks, if not months. A long, public, romantic courtship struck me as the perfect antidote to rural ennui.

"The Gauges is actually much closer to the scene of the crime than is Belle Terre," I observed. "I don't suppose Freeman has bothered to question your staff about any unusual comings and goings or strange lights moving about in the woods?"

Pamela smiled. "He asked me about that very exercise when he greeted me not ten minutes ago. Once he has humored your frolic in the woods, he'll begin interviewing my outdoor staff. How much longer before you return to Town, my lady?"

Rude of her, but then, rude of me to impose on her. "I don't know. I'm sure I'll be welcome to stay at Belle Terre if you'd like me to leave." And wouldn't that just be the most awkward situation ever contemplated?

"No need to leave, but one does worry for you. Enjoy your frolic in the woods. I have correspondence to tend to and bills to pay." She swanned up the steps, though her tread appeared less than sprightly. I did not think she was warning me of physical danger. She simply preferred that I bide at The Gauges, lest she have to rely exclusively on housekeepers to spy on me.

Pamela and Holly had supposedly been quite chummy. I concluded that surmise was in error, or offered by Freeman as an intentional misrepresentation. Pamela had all but labeled Holly a self-absorbed featherbrain, which if true was not the sort of company Pamela would keep.

If false, that characterization proved I would get no honest answers from my hostess.

I found both Sebastian and Freeman at the stable, though Biddle informed me that my mare was still being saddled. I strolled idly back and forth before the carriage house, where somebody had done a particularly fine planting of rosebushes that were not yet devoid of all blooms.

Sebastian escorted me, and how like him that he neither renewed his proposal nor stared at my waist. Last night, he had parted from me on the sweetest, most comforting hug and told me that whatever course I chose, the child and I would have his support.

Had he bludgeoned me with reason or threats of dire social ostracism, I would have ordered him from my room. But he absolutely had not.

"Upjohn doesn't care for this household," Sebastian said as I bent to sniff a rose. "He took a wrong turn last night after playing a round of cards with Miss Hewitt, and the butler nearly tossed him from a window for it."

"That's odd. A marquess's valet should be shown considerable deference by the staff of any household." I regarded the efforts of a pair of grooms across the yard as they scrubbed the wheels and fenders of a stylish carriage.

"Odd indeed, but perhaps the fellow was developing aspirations in Miss Hewitt's direction. She is comely. What are you staring at, Violet?"

"Yesterday was the first rain they've had around here for a week, if the gardeners are to be believed, and yet, that town coach is muddy."

"Any coach that was abroad last night will be muddy. I expect they will wash off my own conveyance next. What troubles you?"

Over in the stable yard, Biddle led out my mare. Time to frolic in the woods, as Pamela put it.

"Our hostess told us she needed an early night last night, and yet, that is her carriage, covered in mud. Somebody from The Gauges went somewhere after dark, and Pamela would not send her staff abroad in her town coach."

"She might..." Sebastian's gaze traveled down the bays of the carriage house, which held a serviceable dog cart, a stylish phaeton, and a venerable closed calash. A pony cart occupied the fourth bay, which was probably the housekeeper's to use or lend to other servants. The calash doubtless took the upper servants to services or market in inclement weather, and the phaeton was Pamela's vanity piece.

One bay—for the town coach—sat empty, suggesting that the household's heavier, slower traveling coach was reposing at the home farm, a practice my father observed for vehicles that saw little use.

I considered that empty bay and the men so assiduously washing off the town coach. "What errand could be so pressing that her lady's maid or housekeeper would be given the use of the carriage?"

"A daughter's lying-in?" Sebastian said, brow furrowed.

Talk of such an occurrence would have made the rounds in the servants' hall, and we could easily ask Lucy and Upjohn if they'd heard any such news.

"Perhaps, though domestics seldom marry. Maybe Pamela herself was using that coach."

Sebastian finished the thought for me. "Using it to move a body."

~

Freeman swung onto his gelding and hailed us, and I prepared to once again fence with a magistrate who'd sought to learn all I knew without showing me the reciprocal courtesy. How much less forthcoming would he be if he became aware that I was carrying his prime —his only—suspect's child?

As we approached the stream bank from the side closest to The Gauges, we came upon three young ladies. One was trailing a stout stick through the still depths near the bank, and another gazed at the water from a perch on an obliging rock. The third was pacing along the water and using another stick to poke at the undergrowth.

The magistrate called a greeting to them. "Miss Bellamy, Miss Faraday, Miss Thetis, good day."

His salutation told me that we'd come upon Squire Bellamy's oldest daughter, Holly Faraday's sister, and based on the appearances of the third young lady, probably a younger Faraday sister as well. Only the oldest daughter would be referred to by the family name, if both daughters were out in company.

The one plunging her stick into the water turned out to be Miss Selene Faraday, and though the young lady was named for a goddess, her figure was that of a particularly robust dairymaid. She was tall and broad-shouldered, and her features could most charitably be described as plain.

She had a lovely smile, though, and left off trawling the stream at Freeman's greeting.

"Mr. Freeman, good morning. Thetis was of a mind to hunt morels. Might you introduce us to your guests?"

The young ladies were eyeing Sebastian as if he were the most succulent morel ever to be discovered in the mortal sphere. Freeman dismounted, so Sebastian and I did likewise. The introductions confirmed at least one of my suspicions: Holly Faraday had not been the oldest sister, but she'd been the prettiest, if Giles Bellamy's description of her was accurate.

Selene, the oldest, was plain, and too tall. Thetis was nearly as tall, a trifle spotty, and had rabbit teeth. She, too, though, had a genuinely friendly smile.

Miss Elizabeth Bellamy was something of a puzzle. Her father had described her as a hoyden, but her mannerisms were nervous rather than confident. She curtseyed to Sebastian at least three times and to me twice, the whole time still holding the stick she'd been using to poke at the bracken and ferns.

In appearance, she resembled her brother. Sandy hair, blue eyes, which were shown to good advantage by her blue riding habit. She was well formed, with a few fetching freckles sprinkled across her cheeks, but no great beauty by London standards.

"I've been meaning to call again at Timberlane," Freeman said, "and I specifically meant to speak with you young ladies. Sisters, I'm told, sometimes notice what parents do not."

He was making a hash of this. He ought not to announce his intent to question anybody. He ought to simply show up, begin a friendly conversation, commiserate a bit, let silences stretch to awkward lengths, and leave some won't-you-please-help-me innuendo floating off to the side.

"While you chat with Miss Faraday," I said, "perhaps Miss Bellamy and Miss Thetis might walk with the marquess and me? The woods are so lovely on a summer morning." Nothing less than the truth, of course.

The looks that volleyed between the young ladies at my suggestion were interesting. Miss Thetis Faraday clearly longed to brag of walking in the company of a marquess. Miss Bellamy looked more flustered than flattered at my invitation, and Miss Selene Faraday's smile faltered.

Divide and conquer. My strategy was hardly subtle, and Selene apparently grasped what I was about.

"Don't go far," she called. "We still haven't found any morels."

To the best of my knowledge, morels never grew under water. Sebastian winged his arm at Thetis, which left me in the company of Miss Elizabeth Bellamy.

"You will think us ridiculous," she said as we meandered along the stream. "We are ridiculous. No chaperones, no groom, but how much trouble can we get into here?" She gestured with both hands as if a gloriously green wood were no more interesting than a dusty schoolroom.

"Holly Faraday certainly got into trouble." Or Giles wanted us to think she had.

"So she did. Papa thinks I'm stubborn, but compared to Holly... I ought not to speak ill of a friend, but you cannot tell that woman anything. Giles despairs of her, and Mrs. Bonaventure has said the London hostesses would eat her for breakfast.

"Pamela said that to Holly directly," Miss Bellamy went on. "I suspect Pamela was trying to diminish the appeal of Town for us, because we are lucky to pop into London for a shopping trip every two years, but Holly lacks sense. The things you think but don't say she says, then tries to pretend she offered them as a joke, but we only laugh to be polite."

"London hostesses can be formidable." And a young lady in the country, celebrated for her beauty and boldness, might be formidable as well—offensively so.

Dangerously so.

Holly had apparently been the sort of young lady in whom a girl should never confide, because Holly's discretion could not be trusted. That same girl might nonetheless repose another's secrets in Holly's keeping, hoping to gain Holly's approval with that offering.

I pondered those possibilities—whose secrets might Holly have learned?—while Sebastian daundered along several yards behind us, Thetis barnacled to his arm. He could be charming when he chose to exert himself, and I had always found his burr delightful. Thetis appeared to be hanging on his every word, as well as on his person, though the object of the exercise was for Sebastian to listen far more than he talked.

"London hostesses *are* formidable," Miss Bellamy said, "but you should hear Papa on the subject of new bonnets. I am so out of fashion I dare not leave the shire."

She was out of fashion by a good three years, though her habit fit well. The Faraday sisters, while equally behind the mode, were apparently not as skilled with their needles.

"Far better, Miss Bellamy, to cultivate good taste than to slavishly follow the whims of fashion. Did Holly long for excursions to Town?"

"Giles said you were smart. Giles is smart. He doesn't let on, because Papa never listens to anybody, but Giles knows a few things. We all long for excursions to Town, but Papa refused to send Giles to university for more than a year—said it was money wasted. If Papa won't pay for a gentleman's education, he's hardly likely to pay for a Season, is he?"

Very possibly, he *could not* pay. "Might Holly have decamped for Town on the arm of a half-pay officer or cit enjoying a nearby house party?"

Miss Bellamy glowered at me. "My brother is not fanciful, my lady. He might affect the role of the featherbrained bachelor when it suits him, but if Giles said he found Holly expired in these woods, then he did. Perhaps wolves dragged her body away, or dogs. We have feral dogs in the countryside."

No, *we* did not. I'd been raised not twenty miles to the west, and a stray dog on the loose was subjected to summary justice. Not only was he a direct threat to game, chickens, pets, and humans, he could be rabid or interfere with some huntsman's prize bitch.

"I do not impugn Mr. Bellamy's veracity," I said, "and I apologize if I gave you an impression to the contrary. You've not spoken of Holly in the past tense, Miss Bellamy. Why is that?"

"Shock, I suppose. And we've had no funeral. The inquest isn't until tomorrow, but without a body... It's all quite appalling."

That St. Sevier had been arrested—not arrested, but *detained*, rather—was more appalling still. The farther we walked, though, the more I grasped exactly how majestic his woods were.

And how valuable. Timber was available here in quantity. Game doubtless abounded, as did raspberries, blackberries, and bilberries. I'd spotted two hazelnut trees, Miss Selene had mentioned that the habitat featured edible mushrooms, and the stream was large enough for trout. Given time and a few tools, an enterprising hermit could live abundantly in this wood—or a lot of families could enrich themselves by exploiting the bounty here.

"Why do you think Holly was alone at the wading pool?" I asked.

"We do more than wade there. Has Pamela told you?"

"You swim. Very daring, but on a hot summer night, who could blame you?" At the select academy charged with finishing my education, I'd certainly enjoyed a few dips by moonlight in the nearest millpond. "I trust you don't swim alone, though."

"We do not. I have no idea why Holly was here by herself, unless she was meeting a fellow. I am not being unkind when I say that she was the sister likely to marry first, if any of us ever marries."

How well I recalled the years of schoolgirl speculation about who would marry whom. Who would be consigned to the Promethean suffering of eternal spinsterhood, who would marry down, and who would be forced to marry as a result of scandal or—the temptation to whisper the words still tugged at me—*precipitous passion*.

We were so innocent and so *bored*. And though I'd thought the lot of us silly beyond words, I was now a lady facing ruin as a result of precipitous passion.

"Holly did meet a fellow," I said slowly. "Giles arrived at the same trysting place as Holly. Were they interested in one another?"

"Giles is too busy panting after Pamela. She's years too old for him, but men don't care about that. She's rich, she's pretty, and she's connected. She's also sophisticated, but since she broke it off with Mr. Freeman, she's had nothing to do with the local fellows. I expect she goes up to Town or to the house parties for her entertainment." Miss Bellamy slanted a look at me. "She knows the marquess."

Not news, but my mind reeled with the ramifications of Miss Bellamy's other revelations. *Pamela and the magistrate were former lovers.* Was Freeman still sufficiently devoted to her that he'd see an innocent man hanged for a crime *Pamela* had committed? Was Giles protecting Pamela somehow?

Was Pamela protecting either a young man smitten with her now, or the magistrate who'd been to war, seen much violence, and done little to catch the real culprit?

Had Pamela been out seeking entertainment last night, and if so, with whom? That question now seemed relevant to St. Sevier's difficulties.

"Do you believe St. Sevier killed Miss Faraday?" I asked as we turned to retrace our steps.

"He is so charming..." Miss Bellamy said wistfully. "But then, aren't the worst villains always charming?"

"This is not a Gothic novel." Besides, Gothic novels required incessant storms, sniveling villains, fortune tellers, and dark castles, none of which were to hand. "A man could lose his life and see his family ruined. A woman is presumed dead. I genuinely want to know who you think sought to harm Holly Faraday, because Monsieur St. Sevier does not, to my mind, number in that group."

Miss Bellamy paced along the stream bank for a few yards before stopping to stare at the water burbling past.

"Monsieur was furious with Papa, my lady. Furious with all the papas hereabouts. In the churchyard, Monsieur was always polite, and my own mother sought his advice about her rheumatism, but he was angry. You could tell he was angry. We can be backward, I know that, but what is more backward than refusing to enclose common land? Papa says that's not only backward, it's treasonous."

Treasonous for a landowner to do as he saw fit with his own acres rather than bow to the collective greed of his neighbors? To me, St. Sevier's exercise of choice was the essence of the property rights English law went to such lengths to protect—for Englishmen.

"Your father makes accusations of treason, but what do you say, Miss Bellamy?"

She scooped up a pebble and tossed it into the water, causing rings to ripple out across the surface. "A doctor would know all sorts of ways to kill a woman."

More of her papa's vintage bile, or perhaps a theory on loan from the Belle Terre housekeeper.

"A gamekeeper, a butcher, or *any* former soldier would also be skilled at ending lives, but I don't see anybody from those walks of life enjoying Mr. Freeman's dubious hospitality." If Freeman's questioning of the gamekeepers had resulted in any useful information, he'd not shared that with me.

"Papa says Monsieur's guilty."

"Your father says that loudly, at every opportunity, though he has yet to present any reason why a man of means and standing—a dedicated healer—would harm a young woman whose greatest crime was nothing more than swimming naked with her friends after sunset. You share in that villainy, and yet, I find you and her sisters wandering the woods without escort, which suggests you do not fear to become St. Sevier's next victims."

"Freeman won't let him go before the inquest. Monsieur would scarper to France, and then Freeman would look a fool. Men hate to look foolish."

For a backward country miss, Elizabeth Bellamy exhibited a fair degree of common sense, when she wasn't quoting her father.

"Then you don't think Holly has merely staged a prank and nipped off to Town?"

Miss Bellamy tossed another pebble into the water. "I wish she had, my lady, but she hasn't."

Sebastian had said something to make Thetis laugh, and when

she laughed, she lost her nervous air. She was not pretty, but she could be attractive. Could she be jealous enough to kill a sister who stole all the attention? Could she and Selene have conspired to remove Holly from competition for Giles Bellamy's attention?

Now who was conjuring Gothic novels from thin air?

CHAPTER TEN

We wandered back to join Selene and Mr. Freeman, who sat side by side on a boulder, apparently discussing some famous chess game.

"A final question for you, Miss Bellamy," I said as we waited for Sebastian and Thetis to catch up to us. "Where are your horses?" She wore a riding habit, and she'd mentioned the lack of a groom, but I saw no trusty steeds.

"We always leave them up the trail, closer to the part of the wood that borders my papa's land. Horses *do things* that draw flies, and flies are exceedingly nasty. We also don't want our horses neighing at the approach of other riders and signaling our precise whereabouts. We enjoy swimming after sunset, but we aren't completely lost to modesty."

Yes, they were, if they were swimming naked when St. Sevier or any other gentleman could come upon them. I had to admit, though, that tying the horses elsewhere was shrewd, not a precaution I would have thought to take.

The young ladies curtseyed their farewells to us a few moments later, and when I expected Mr. Freeman to undertake the inspection of the stream bank that had occasioned this excursion, he instead resumed his perch on the boulder.

"The young ladies obliterated any possible trace of evidence on this side of the stream," he said, scowling at the undergrowth. "One wonders why, precisely, they had come looking for mushrooms in this location, this early in the day, on this specific occasion."

"We ought not to underestimate them," I said. "They are hiding something."

Freeman turned his frown on me. "What makes you say that?"

"Morels went out of season weeks ago, sir. Then too, Miss Bellamy claimed that they never brought their horses this close to the pool, but rather, tied them nearer to Bellamy property. If Holly was found here—note the conditional—then her horse would have been tethered well out of sight. You did not report that the horse arrived back to her barn without a bridle, or with her reins snapped off, such as can happen when a tied beast panics."

Freeman's scowl had faded to puzzlement. "You think whoever harmed Holly turned her horse loose?"

"Or Holly took a fall. That explanation makes much more sense than accusing St. Sevier of murder merely because he remonstrated with a young lady who was behaving scandalously on his property. Every parent in this shire doubtless disapproves of how Miss Faraday and her friends behave."

Freeman smiled and rose. "They do, but they also take a certain pride in having raised young women of substance. Selene would have made a talented code breaker—she's that well-read and that mentally tenacious. She's also an unconventional thinker, which is an asset to a code breaker."

He ambled toward the horses as he continued his discourse. "Elizabeth Bellamy took over her father's books five years ago, and between her and Giles, Anthony finally gave up the sheep, probably in the nick of time."

"And Thetis?" I asked.

"A keyboard virtuoso, not that she can perform publicly. She and

Holly are—were—much in demand to play duets at any local gathering, though. Thetis longs to study music in Paris, where young ladies have more options than they do here, but her parents won't hear of it."

Sebastian checked my mare's girth, though we were less than a mile from The Gauges. "Did Holly Faraday have a particular skill?"

He boosted me into the saddle with an ease that spoke both of his fitness and of our familiarity. Sebastian had been boosting me into saddles since I'd ridden ponies, and for whatever reason—my condition, St. Sevier's peril—his display of courtesy caused me a pang of sentiment.

Overwhelming tenderness, homesickness, I knew not what to name it, but the emotion was deep and private. He was willing to risk that St. Sevier's son would inherit the Dunkeld title and all the wealth that went with it simply because I might need a husband.

Freeman climbed onto his horse with surprising grace for a man with only one arm at full strength.

"You ask me about Holly," he said, taking up the reins. "The Faradays have no sons, and Holly became her papa's darling. He is our master of foxhounds, but Holly has the instinct for where to cast the pack, and when they are running riot, she can ride circles around any man in the shire, which is saying something. We've former cavalry among our number, though most of them are long retired and —I might add—no challenge at all over a chessboard."

"I gather Selene can hold her own?"

"She's beaten me more than once, and I suspect she's pulling her punches." He spoke with genuine admiration, though I doubted he'd conveyed that admiration to his opponent.

Nor did he seem particularly vexed that she'd lied to him, straight-faced—the ladies had not been searching for morels. She had then apparently changed the topic from a murder inquiry to a subject sure to distract the king's man from his stated purpose.

Sebastian climbed into Hannibal's saddle and led the way back to the bridle path.

I let my mare amble along beside Freeman's gelding. "Did Miss Selene have anything to say regarding who might wish her sister harm, or what Holly was doing alone in the woods at dawn?" I asked.

"She said Holly has been increasingly bold of late, but the young ladies are agreed that nobody should ever swim alone. I don't believe they fear drowning, but rather, fear what would happen to a woman on her own should the wrong sort of man come by."

More shrewdness. With a witness to back her up, a young lady's accusations of harm might carry weight. Her word alone, pitted against a man swearing his innocence, would see her branded a liar and a flirt who deserved any harm that befell her.

I applauded the fairly recent development in criminal law that maintained that the accused was innocent until proven guilty. That singular point of jurisprudence might save St. Sevier. And yet, women were not innocent until proven guilty. They were convicted of low morals, dishonesty, stupidity, hysteria, and all manner of faults by virtue of gender alone.

Those thoughts occupied me as we made our way in silence from the wood.

"Did you learn anything of interest from Elizabeth Bellamy?" Freeman asked as we crossed the lush green expanse of the deer park.

"Mostly a general impression," I said. "The young ladies took a certain pride in Holly's forthright nature, even though they did not confront her on some of her more unkind comments or actions. The same dynamic springs up at girls' schools, where a pack leader is granted latitude, but whispering about her behind her back creates a sort of cohesion in the ranks. I assume the military had echoes of the same trait."

Freeman nodded. "I was removed from most of it, being consumed with an arcane and pressing task. Dunkeld probably saw much jockeying among the officers for approval from generals those same officers considered dunderheads."

Who was the general in this case? Giles Bellamy, as the most eligible bachelor? Why wasn't Freeman cast in that role? All of

England suffered a paucity of bachelors and husbands thanks to the Corsican's rapaciousness, and Freeman was comely, landed, respected, and well mannered.

Selene had certainly offered him a brilliant smile to go along with her lies.

I had much to ponder as we rode into the stable yard, and I wanted privacy with Sebastian while I pondered it. He had disclosed nothing of his conversation with Thetis, and he had a perspective on Pamela Bonaventure that I lacked.

"I'll wish you good day," Freeman said, touching a finger to his hat brim after Sebastian had assisted me to dismount. "I'm sorry our outing yielded no further insights into who might have wished Holly Faraday ill."

"Oh, but it did," I said. "By the admission of her closest friend, she was a disgrace to her upbringing, a threat to any young lady with marital aspirations, and reckless in the extreme, wouldn't you say?"

"I would," Sebastian muttered. "Goading her sisters to swim naked by moonlight, eschewing a groom no matter the hour, directing the hounds in the hunt field... I admire her independent spirit, but the local society doubtless accounts her six kinds of bad example. St. Sevier, who only visited his property to manage it, had no cause to quibble with her beyond any landowner's objection to trespassers intent on a frolic. Every parent in the shire, by contrast, doubtless despaired of her."

"She is deserving of justice nonetheless," Freeman said, a bit severely.

"I agree," I said as Freeman aimed his horse in the direction of the park, "which is why I wonder where you are off to when questioning the staff at The Gauges was supposed to figure prominently on your morning schedule."

I smiled sweetly at him—he had the grace to look chagrined—and took Sebastian's proffered arm. As we made our way from the stable yard, I heard Freeman yelling for a groom to please come fetch his gelding.

"Are you in need of rest?" Sebastian asked as we strolled back to the house, arm in arm.

"I am in need of answers."

"I heard your conversation with Freeman, about jealousy in the ranks. I hate to think that some young lady is willing to kill for a better chance at Giles Bellamy's hand."

I gestured in the direction of the bank of rhododendrons. "Might we enjoy the fresh air a while longer, my lord?" Later in the day, I would call on the vicar, though the vicar's wife was my objective.

We passed down the shady path, birds flitting overhead, sun slanting through the towering maples. The Gauges was a gorgeous property, even if the house could have used a little more dusting, and conduct in the servants' hall was apparently less than respectful. The grounds, by contrast, were lovely, and the stables would be the envy of many a squire. Pamela had once told me that she genuinely mourned her late husband, still, years after his death, and I believed her.

She was not a happy woman, but this property should have been as much consolation as any widow could wish for.

We reached the clearing, and I settled onto the bench, which at this hour was in shade. "You can joke about young ladies desperate to secure a match, Sebastian, but to them and to their parents, matrimony is very serious business."

"Emphasis on the business," he said, coming down beside me. "At least from the perspective of the parents. These young ladies don't strike me as very fanciful either."

Young women, by reputation at least, were supposed to *be* fanciful—I certainly had been—but I shared Sebastian's opinion of The Gauges's neighbors.

"A lady who fails to find a husband is a charity case for life," I said. "One who marries well is fixed for life, and one who marries a cruel man is doomed for life."

Sebastian took off his top hat and set it on the bench beside him. "You are saying matrimony is a life-or-death proposition for a girl whose family has modest means. Don't marry me because you are desperate, Violet."

I had thought much about Sebastian's proposal since he'd left me the previous night. He had seen to the heart of the matter immediately: I was already fiercely protective of my child.

For myself, I could dodge outright scandal by claiming to spend a year traveling on the Continent, but there would be talk. When a widow undertook an extended journey for no reason other than her own diversion, there was always talk, even if she was chaperoned by four aunties, two uncles, a doting brother, and a brace of mastiffs.

And if heaven were benevolent, I would bear a child, which would fuel more talk, no matter the story I concocted to explain the addition of an infant to my household.

For me and even for my family, the talk did not signify—much. My father was an aging rake whose flirtations were excused because he hailed from an earlier generation. My two unmarried brothers were certain to marry well, if they bothered to marry at all, because they were the offspring of an earl. My oldest brother was apparently already supporting one illegitimate son.

But for *my* child, my choices mattered, especially if I bore a girl. My decisions would matter as well for my unmarried cousins and my nieces.

"I am not desperate," I said.

Sebastian rested his arm along the back of the bench. "You want to discuss the matter with St. Sevier, not only because he is the father of your child, but because he is your confidant of choice. You also don't want to burden him with a concern he can do nothing to address and one—might I had—which he had a hand in causing. Finally, you are worried about how the whole business will sit with Ann, who might arguably have two reasons to hate you now instead of one, and hatred is not a sentiment you will bear with ease."

This recitation reminded me that long ago, before St. Sevier had become my confidant, Sebastian had had that honor.

"Ann and I do not hate each other. If anything, we are respectful. I poached on her preserves unwittingly. She unwittingly exposed me to heartache. What matters is that St. Sevier must survive to play some role in the life of his offspring—all of his offspring—assuming my travail concludes well."

Sebastian squeezed me in a gentle, one-armed hug. "The child will be obnoxiously healthy, Violet. You are not drifting about London Society, deeply vexed by a philandering sophisticate who failed to treasure your devotion. You are hale, vigorous, and happier than you were as Belmaine's wife."

Sebastian let his arm rest around my shoulders, and the contact felt good—fortifying and steadying. He'd been an affectionate boy, which had meant much to a girl whose menfolk had had no use for her.

"I am in good form, you are right about that." My robust health was largely the result of Hugh St. Sevier's guidance, badgering, and inspiration. "I want a country home, Sebastian. A respite and a haven."

"My family owns some islands in the Inner Hebrides. If you seek only a respite and a haven, you could disappear there for years, nobody the wiser. My aunties would get you settled, and our people are loyal. When you returned to Society, or to your manor house in the south, nobody would know where you'd been or how you had acquired a young ward."

Women did not have wards, but they did have godchildren. They had second cousins left orphaned. They took in foundlings.

"You are offering me options. Thank you." Though those options meant illegitimacy for my child, for which that child would never thank me.

"I could not abide the notion that someday you might resent becoming my marchioness."

Sebastian was proud. I liked that about him. "You would not resent that St. Sevier's child inherited your title?"

The air was soft, the breeze mild, the birdsong a lovely lullaby. I closed my eyes, wanting the peace of the moment to sink into my heart. I had a friend in Sebastian. A dear, gallant, sensible friend. That was a boon I'd not enjoyed for too long when he'd gone off to war, and I had married at my father's direction.

"I never wanted the damned title," Sebastian said. "The title is why I was parted from my family in childhood, subjected to the whims of a lot of prancing, priggish tutors determined to beat the burr out of me. The title is why my own aunties look askance at me. 'Too long among the heathen English,' they say, as if I've contracted a wasting disease."

"The title is why I got to know you," I murmured, closing my eyes. "If your uncle hadn't sent you south, we would never have met."

"A singular consolation. Are you falling asleep?"

"I am resting my eyes. I did not sleep well. Too much on my mind. My former fiancé faces the noose, and I face motherhood."

Sebastian muttered something in Gaelic. My last coherent thought was that if he and I married—a purely theoretical sort of *if*—I would have to learn his native tongue. He referred to me by all manner of terms— *mo charaid, mo chridhe, mo ghràidh*—and for all I knew, he was calling me names reserved for fools and sluggards.

I woke much refreshed—and plastered to Sebastian's side—when Ann St. Sevier called out to us from across the clearing. As she approached, I could see that she, a woman of notable reserve, had been crying.

"Walk with us," I said, for we needed to find a place where no obliging bushes might hide an eavesdropper. Whatever Ann had to tell us, the news was clearly bad.

∾

Sebastian offered Ann his arm, and she accepted his escort, which I took for a symptom of her upset. We followed the path away from the house and stable yard and came upon another, larger clearing. The rhododendrons rose to at least fifteen feet here, and across a patch of grass much in need of a few hungry sheep sat a tidy half-timbered cottage.

The structure was too commodious to be a pensioner's home, having two floors and an abundance of mullioned windows. Roses vining all about the front porch completed a fairy-tale picture of the snug woodland abode drifting quietly into the mists of enchantment. A steward might be given such a house, or a very lucky gamekeeper or head gardener, though the place was in want of maintenance.

I could not see this part of the property from my windows, enclosed as it was in trees. Perhaps this was the dower house, out of sight but close enough that servants could come and go easily from the main house.

In any case, nobody appeared to occupy the dwelling. No flowers adorned the window boxes or porch steps, the grass desperately needed scything, and on this lovely day, nobody had tied back a single curtain. The cottage had a timeless quality, as if a touch of magic would keep the roses eternally blooming and the birds forever singing in the surrounding wood.

"I asked the grooms to saddle your horses," Ann said, "because I want to show you what I found back at Belle Terre."

"Freeman is at The Gauges," I replied. "He will doubtless be informed of your arrival. Should he see what you are about to show us?"

Ann paced off a few yards through the long grass. "I don't know. My instincts say no, but my instincts have been notably in error on occasion."

Such as when those instincts had prodded her to abandon her French husband all those years ago? "What have you found?"

"Proof of an assignation, at least." She closed the distance between us, the skirts of her habit dragging through the overgrown grass. "Belle Terre is as self-sufficient as Hugh could make it. We don't have our own blacksmith, and we buy some of our candles, but in many regards, it's an old-fashioned estate."

My family seat, Derwent Hall, was the same sort of property, where the old ways were still the best ways, to hear most of the staff tell it.

"And the significance of this self-sufficiency?"

"We have a cheese cave," Ann said. "It's big. Hugh showed it to us when we first arrived, because it's the sort of place Fiona might discover on her own. Hugh has had the smaller passages bricked up, though. Fiona can't get lost there."

I wanted to take Ann's hands and shout at her to get to the important part, but she was a mother. To her, Fiona's safety would always be the important part.

"Go on," I said as Sebastian appeared to study the cottage.

"I went to the cave this morning—it's not that far from the house."

The summer morning acquired an ominous chill. "Did you find a body?"

Ann shook her head. "No, but somebody was there. Two somebodies, at least."

Sebastian peered at her. "A maid and a footman?"

"You have to see it," she said. "The cheese is all along one wall, in a sort of birdcage arrangement. The cave is not locked or gated, but nobody has any reason to go there except Belle Terre staff."

"In fact," I said, "nobody has any *right* to go there, except the owners of Belle Terre or their staff upon direction."

Ann made a face, suggesting the rights of the Belle Terre property owners were more often honored in the breach. "I want you to see what I saw, because I do not trust my own eyes."

"Has somebody been using the cave for a trysting place?" Sebastian asked.

"That is the logical conclusion," Ann replied, "if the tracks I noted were those of a man and a woman. One set of boot prints is larger and deeper than the other, and they are well away from where the cheese is aged."

When we returned to the stable yard, Biddle led out a gray mare for me. She was elegant and rangy, probably a prime goer in the hunt field.

"Artemis isn't everybody's cup of tea," Biddle said, stroking a hand down the mare's neck. "She takes a tactful hand, if you know what I mean. Missus keeps her as a guest horse—Mister were quite attached to Artemis—but not too many ladies care for spirit in a mount."

"I'm sure Artemis and I will get on famously."

He looked unconvinced, but led the horse to the ladies' mounting block. The mare stood calmly while I lowered myself into the saddle, then she tried to dance away as soon as I had my foot in the stirrup.

"Settle, madam," I said pleasantly. "Biddle, you may release the reins. Artemis and I will have a civilized chat about our respective roles, and all will be well."

Sebastian boosted Ann onto an elegant bay mare, then swung up onto Hannibal.

I had not ridden a spirited mount for years, but as a girl, I'd been intent on keeping up with my brothers. Aurora, the mare who'd taught me so much, had never been shy about stating her opinions. I'd soon learned that when it came to footing, distances to a fence, or hidden hazards, her expertise was superior to my own.

Biddle stepped away, his expression a testament to polite skepticism. "She likes a loose contact, ma'am," he said. "You pull on the bit, and she'll pull right back twice as stoutly."

"I know the type," Sebastian said, gathering up Hannibal's reins. "Ladies, shall we be off?"

Sensible horsemen knew that somebody at home should always be apprised of the rider's destination, no matter how trivial the excursion. We neglected to observe that bit of protocol, and Biddle watched us go in silence.

The cheese cave sat a good fifty yards off any bridle path, the opening a yawning gap in the wooded hillside. I did not care for caves generally, having had a very bad experience as a child with one of the priest holes at Derwent Hall.

Sebastian took down a lantern Ann had apparently left lit earlier in the morning and held it high as we entered the cave. The scent was of damp earth and chalk, but the space was, as Ann had noted, large. The ceiling soared at least twenty feet overhead, the lantern's shadows flickering along the walls like dancing spirits.

A good distance back from the opening on a shallow ledge about two feet above the cave's natural floor, wire-enclosed shelves held wheels of cheese, the rinds progressing in color from white to a mottled brown. The cheese added an astringent note to the cave's scent.

"They probably found flint in here in the old days," Sebastian said, considering the pale stone walls. "And they certainly found shelter from the elements."

"Somebody else found privacy in this cave." Ann walked past us to the far side of the cave. "The footprints are over here. Please bring the light, and mind where you step."

Moving farther from the mouth of the cave sat ill with me, but I rounded a bend into the deeper reaches of the cave.

"There," Ann said, pointing to the ground along the far wall. "Boot prints. My housemaids don't wear boots, they wear house slippers. A dairymaid or laundress might have come this way, but the smooth sole suggests a lady's riding boot."

Sebastian knelt, setting the lantern on the floor. "You can almost see the maker's mark on the larger footprints. Not Hoby."

Hoby, bootmaker to four royal dukes and—more significantly— His Grace of Wellington, ran the premier London cobbler's shop. He did substantial business by mail, sending out instructions for how to measure the foot and accepting payment by post for the finished product. Any rural gentleman of means could wear Hoby boots and many of them did.

"If not Hoby, then who?" I asked.

Sebastian bent low and moved the lantern. "Looks like... Dern?

They're a French firm, if I recall. The proprietor is an émigré..." He knelt up and peered at Ann. "Does St. Sevier use them?"

He did. I held my tongue because I had no business knowing such a thing about Ann's husband.

"Wherever possible," Ann said, "Hugh patronizes the émigré businesses. I don't know about his boots in particular, but I know his general thinking on the matter. He says the émigré is likely to do better work and charge less because his business must compete with established London firms."

"It might not be Dern," Sebastian said, rising. "London has a hundred bootmakers and cobblers."

I lowered myself to my knees and peered at the boot tracks. The D of the maker's mark was clear enough to me. "The lady's boots have no identifiable mark, suggesting the boots were resoled locally."

Sebastian gave me a hand up. "You also think it's a lady's riding boot?"

I carefully placed my foot parallel to one of the clearest tracks and bore down. My imprint was narrower than the older one, but the same length and nearly the exact same contour.

"Riding boots have no tread," I observed, "because the wearer has no need for traction on slippery ground, and because the boot must easily come free of the stirrup. The pointed toe aids in locating the stirrup with the foot if the stirrup is lost. That certainly looks like a riding boot to me."

"Hugh rode out after supper at least twice a week," Ann said miserably. "I do not mean to imply that he would be unfaithful, but how many men in these surrounds will patronize a French London bootmaker?"

"My glovemaker is French," Sebastian said. "St. Sevier's reasoning, about the lesser establishments offering the better bargain, has merit. I buy my champagne from a former cavalryman who's French on his mother's side. I buy all my claret from a Frenchman. If St. Sevier was in this cave, that in no way proves he did violence to Miss Faraday."

True enough, but right now, that was not the point.

~

I marched up to Ann and took her by the arms. "St. Sevier would never be unfaithful to you. If he meant to betray his vows, he'd betray them with me. From the moment he grasped that you yet lived, he has steadfastly refused anything approaching impropriety with me."

Ann regarded me by the dim light of the lantern. "You have refused impropriety as well, my lady."

"We are of the same mind. Vows are vows. You made the effort to travel hundreds of miles to introduce Fiona to her father, so you must be in agreement with us as well. Your husband is honorable, and while I admit the evidence is damning, we are in a cave. No wind or rain disturbs this place from year to year, and those tracks could be months old."

"We have to ask him about them," Ann said, gaze on the maze of tracks, "and do it when Freeman isn't listening at the nearest keyhole."

Freeman, whatever his other faults, apparently did not listen at keyholes.

Sebastian bent to pick up the lantern. "Send a note 'round to Freeman telling him you'll bring fresh clothing by for Monsieur before the inquest. Insist on a few minutes alone with your husband, but don't balk if Freeman observes you from a distance. Assume he can understand any language you use and assume he can read lips."

Sebastian could be ruthless. I liked that about him too. "I don't know as we've discovered anything of material interest here," I said, wanting to be away from the darkness and the implications of those boot prints. "Dern likely has hundreds of patrons, Hugh owns this property, and perhaps he was down here with the cook."

"Cook is roughly fifteen stone," Ann said. "Those are not her boot prints. They aren't mine either, in case you're wondering. My left foot is larger than my right, and both of the smaller set are the same size."

I peered again at the impressions in the dirt, and something caught my eye. "Sebastian, may I have the light?"

He passed it over, and I again knelt. I could not decipher what about the tracks was bothering me, then I raised the lantern, hoping to reveal some additional detail.

"What's that?" I leaned closer, my gaze on a streak darkening the pale wall of the cave.

"Dirt?" Ann asked.

"Could be." Sebastian took the lantern and held it higher, revealing what looked like half a handprint—the heel and four fingers.

"Compare that to your own hand, my lord," I said.

Sebastian's handprint dwarfed the pattern on the wall, but my own hand nearly matched it.

"I know what you're both not saying," Ann muttered as we moved toward the mouth of the cave. "That might have been a muddy handprint, and it might have been made by blood. Do we tell the magistrate? My staff knew I was coming here this morning, and Freeman will know I retrieved you from The Gauges."

"Freeman has been neither forthcoming nor thorough in his investigation," I said. "You say nothing until you've discussed the matter with your husband. You cannot be made to testify against St. Sevier, so you are the person who must raise the topic with him."

"You and the marquess can be made to testify," Ann observed as we emerged into dappled sunlight. "My housekeeper, the grooms... They will all stick their oars in, and Hugh will not dignify their accusations with a rebuttal. This is my penance, for not searching for him longer, for leaving him, for not troubling to learn if he had any family... I am to lose my husband just as I've found him, and Fiona will have a convicted felon for a papa instead of a brave French physician."

The thought popped into my head: *At least Fiona isn't illegitimate.*

"Tell St. Sevier how you feel," Sebastian said, untying Ann's horse and assisting her to mount. "Tell him that you blame yourself, that you do not want to lose him, that Fiona needs him to clear his name."

"I have, when last we visited him. He smiled and kissed me and said he would not trade the past few weeks with me for all the champagne in France. I am to tell Fiona he loves her. I wanted to hit him."

So did I. "There's such a thing as having too much honor." I approached my mare, who displayed a nervous eye and pricked ears. "Artemis, you will stand like a lady and cease your silly displays."

The mare deigned to hold still long enough for me to climb aboard. Sebastian stroked her shoulder while I arranged my skirts.

"She tests you," he said. "Be careful with her."

"She tests me because few are worthy of her respect. If Freeman should ask, what was the purpose of this outing?"

Sebastian swung onto Hannibal's back in one lithe move. "We were doing as half the shire apparently does and enjoying the sylvan beauty of Belle Terre's woods. Madame is not well versed in cheese-making and wanted your opinion on the aging of her cheddars."

"Might we enjoy the lanes on our return journey?" I asked. "Artemis has had enough of mincing along the bridle paths. Clearly, nobody gives her the opportunity to gallop."

Sebastian sighed, and Ann's gaze bounced between us. I knew what troubled Sebastian. I was with child, and a fall from a horse was the last thing a woman in my condition should risk. But soon, I would be denied the saddle altogether, and I craved the exertion of a more energetic ride.

"We will canter," Sebastian said, "and you will not goad Hannibal into racing."

Sebastian led the way back toward Belle Terre's stable yard, but before we reached that destination, Ann drew her mare even with Artemis.

"You call him Sebastian." This was a question.

"I've known him since I was a child."

"Ah."

"He proposed to me last night."

I wanted to tell her the rest of it, but felt Hugh should hear the news first. But when would I have an opportunity to tell him? Once the inquest was held, Freeman could bind his prisoner over for the assizes with very little additional effort.

"This grows awkward," I said.

"You and I passed awkward a good twenty miles ago, my lady, dragging Hugh between us. My husband—to whom you were all but engaged—is accused of murder, I'm hundreds of miles from home, and a vindictive jury could see me and my daughter turned out penniless on the road."

"I would never allow that, and neither would his lordship."

"Whom you call Sebastian."

I did not want to like Ann St. Sevier. I could reconcile myself to respecting her and even to wishing her well, but liking...?

Botheration. "I suspect I am with child, and the only possible father is your husband. I am torn between informing him of this development in hopes that he will abandon his posture as a noble victim of injustice and the temptation not to burden him with what could only be a further regret."

Sebastian, riding some yards ahead, either did not hear us or was pretending not to hear us.

Ann muttered something in her native language. "If we had concocted a farce with every convolution ever penned by the most gifted playwrights, we could never have contemplated the situation we find ourselves in now."

"Verily."

"Hugh will deduce your condition," Ann said, "if he lives. He can use a calendar, he knows all about midwifery, and a marquess cannot keep his firstborn child's date of birth a secret for long."

"I haven't agreed to marry Dunkeld."

Though watching Sebastian ride before us, his posture so straight, I was tempted. The intimacies were awkward to contemplate, but not... not *impossible*. As a girl, I had fancied Sebastian mightily. He had been the first fellow I'd practiced kissing, an occasion he bore with stoic humor. As a widow... I had been very glad to make my peace with him.

A conundrum for another time.

"Shall I tell Hugh your news?" Ann asked.

"I don't want to ask that of you."

"He will take it better coming for me. I can scold him for feeling guilty and assure him you are in great good health and tell him of Dunkeld's proposal. He will take comfort from Dunkeld's offer, even if you do not."

"I do. I very much do."

"Come in for tea," Ann said. "The servants will report that our outing was social, and we can work out our next steps."

I wanted to protest: *Thank you, no, I must be getting back to The Gauges... Very kind of you, but I hadn't planned on revealing my deepest secret to my former fiancé's wife just yet...*

Except that Ann was being more than decent, the servants should be thrown off the scent, and a cup of tea sounded wonderful. I agreed to stay for tea, and as we walked with Sebastian up to Belle Terre's terrace, I had occasion to ponder why that should be.

Ann had said that we could never have contemplated the situation we found ourselves in now, and her word choice was appropriate. *We* were in a situation—her, me, St. Sevier, Sebastian, even Fiona and the baby.

We were in that situation, and it was dire and complicated, and refusing a cup of tea from St. Sevier's wife would have been churlish and silly. I enjoyed a good cup of tea, and though my admission was a trifle grudging, I departed from Belle Terre well aware that Ann St. Sevier was in her way a likeable sort too.

CHAPTER ELEVEN

Sebastian and I took the lanes back in the direction of The Gauges, and when I gave Artemis her head, her speed was astonishing. She was by no means a young horse, but her ability suggested bloodstock in her lineage.

The exhilaration of an all-out gallop cleared the worry cobwebbing my thoughts and resulted in a far more relaxed mare.

"That was not a canter," Sebastian said as Hannibal puffed along at the walk beside us. "And now we will have to walk for at least a mile lest the grooms be wroth with us."

"Artemis is not wroth with us. I believe she feels like herself for the first time in ages." I patted her sweaty neck, and she tossed her head. Bad manners, that, though in a stallion, it would be referred to as high spirits. The fidgets, nothing more.

"Let's meander through the village," I said. "I'd like to drop in on the vicar of St. Ivo's."

"Any particular reason?"

"General reconnaissance. The shepherd of the local flock hears much, and his wife hears even more." Sebastian had no rejoinder for that, and I peered over at him. "What aren't you saying?"

He gave Hannibal a loose rein, and I did likewise with Artemis. We were to daunder along until the horses had recovered their wind.

Sebastian gazed about us, at fields and pastures ripe with high summer's bounty. "I rode dispatch."

"For a year," I replied, "which I gather is some sort of record. Felix says you took foolish risks and became something of a legend. You never failed to come through the lines, despite frequently cutting through territory held by the French."

"Being Scottish helped, though being Irish would have been a greater boon. The French well knew that not all Britons were enthralled with Mad George and his causes."

I took a moment to parse that politesse. "You're saying you could have passed for a deserter if a French patrol came across you." I wish I knew more about Sebastian's years at war. They had changed him, turned an imaginative, quiet boy with a kind sense of humor into a taciturn and serious man. The humor was still there, but buried deep beneath pragmatism and privacy.

The kindness was there too, thank God.

"I did pass for a deserter more than once, and the ruse served me well. I also learned something of a tracker's skills, because I needed to know how recently a patrol had passed through a crossroads or how long ago the French had stopped to water their horses."

And this was relevant, because... "The tracks in the cave told you something that you did not mention in front of Ann."

"I am not expert enough to know how the humidity or darkness in a cave would affect footprints in soft earth, but the tracks were very clear—clear enough to show most of the maker's mark on the larger prints. No minute deposits of dust obscured the outlines."

This was not good news. "They were fresh."

"Again, I cannot say how fresh, but they certainly were not made months ago."

Drat and blast. "Were they made days ago?"

"Possibly. As you noted, even if St. Sevier met a woman in that cave, that does not prove he subsequently did that woman—or another woman—harm."

"Hugh is not a sneaking sort of man. He will honor a confidence to the grave, but he would never engage in clandestine assignations." Even as I said the words, I recalled the nights—wonderful at the time, bittersweet in hindsight—when he'd shared a bed with me.

We had exercised discretion when indulging our passions, not the same thing at all as sneaking, was it?

"St. Sevier is canny," Sebastian said. "If some woman wanted privacy to consult with him in a medical capacity, the cave would do. The entrance isn't readily observable from the bridle paths, and he could meet her there with nobody the wiser. The young ladies of this shire charge about on horseback heedless of propriety. They would not hesitate to meet with a physician privately."

"Hugh would hesitate to meet with them." Or would he? "He is all but reviled by his neighbors and well knows the danger untoward rumors can present." But then, even Mrs. Bellamy had appealed to him for use of his medical expertise. Had some other lady—or gentleman?—sought St. Sevier out privately? Freeman had confirmed that no physician bided in the neighborhood.

Any apothecary could supply mercury pills to a man suffering the Covent Garden ague, but what country gentleman would want his apothecary knowing of that affliction?

"An assignation or medical consultation does not explain a muddy handprint," I said. The morning after a hard rain, the cave floor had been more or less dry. No moisture seeped down the walls either.

"Murder explains a *bloody* handprint," Sebastian replied as the bell tower of St. Ivo's came into view.

"St. Sevier is no murderer."

"Perhaps not, Violet, but he is keeping something from us. We know he views the role of physician as a sacred trust. I expect he regards the roles of husband and father with equal seriousness."

The village green was a peaceful expanse of grass measuring

about two square acres. On market days, tinkers, shopkeepers, and craftsmen would offer goods and services to the local families. Everybody would catch up on the gossip and the news, the posting inn would do brisk business in the common, and children would play away the daylight hours with neighbors.

St. Sevier sought to protect that way of life, where a village was a village, not merely the dormitory for the pensioners and day help from the nearest stately home. All over England, "progress" had resulted in empty villages and abandoned markets.

Was that really what the Squire Bellamys of the shire wanted?

I probed around the edges of that question when we were ushered into the vicar's cluttered parlor by Mrs. Abel Cooper. Mr. Cooper, pipe in hand, greeted us genially and directed his wife to fetch the tea tray with all due haste.

Cooper fit his role, right down to kindly blue eyes, a thinning mane of white hair, and the ruddy complexion of a man used to paying calls in all weather. I'd put his age at a vigorous, lanky fifty and his intelligence at far more shrewd than he appeared.

And if he was shrewd, his comfortably rounded, be-shawled and bespectacled wife was probably shrewder still.

"You are visiting the Widow Bonaventure," Mr. Cooper said when the tray had been brought, and Mrs. Cooper had poured out. "We are glad to see her having company. She seems to prefer to pop up to Town or take in the house parties."

"Not that we're criticizing her," Mrs. Cooper added, passing me my cup of tea. "She was quite devoted to her husband. We all held Mr. Bonaventure in considerable esteem."

"Not high in the instep," the vicar said. "Though he went up to Town and got himself an heiress for a wife, in the grand tradition. Still, I do believe it was a love match, for all the young lady came from means."

Ancient history was not exactly what I'd come to hear. "Mrs. Bonaventure speaks quite highly of her late spouse. Do you suppose she might consider remarrying?"

"She'd best be about it, if that's her plan," Mrs. Cooper said, serving Sebastian his tea. "A woman's looks don't last forever, and heaven knows we have an abundance of young ladies without spouses in our congregation."

"Tilly," the vicar said, "her ladyship might like a tea cake or two."

"Vicar is scolding me," Mrs. Cooper replied, holding up a plate of tea cakes to me. "I'm only being honest. Mrs. Bonaventure is the closest thing we have to a grand lady hereabouts, and while she's gracious and pleasant and all that other whatnot, the young ladies need husbands. In my opinion, our grand lady ought to be assisting in that endeavor."

"A widow often loses touch with greater society," I said, taking one tea cake. "If you are looking to Mrs. Bonaventure to host the young ladies in Town, her connections might not be all that useful."

Though, Pamela's connections included Sebastian, a marquess, and I'd seen her tooling through Hyde Park at the fashionable hour and at the opera. Compared to Mrs. Cooper's resources, Pamela had marvelous connections.

"If Mrs. Bonaventure doesn't want to go up to Town, why not hold a house party?" Mrs. Cooper went on, gathering momentum, even as she offered the cakes to Sebastian. "Our girls need to meet *eligible* young men if they are to marry well, and Mrs. Bonaventure is their best hope, my lady. She's connected to some title or other on her mother's side, and clearly, she has means."

"Matilda." The vicar's tone was pleasant. "Perhaps your husband would enjoy a tea cake or two, hmm?"

"Lady Violet grasps my concern, Mr. Cooper." She held the plate out to him. "It's fine for the gents to ride to hounds and gossip about the crops from year to year, but Giles Bellamy is the only marital prospect worth mentioning. He's too busy nipping up to Town to hobnob with his university chums to bother settling down."

And to think I'd been mentally venerating the bucolic traditions of English village life not a quarter hour before.

"Could a lovers' quarrel figure into Miss Holly Faraday's demise?" I asked.

The vicar choked on his cake, and Sebastian stared pointedly at his tea, but really, Pamela's inability to find husbands for a lot of hoydens on horseback was not germane to St. Sevier's situation.

"Men," Mrs. Cooper said. "Such delicate sensibilities. You will think me unkind, Lady Violet, when I tell you that Holly Faraday was galloping toward ruin. She was headstrong, outspoken, and convinced of her own brilliance. Her father indulged her, her mother deferred to her, and she set a bad example for sisters and friends alike. She did not deserve a bad end, but she courted one all the same."

"Matilda, our guests will think us unchristian."

"Speaking of unchristian sentiments," I said, "does everybody share Squire Bellamy's enthusiasm for tossing St. Ivo's poorer families off Belle Terre's common land?"

Sebastian winced at that question.

"No, they do not," Mrs. Cooper said, sitting up straighter. "The shopkeepers and laborers are in accord against the notion, and Vicar preaches as often as he dares on who-is-my-neighbor and thou-shalt-not-covet. Our last living was in the Midlands, and we've seen what happens when village folk are reduced to trudging to the cities to find work. Children go into the factories when they should be learning their letters, gin obliterates decency, and young people with any gumption leave for foreign shores."

I liked Mrs. Cooper. She'd summed up the realities of "progress" for the poor in a few sentences. "What does Mr. Freeman think of the squire's ambition?"

The lady chose then to pour her own cup of tea, which I took for a willingness to toss the conversational ball to her husband.

"Mr. Freeman keeps himself to himself," Mr. Cooper said. "He's friendly enough to his neighbors, but war can knock the frivolity right out of a man. Got out of wool and into corn. Went to four-crop rotation when some of the older men are still using the three-crop system.

Hasn't become obsessed with breeding bloodstock. Plays a fine game of chess. He even occasionally beats Selene Faraday."

"She got the brains in that family," Mrs. Cooper said, "and spare me that I'm-disappointed-in-you look, Abel. If her ladyship has met Selene, she will doubtless agree with me."

"My love, I could never be disappointed in you. The Lord could not have given me a finer helpmeet, nor one better suited to ensuring my ongoing humility."

"How I do treasure you for that humility, Mr. Cooper." They regarded each other with fine good humor, and Mrs. Cooper held the plate of cakes out to her husband.

Without warning, tears again threatened. The Coopers were a *couple*, a man and woman joined by long years together, high mutual regard, humor, acceptance, affection, respect... They were partners in a way I had never been with my own husband. I wanted what they had for myself, but doubted I would ever have it.

Sebastian watched me, his gaze knowing, his mouth curved in a faint smile. He winked at me, the gesture so subtle I almost missed it.

"I will make it a point," he said, "to suggest to Mrs. Bonaventure that her lovely house should see more company. Freeman's murals are unique, and The Gauges is beautifully situated."

That was the precise right thing to inspire Mrs. Cooper into beaming at us all the way to the vicarage's front door. She and I stood on the porch chatting as Sebastian and the vicar crossed the green to the livery where our horses had been stabled.

"I will be honest with you, Mrs. Cooper. I am in the area at the invitation of Madame St. Sevier. She believes her husband is innocent of all wrongdoing and in danger of a miscarriage of justice."

"I hope he is innocent," Mrs. Cooper said. "I cannot tell you how tedious it is for Abel to be called to one sickroom after another, and all we can offer to alleviate suffering are herbal cures, patent remedies, and prayer. Prayer has its place, but the good Lord has seen fit to give us learned men and women in addition to the lilies of the field."

"You *want* St. Sevier to reside at Belle Terre?"

"He won't, not after this. We have much illness hereabouts, my lady. Some of it is simply poverty, old age, or excessive drink, but we are also prone to human frailties and failings. I like Monsieur St. Sevier—he seems devoted to his wife and daughter—but again, I hold the minority opinion. Abel says I excel at that, and my husband is an astute observer of the human condition."

"If St. Sevier did not kill Holly Faraday, who did, and where is the body?" Or where was a young lady recovering from what might be a very serious injury?

"Good questions, my lady. Here come the gentlemen with the horses. Enjoy your stay at The Gauges, as much as you can under the circumstances. I will be besieged by callers now that you and yonder marquess have graced us with a visit."

"If you hear of anything that might aid St. Sevier's situation, will you let me know?"

"I will, my lady. Holding a minority opinion becomes a habit, but it's a habit based in truth. Abel relies on me to be honest, and I rely on him to be kind."

The men came directly across the green with the horses in tow. I hoped Sebastian was learning something useful from the vicar. I wasn't sure my call at the vicarage had been productive, but I had been reminded that marriage could be a partnership, and that was worth remembering.

Sebastian recounted only pleasantries exchanged with Mr. Cooper, and we returned to The Gauges's stable yard in thoughtful silence. The peace of the summer day was broken by a raised female voice coming from inside the barn.

"Not Pamela," I said. "She would never..."

Elizabeth Bellamy stalked out of the stable and came to an abrupt halt. "My lady, my lord." She popped two perfunctory curtseys. "I hope you've had a pleasant outing?"

"Very," I said as Sebastian assisted me from the saddle. "We called in at the vicarage after taking tea at Belle Terre. What brings you to The Gauges?"

Biddle stalked out of the barn and took Artemis's reins, then collected Hannibal as well. A fulminating look passed between him and Miss Bellamy.

Oh. *Oh.* "My mare was thirsty," Miss Bellamy said. "I'll be on my way now that she's been watered."

Utter balderdash. The stream in the woods was readily available for any rider whose mount was thirsty. Sebastian performed the mounting-block courtesies, and Miss Bellamy was soon cantering off across the deer park.

"Intrigue and drama on every hand," Sebastian murmured, watching the young lady disappear into the trees. "The inquest is tomorrow, and we seem to be no closer to any useful answers."

"While we have an abundance of questions." I was struck by an impulse to slip my arm around Sebastian's waist and merely lean against him. That would not do, not here in the stable yard.

Time to change out of my habit, re-pin my hair, and make myself presentable for another luncheon on the terrace. I was staring at the ground, steeling myself for those tasks, when I noticed a boot print near the mounting block.

I took the few steps necessary to put my foot down next to Miss Bellamy's perfectly clear track.

"Miss Bellamy's boot is a trifle wider than my own." In other words, her footprint was a very close match with the ones we'd found in the cheese cave. Moreover, we had just heard her having what appeared to be a lovers' quarrel with a fellow who could not possibly be courting her—could he?

Had Biddle flirted too much with Holly Faraday? Had Holly insulted Biddle's lady love once too often? I recalled again how emphatically Biddle had warned me to stay away from the woods and to mind my own business.

Gracious, life in the country could grow complicated.

～

"St. Sevier said he hasn't been to the cheese cave since he showed it to Fiona and me." Ann kept her voice down as she and I promenaded on the green. The inquest would begin in less than a quarter hour, and every soul in St. Ivo's was apparently to attend.

Vicar and Mrs. Cooper were on the steps of the posting inn, chatting with Giles and Anthony Bellamy. Sebastian was escorting Pamela into the inn, where the proceedings would be held. In a typical murder inquest, the body would be on hand for an examination by whoever served locally in the capacity of coroner.

But then, nothing about the situation was typical. "Did you tell St. Sevier that he's to be a father again?" I asked.

"The London solicitors were hovering, and the time wasn't right."

When, pray tell, was the right time to convey such a development? "Within seventy-two hours, St. Sevier might well be bound over for the quarter sessions. He'll be removed from Freeman's home, tossed in with a lot of English suspects. Some of them have committed violent crimes, others are deathly ill, and still others bear a rabid hatred of the French. If he's to avoid that fate, he needs to help us fight, Ann."

"Does he want to avoid that fate?" Ann sounded despondent rather than philosophical, and I was reminded again that she was far from home, facing possible penury in addition to unavoidable scandal, and she was the mother of a small child.

"Let's take a bench. Freeman has yet to arrive with the suspect." I had no wish to join the crowd inside, no wish to see the local folk entertained by injustice.

"Freeman won't bring Monsieur in the front door," Ann said. "Hugh is to be sneaked through the kitchen, supposedly for his own safety, but such theatrics only make him look more guilty."

In theory, St. Sevier was just another witness at this stage of the proceedings. In fact, Ann's conclusion was spot-on. No other "witness" would arrive in the magistrate's custody, or be hustled through a back entrance into the common.

"Why do you think Hugh is surrendering without a fight?"

"To win security for me and Fiona. If he confesses, the jury is more likely to follow the usual course and account him a pauper."

Logical and entirely like St. Sevier to think in those terms. "Any other reason?"

"I knew him in Spain, my lady. He was fanatical about his calling. He'd take all manner of risks to bring the wounded in from the battlefields, and he would go toe to toe with colonels and generals when he thought their decisions medically foolish."

"You describe a hero." Or an imbecile. A dead physician killed by a French sniper could save no lives, but any healthy private could bring bodies in on a stretcher.

"Two of his brothers died in battle, one in an English army camp. He saw every wounded soldier as somebody's brother, father, son, or husband. Hugh would not rest until... Suffice it to say, he can be heedless of his own welfare. I've seen him spend forty-eight consecutive hours in the surgery tent, nap for two hours, then go right back to work. He would make no compromises for the sake of his own convenience or the sake of his own life."

"Might he believe he ought to have died along with his brothers?"

Ann gazed across the green to the inn, where people were filing up the steps as if in preparation for divine services.

"In France, conscription was the normal practice," she went on. "Nobody had a choice. If France called—and her demands for soldiers were relentless and voracious—any man was honored to serve, and any man could be promoted for his courage and skill. Hugh's brothers had no choice, and that tore at him. He'd been sent to London for safekeeping, while they..."

Had not been ripped away from home and family at a young age, cast into the keeping of strangers in a strange land, cut off from all contact with loved ones... No wonder Sebastian and St. Sevier understood each other so well.

"Is this part of why you left him? You did not want to be widowed again?"

She gave me an odd smile, as if I'd guessed a riddle that had long eluded her own understanding.

"My first husband took the king's shilling," she said, "knowing that disease or battle might see him dead. He was brave, also reckless, but then, nineteen-year-olds are put in uniform for precisely those qualities. Hugh was... He *is* like no other man I've known. That he'd put himself in the way of French bullets—or English bullets, for that matter—was obscene."

She rose, and I had no choice but to walk with her across the green. "When I remonstrated with Hugh, when I begged him to be more careful, he would smile and tell me I'd be well provided for in the event of his death, which made me all the more angry with him. I was coming to care for him too much. A child was inevitable if we continued on the course we'd set. I left him, but without realizing I'd deserted too late to avoid the calamity of motherhood."

All of this had unfolded before Ann had reached her legal majority. At that same age, I'd been breathlessly anticipating marriage to Freddie and consumed with cataloging my enormous trousseau.

"Was motherhood a calamity?"

Ann stalked up the steps to the inn's front doors. "Fiona has saved my life, my heart, and my soul more times than I can count. Now I'm hoping she can save her father's, but that hope is faint and weary, my lady."

This recounting of St. Sevier's history helped me better understand the charm he deployed as camouflage and his unwillingness to entirely abandon a medical calling despite having the means to live a life of idleness.

"You are saying he would never take a life intentionally," I observed as Sebastian motioned us over to seats at the side of the room.

"Hugh risked his life countless times for strangers and enemies, my lady. Hugh is the last person who should ever be suspected of murder."

More people crowded in, for this was high theater to most of the village denizens. Some of them might have been genuinely interested in seeing justice done—a young woman was missing, after all—but most were seeking a diversion, something to gossip about. The publican, who would do a brisk business before and after the inquest, was only too happy to accommodate them.

"The Williamses, Grants, and Donohues have turned out in force." Ann nodded to a ragged assortment of people standing along the opposite wall.

A contingent of The Gauges staff was also on hand, Biddle not among them.

The din in the room rose around us until Sebastian nudged my arm. "He's here."

Freeman emerged from the kitchen entrance behind the bar, St. Sevier behind him. I was relieved to see that Hugh's hands were not bound, and he was turned out as a fashionable country gentleman ought to be.

I saw the moment when Hugh's gaze lit on Ann. His smile was slight and pained, but he bowed to her as courteously as if they were acquaintances meeting in the churchyard. He nodded to me and to Sebastian, then took a seat set apart from the table Freeman occupied.

The physician Freeman had recruited from the next shire spoke first. In quick, clipped tones he reported that based on the quantity of blood described at the scene, the young lady's competence in the saddle, and her continuing absence, foul play was extremely likely. Moreover, "if a man knew where to strike," a single hard blow to the head could cause death.

At Freeman's request, the doctor confirmed that Hugh—*being a physician*—would know exactly where to land such a blow. Freeman's medical authority went on at ghoulish length about the brain twisting, blood gushing into the skull, and the humors congesting, which no doubt delighted the gallery enormously.

I began to regret attending, then Sebastian, who had at some point taken my hand in his, squeezed my fingers gently.

Right. *Noli desperare.*

Giles Bellamy averred that he'd come upon Miss Faraday's dead body, but Freeman was careful to establish that Giles had never checked for a pulse, never listened for a heartbeat, never even touched Miss Faraday to know if her skin was warm or cold. Further, Giles admitted that he had no medical training, was terribly upset at the time, and had never, in fact, seen any dead human bodies prior to the occasion in question.

All Giles could say was that he'd seen Miss Faraday prone and unresponsive to his shouting and that he'd then gone for the magistrate. When he'd returned more than an hour later, the clearing had been empty.

Holly Faraday's father testified that his daughter had been in the habit of riding the bridle paths at all hours and had done so safely *for years.* The import of that last statement was that she'd done so safely as long as St. Sevier had not been in residence at Belle Terre, of course.

Anthony Bellamy added that St. Sevier had been extremely wroth with him in the churchyard, threatening to take stern measures if Bellamy did not cease making the very reasonable request to enclose the last of the common acreage.

"I have never seen a man so violently gripped by temper," Bellamy said, "and over mere words, and reasonable words uttered on holy ground."

A righteous murmur of agreement went through the gallery, though the Williamses, Grants, and Donohues looked disgusted, and Mrs. Cooper regarded Bellamy with a flat stare.

Bellamy waited for the room to come to order before delivering his final blow: He'd heard St. Sevier and Miss Faraday arguing in the woods, heatedly, just days before the young lady "came to grief."

The London solicitors did what they could after that performance.

Why had Giles gone to that clearing at that hour of the day? Had he been planning to meet Miss Faraday, perhaps? Had he and Miss Faraday quarreled recently?

Had Anthony Bellamy raised his voice at St. Sevier, and had Bellamy himself been the party to broach the topic of the enclosure? So *Bellamy* had started an argument on holy ground, hadn't he?

If Bellamy was so certain Miss Faraday and Monsieur were arguing, what precisely were they arguing about? Perhaps about Miss Faraday, Miss Bellamy, and other young ladies of the shire making free with Monsieur's woods in an improper manner?

An amused murmur went through the assemblage at that question, while Bellamy was left to sputter and glower and sniff.

St. Sevier was called to testify, though by law he could have declined to incriminate himself—which was, of course, precisely what a culprit would do. He reported that he and Miss Faraday had had words about the risks she and her friends took when they trespassed at all hours in his woods. He had no issue with their use of the bridle paths, but they *strayed* far from those byways.

His concern was for their safety, and his concerns had apparently been justified.

The room got quiet at that delicate scold, and I took heart. Happy to seek entertainment at another's expense these people might be, but they were not convinced St. Sevier was the guilty party. Moreover, most of those in attendance were adults with children of their own.

The young ladies had been overly indulged, and every person in the room knew it. St. Sevier had been expressing a reasonable fear for their wellbeing, something nobody else had done.

When asked if he had anything more to say on the matter, St. Sevier looked thoughtful. "Any absentee property owner must accept that, despite a vigilant gamekeeper, poaching is a possibility. Mr. Bellamy's discovery of blood by the stream suggests my concerns in this regard are well-founded too. Poaching is a violent undertaking and carries serious consequences if discovered. I pray Holly Faraday did not find herself in the wrong place at the wrong time observing the wrong sorts of activity."

That Banbury tale was worth airing.

Poachers were like fairies—ever handy for explaining the inconvenient. If the population of game was declining, poachers—not a loss of habitat from enclosures—was responsible. If game had grown more wary, poaching—not excessive shooting—was to blame. If somebody's livestock had been turned loose beneath a quarter moon, clearly poachers setting up a distraction—not drunken youths—were at fault.

Why not blame poachers for Miss Faraday's situation?

And yet, the crowd in the common appeared to take St. Sevier's suggestion seriously. Poachers were a fact of rural English life, much as press-gangs had been a fact of life in the port towns for generations.

Though poaching struck me as precisely the sort of crime Freeman and the local landowners would delight in prosecuting vigorously.

I was beginning to hope the jury might return a verdict of death by misadventure when the Belle Terre housekeeper was called to testify. Mrs. Dorrance was a woman of perhaps thirty-five years, with refined features. She wore her blond hair under a lacy cap and held herself as if her post at Belle Terre were tantamount to the same appointment at the Court of St. James's.

Everything about her, from the confection passing for her cap, to her gliding walk, to her imperial disregard for her neighbors, proclaimed her to be a superior exponent of the domestic class.

She took the appointed chair with all the pomp of a queen holding court, even to arranging her skirts and shawl at tedious length. I was prepared to hear that her employer and his wife had occasional spats—more proof of an ungovernable temper?—or that St. Sevier had threatened to sack some footman for slacking.

The reality was far worse: Mrs. Dorrance had seen Holly Faraday meet with a gentleman in the Belle Terre cheese cave. She could not say for certain who the gentleman was, but he was dressed as a gentleman in top hat, riding boots, and riding jacket. He arrived on foot from the direction of the bridle path, staying for a good half hour and waiting until the lady had departed first before leaving himself.

The only other detail Mrs. Dorrance could add was that when she'd made her way, *shocked and aghast*, back to Belle Terre, St. Sevier, attired for riding, had been coming up the path from the stable, and his air was most distracted indeed.

In that moment, if somebody had handed me a riding crop, I would have cheerfully striped Mrs. Dorrance with it until my arm fell off. St. Sevier, by contrast, sat as calmly as if he were attending some lecture on the medical uses of roses.

The jury returned a verdict of murder by person or persons unknown. They might as well have ordered Freeman to lead St. Sevier away in chains.

CHAPTER TWELVE

"Something bothers me," Sebastian said as we trod the same path Ann and I had taken earlier in the day.

"I am a temple to botheration," I retorted. "Freeman was surprisingly evenhanded, the solicitors did yeoman work on cross-examination, and the jury—without a body—is determined to see St. Sevier hanged nonetheless."

"But they can't," Sebastian said. "The problem all along has been the Campden Wonder. Freeman can hold six inquests, but conviction for murder without a body isn't possible under English law."

I was so busy mentally thrashing Mrs. Dorrance that Sebastian's words took a moment to make sense. "Then why detain anyone? If no conviction is possible, why create all this uproar, and what is the Campden Wonder?"

"I am no lawyer," Sebastian said, "and English law and Scottish law are different, but I put my question to the solicitors just now, and they were quite clear on the matter. Some old case from the 1660s, now referred to as the Campden Wonder, resulted in three people being hanged for murder. The head of the household went off one evening to see a tenant and didn't return, though a few of his effects were found along the roadway the next day."

"Was he murdered?"

"The jury said yes. The family employed a mother and her two grown sons as house servants, and one of the sons implicated his mother and brother. He testified that the three of them had schemed to rob their employer, had been stealing from the household for some time, and had decided to do him in."

Sebastian's gaze lit upon Ann and St. Sevier, who tarried beneath an oak beside the blacksmith's establishment. Freeman stood some paces off, pretending to study St. Ivo's tower.

"As magistrate, would Freeman know of this case?" I asked.

"Apparently not, but then, magistrates are not lawyers. They are simply landowners handed a few manuals and charged with resolving petty squabbles. Freeman has never investigated a murder before."

I could not fathom what Freeman had been about at the inquest. He'd been more thorough and fair than I'd expected. But had his efforts been simply for show, a sop to his conscience when he'd known all along what the jury would do?

"So how does hanging three culprits bear on St. Sevier's position?"

"Sometime after the executions, the supposed victim came jaunting along, spouting a tale of having been abducted and sold into slavery to some Barbary potentate. He was hale and whole and most assuredly alive."

"Have the London solicitors discussed that case with Freeman?"

"I asked them to do exactly that before they return to Town tomorrow."

St. Sevier and Ann embraced, and such was the difference in their heights that Hugh could rest his cheek against her hair. They held each other, and never had I seen a more eloquent portrait of tenderness and despair.

"Why is St. Sevier not free?" I asked. "If he cannot be convicted, why charge him?"

"*That* is what bothers me. Is this all just a tactic to harass him into selling Belle Terre? A warning that even he dare not ignore. This time, the charges can't result in a conviction, but they can certainly see him jailed, tried, and humiliated. They can see his wife and daughter covered in scandal. As a warning shot across the bow, a murder trial serves nicely."

St. Sevier's posture as he embraced Ann was protective, and I thought of all the times he had interceded on my behalf. He'd risked his life for me, pulled me from a raging river, and pulled me from equally dangerous depths of melancholia. He'd reluctantly escorted me through the solutions of several potentially dangerous puzzles, ever unwilling to see me in harm's way.

"He's protecting somebody, Sebastian. I know it."

"His first obligation is to his wife and child."

His wife and *children,* did he but know it. "He might well be thinking Ann and Fiona managed handily without him for years. She left him rather than fall in love with him, but I do believe her strategy failed."

"Are you jealous?"

I inventoried my feelings as Freeman glanced over his shoulder at a husband and wife who might well never hold each other again.

"She has been through hell, Sebastian, and some of that hell was of St. Sevier's making. He rescued her, but he also subjected her, a new widow, to unpardonable neglect and anxiety. I hope he is a different man now, but I suspect he's not different enough."

I decided in that moment that I, too, would have a private word with Hugh St. Sevier, and I might bring my riding crop along to the interview. For whom would St. Sevier offer his life? I thought of the Grants, Donohues, and Williamses, standing silent and grim along the wall of the inn's common room. Their children were ill. The wives could not afford medical care in childbirth.

St. Sevier was refusing to petition for an enclosure act because of them and the other families like them.

"If St. Sevier is hanged," I said, "what happens to Belle Terre?"

"The property either passes to his heirs, if the jury finds he's a pauper, which juries have been routinely doing for convicted felons for years. They do this both out of compassion and out of disgust for the crown's excesses. In the alternative, the estate reverts to the crown. After a suitable interval of looting for royal purposes, Fat George will probably award Belle Terre to some lackey in exchange for an unrepaid loan."

And the royal looting would take years, during which nobody would bother petitioning Parliament for the right to enclose the land because both the petition and the fencing cost dearly. Years, during which the poor families of the shire could run their chickens and pigs over those acres, or graze enough sheep to spin the wool needed for decent clothing.

"I must speak with St. Sevier."

"Now is not the time, Violet."

"We are out of time. Freeman could bind him over tomorrow morning, and then St. Sevier is off to be killed by jail fever or in some contretemps among his fellow prisoners."

Sebastian took me by the wrist, for I'd marched off in the direction of the couple under the oak.

"*Not now.* For all you know, Ann has also conceived St. Sevier's child. They will never hold each other again, never touch each other again."

"And I cannot permit that tragedy to befall them. Wash your hands of me if you must, go back to London or Perthshire and try to forget this situation if you can, but I will not rest until I've reached the bottom of it."

Sebastian gazed down upon me, his expression unreadable. Just when I thought I might have to make a scene, he smiled.

"Stay here." He stalked past me and approached Freeman, while I waited some yards off, wishing I had my riding crop.

Puzzle pieces taunted me from every direction. Where was Holly Faraday, or where was her body? If she was seriously injured and had no physician to tend her, she was as good as dead. Then too, if getting away with murder in England was as simple as hiding the body, why was Freeman so intent on seeing St. Sevier charged with the crime?

Who was St. Sevier protecting?

Who had met with Holly Faraday in that cheese cave—if not Hugh?

What if the objective was, as Sebastian said, to prompt Hugh into selling? Who in the area could afford to purchase the property at even a bargain price?

The answer hit me like a wave of vertigo: *Freeman could.* He was clearly one of the best set-up in the neighborhood, and he'd know exactly how to wrest every drop of revenue from so much acreage. If he intended to buy the place—from Ann, should St. Sevier be hanged, or from St. Sevier, should the murder charges come to naught—then an appearance of evenhandedness in his investigation was mandatory.

Sebastian stood in conversation with the object of my suspicions. Freeman glanced at me, then at St. Sevier and his wife, who had stepped apart, but continued to hold hands. Freeman nodded, though he did not look happy.

And neither did Sebastian.

"I will escort Ann to Belle Terre," Sebastian said when he returned to me. "You will be permitted to ride with St. Sevier in Freeman's coach back to Freeman's manor. He will ride on the box, and I will collect you when I've seen Ann safely home."

"Thank you." I did not want to know how Sebastian had effected this minor miracle, but I hoped the process had involved putting the fear of a powerful Scottish marquess into Freeman. More likely, Sebastian had appealed to romantic gallantry, which—oddly—had no place in my motivations at present.

"There's something else, Violet."

"Bad news." What could be worse than seeing St. Sevier charged with murder?

"Earlier today, the solicitors explained to Freeman the general holding resulting from the Campden Wonder: No body means no murder conviction. Freeman inquired of them if kidnapping charges also required the production of the kidnapping victim, and the solicitors allowed as how it did not."

"Then St. Sevier will be charged with *kidnapping* Holly Faraday?"

"Freeman's considering it."

Which meant Hugh would be hanged, though no proof had been produced of either murder or kidnapping.

"Take Ann home," I said, "and have a look at the boot prints of as many of her domestics as possible, starting with the lovely and catastrophically disloyal Mrs. Dorrance."

❧

"How many days have we spent sharing coaches, St. Sevier?" I fired my question at him as he moved to the rear-facing seat in Freeman's commodious conveyance. "You need not stand on ceremony with me at this late date."

"I am not standing on ceremony, my lady. I am sitting such that the lovely aspect of your countenance is fully before me and not obscured by your millinery. How are you?"

Oh, to hear that slight, tart, confiding note in St. Sevier's voice. To know his spirit was not yet vanquished and his gallantry in fine repair.

"Do not attempt to cozen me, sir. I am trying to save your life, while you are making your final arrangements. What in God's name are you about?"

"You need not save my life, Violet, though I thank you for the sentiment. I am in no danger of being convicted. Some old English case which demands a body be produced to prove murder protects me."

"And if somebody stumbles across that body in your wood tomorrow?"

He frowned. "It's been nearly a week. In high summer, human remains are hard to hide for that long."

Ever the physician. "Unless they are buried only to be found by some squire whose lurchers take to digging in the wrong spot. Unless those remains have been weighted with rocks and sunk in your stream, only to be discovered when the next rainy week befalls us. Who are you protecting, St. Sevier? If you know who killed her..."

"If *you* had killed her, or Ann had, I might hold my peace, or doubt the evidence of my own eyes, but you did not, and Ann did not. Fiona, for whom I would gladly lay down my life, is also no killer."

"Then you don't have any suspicions? You were truly arguing with Holly Faraday about her disregard for propriety?"

"Not propriety, my lady, *safety*. The village boys think it a great lark to spy on the ladies at their evening pleasures in my stream. I've caught Bellamy *père* and *fils* on my land after sunset, which is an odd time to wander off the paths in a darkening wood. The grooms and footmen from The Gauges are frequently at liberty in the evenings, and I do not trust Mrs. Bonaventure to curb their mischievous impulses."

"This has to do with Fiona," I muttered, noting that for all St. Sevier's proper airs, strain showed around his eyes. "She has turned you up proper."

"This has to do with gentlemanly honor. Those women are at risk of harm, and they are too young and stupid to know it. Had they seen what fine English officers can get up to with a bit of liquor in them..." He stared past me. "I digress."

"Freeman is a fine English officer."

"He shares my concerns for the young ladies."

"Then he should arrest them for trespassing at your stream, if he can't arrest them for using the bridle paths."

St. Sevier focused on me. "Please suggest that to him. In several evenings of impressive chess, we have not discussed that topic."

"Are you protecting the young ladies?" I was flailing about for answers and thus asking questions nearly at random.

"My efforts in that regard have been unavailing." St. Sevier suffused that statement with all the arrogance a dispossessed French nobleman could cram into a single sentence, which was considerable.

"Who are you protecting?" I wanted to shout my query, but I stated it—again—calmly.

He scrubbed a hand across his brow and sighed. "What do you know of rickets, my lady?"

Ann had mentioned this affliction. "The poorer families suffer from it. Small children show the symptoms, and it results in bowed legs and shorter stature."

"Rickets *hurts*," St. Sevier said. "The simple act of walking, which ought to be any child's birthright, *hurts*. When the condition is severe, drawing a deep breath *hurts*. Wealthy children are seldom afflicted, while the poor are seldom spared. What does this tell you?"

What on earth was he getting at? "That diet might play a role in the disease?"

"Precisely. Diet and fresh air. The children consigned to the mines are never spared, while children along the coasts fare much better. A child in the mines subsists on potatoes and pork fat and rarely sees the sun, while a fisherman's offspring eat many varieties of fish and get plenty of fresh air."

The Grant children were not working in the mines. "What is your point?"

"Mrs. Grant has five children, and they are progressively more sickly. I have insisted that she dose them with cod liver oil, which has been shown to aid in the treatment of rheumatism, but she cannot afford even that remedy. She cannot afford a midwife, though the poorer women all do what they can for one another. To see that penury in plain sight and know that Bellamy and his ilk would happily take away what little those families have offends my honor."

And Hugh St. Sevier's honor was formidable. "It ought to offend anybody," though poverty in the midst of abundance was often excused by recourse to Scripture. *For ye have the poor with you always...*

"The young women of this shire," St. Sevier said quietly, "have nothing better to do than gallop around at all hours, gossiping and lamenting the lack of bachelors. I grasp that for them the situation appears dire. The poor families—their neighbors—face starvationr, cold, illness, and worse, and if I yield to Bellamy's tricks, those poor children will be dead within two years."

"St. Sevier..."

"My lady?"

Did he think to give those children a few more years foraging for nuts in his wood, a few more years of the occasional trout for supper, at the cost of his life? Would St. Sevier abandon his wife and child for limited gain, when he could instead simply employ the poorest families at Belle Terre?

Perhaps I did not know my former intended as well as I thought I did.

The coach rolled around a turn, and the movement sat ill with my belly. "If the welfare of children is what motivates your sacrifice, then you should know that I am to have a child."

St. Sevier regarded me in some puzzlement.

I tried again. "*We* are to have a child. I will see to it that Mrs. Grant and the other families have a steady supply of cod liver oil, warm blankets, and anything else they need, but in your crusade to better their conditions, please don't deprive your children of their father."

"A child?" For a medical man, he posed the question with a quantity of wonder.

"I needed some time to become aware of my own condition, but the signs are consistent."

He took my hand and held my knuckles to his forehead. The gesture was medieval and courtly, also entirely spontaneous. The smile he bestowed on me was full of tenderness and joy, and I was glad I had not left my news for another to convey.

"A child. Well, then." He kissed my fingers and gave them a squeeze, then released my hand. "Avoid strong spirits. Eat plenty of red meat, and don't skimp on your greens and fresh fruit and produce. No lowering diets, Violet. For God's sake, promise me that. Eat variety and eat *well*, rest well, and maintain at least moderate activity. The English know nothing about how expectant mothers should go on, so you must heed my advice to the letter."

I had ambushed St. Sevier, and handing out medical advice was one of many things he did well. He had retreated to solid ground, which proved that my news had affected him.

"Heed my advice as well, St. Sevier: Dying at the end of a rope for the sake of families who will be forced into Town despite your sacrifice puts the welfare of others before the welfare of your own children. I will not tolerate martyrdom from you, no matter how noble your wife is willing to be about the whole matter. If you know anything more than what you've said, you need to tell me now."

"Dunkeld would not thank me for involving you in my difficulties, my lady."

"Dunkeld has offered to marry me, and so far, he has been far more help solving the local difficulties than you have."

The coach slowed through another turn, and I knew we must be approaching Freeman's manor house.

"Violet, you will marry the marquess, please. I beg this of you when I do not beg even the Almighty for mercy. I realize the futility of telling you what to do, but I remind you that to cling to your independence when doing so will result in illegitimacy for the child is to commit the same error of stubbornness that you accuse me of."

I wanted to stick my tongue out at him. "I know."

We rolled along in silence, two people who had once been so joyously close and whose situation was now, as Ann had said, twenty miles beyond awkward. And yet, I cared ferociously for St. Sevier and knew that my well-being mattered to him too.

"I am glad about the child, St. Sevier. Worried, too, because of the miscarriages and because my baby will have a dunderhead for a father, but very, very glad."

The coach passed through high gate posts and into a grassy park.

"You are so brave," St. Sevier murmured. "A baby—of yours. Ann and Fiona do not need me, but they are my family, and now you... Well, you are my family, too, which pleases me. I can tell you this, my lady. Belle Terre's woods are not the peaceful forest they should be. The bridle paths are heavily used, but the traffic frequently strays from the paths too. My own staff watches me every time I take to the woods, and I was cautioned by no less person than Mrs. Dorrance against allowing Fiona to explore the property beyond the gardens."

"I do not care for Mrs. Dorrance."

"Ann wanted to sack her, but we cannot until my situation is resolved."

"Who was meeting Miss Faraday in your cheese cave, St. Sevier?"

The coach horses shifted from trot to walk, and the coachman called out.

"I have no idea, but if it had been me, Mrs. Dorrance would have said so. I might be protecting the poor families from eviction, but she is also protecting somebody."

A groom opened the coach door, and St. Sevier alighted before me, then offered a hand to assist me to step down.

"Freeman can charge you with kidnapping," I said, keeping my voice quite low. "The lack of a body doesn't stop him from arresting you and binding you over on that charge, St. Sevier. I'm sorry." I kissed his cheek and stepped back as Freeman climbed down from the box.

St. Sevier's gaze was bleak. "I suspected as much. I'm sorry too, Violet."

"Can you be a little happy as well?"

He bowed over my hand. "About your disclosure? I am worried, but also ecstatic, despite all. I am transfigured with joy." He offered me a smile that was anything but ecstatic.

The grooms escorted him to the house, the coach pulled away, and I was left standing in the drive with Freeman.

"Will you bind him over?"

"I don't want to."

And there was my answer: In the morning, in a day or two at most, St. Sevier would be arrested for a capital crime and cast upon the further dubious competence of *English justice*, a contradiction in terms if ever I'd heard one.

CHAPTER THIRTEEN

"Ann is preparing to return to Scotland if St. Sevier is bound over," Sebastian said as his coach pulled into The Gauges's stable yard.

"Shouldn't she be on hand for the trial?" I asked.

"Freeman says she cannot be forced to testify against her husband. She's free to take the child north at any time."

The coach came to a smooth halt. Pamela's grooms apparently knew better than to intrude even to the extent of opening the door, but I wanted fresh air, immediately. I unlatched the door and stepped down too quickly for Biddle to offer me assistance.

"If Ann is in Scotland," I retorted as Sebastian descended, "she cannot testify in his favor. She cannot stand by him as a reproach to the vultures trying to see him hanged. She cannot maintain his innocence to any who will listen."

"St. Sevier has asked her not to."

Biddle passed me my parasol, which I would have forgotten in my increasing upset. St. Sevier was prepared to die, and I could do nothing to stop his murder at the hands of the crown.

"He does not want her charged as an accomplice to this so-called kidnapping?" I nodded terse thanks to Biddle and turned to leave.

"Freeman would not dare..." Sebastian did not complete the thought. Freeman had dared much already. "Where are you going?"

"To the woods. I need to be someplace where I can use a great deal of profanity without giving offense." Someplace Hugh owned, someplace he had ridden when he'd sought peace and tranquility for himself.

"The inquest made it real, didn't it?" Sebastian said, stepping closer. "We could lose him."

I did not recall precisely reaching for Sebastian, but when his arms came around me, I tossed aside my parasol and clung to him. I stood in the circle of his embrace and frankly bawled like a disconsolate child.

I had never cried for my husband the way I carried on in The Gauges's stable yard. I didn't believe I had ever cried for anybody like that.

"St. Sevier is innocent, Sebastian," I said—more like croaked—when I could speak. "He's not perfect by any means. He's stubborn and proud and too honorable for his own good, but to think of him put to death for the sake of Squire Bellamy's next morning horse, or a trip to Town for a lot of silly young women... They need him here. He knows things—about fish oil and childbearing—and they will see him killed when all he's ever sought to do is save lives."

Sebastian held me, and never had a man's embrace brought me such comfort. I felt as if he willed into me a portion of his own steadfast courage and indomitable will. He murmured something to me in Gaelic, and though I had no sense of the meaning, he soothed my rage and frustration.

"Tomorrow is the Sabbath," he said. "Freeman won't hold any legal proceedings on Sunday. We have some time yet, and I have not given up."

I did not want to part from the consolation of Sebastian's arms, but I stepped back. "I told St. Sevier my news."

The stable yard activity went on around us, so I spoke very quietly. Sebastian's coach rattled off in the direction of the carriage

house. A sweaty, tired horse trotted in from the main drive, a groom
in the saddle. Biddle stood a few yards off, holding my parasol and
looking mortified.

"Biddle, be a good lad and take the beast," the groom called,
bringing his leg over the pommel and sidling to the ground. "I'm fair
knackered." He stood bent over, hands braced on his thighs, while
Biddle collected the horse's reins.

Biddle passed me the parasol and went about the business of
running stirrups up their leathers and loosening the girth. The
exhausted groom clapped Biddle on the shoulder, nodded to me, and
hobbled off in the direction of the house.

"That was a footman," I said. "That was a footman attired as a
groom." Pamela's male staff was remarkable for their good looks, and
that fellow had been a dark-haired Adonis. Moreover, he was away to
the manor house, when a groom would have slept above the stable or
carriage house.

"Maitland goes to see family on his days off," Biddle said.
"Travels nigh to London and back to see his auntie and cousins.
Missus allows it, provided his duties don't suffer."

Judging from Maitland's walk, he'd be moving slowly for the rest
of the day at least. "Please send my regrets for luncheon up to the
house, Biddle," I said as Maitland disappeared around a bend in the
path. "If I wanted to take Artemis out later today, could you have her
ready for me?"

Biddle petted the winded gelding on his sweaty neck. "She likes
you, Arty does. Missus has no use for that mare, but Arty took a shine
to you."

I doubtless looked a fright, and the cool and quiet of the woods
called to me, but I was pleased to have won Artemis's regard. I also
knew that Sebastian would accompany me on any mounted outing.

"Artemis has excellent training and plenty of bottom," I said.
"Why wouldn't anybody enjoy riding her?"

"Missus blames Arty for Mr. Bonaventure's death. Said if the
horse hadn't been so game, Mr. Bonaventure would never been

following the hounds in all weather. She said he loved that horse more than he loved his wife."

"Sorrow is three parts anger," I replied. "The mare is wonderful. I will gladly buy her if you think she's for sale."

Biddle scratched the gelding's ear, and the horse exhaled on an equine sigh, then shook all over. "She might be. You'd have to ask Missus and catch her in the right mood."

Sebastian took my parasol from me. "Would Mrs. Bonaventure be more likely to sell the mare to me?"

"Arty isn't up to your weight, milord. Not for the duration." That Biddle would remonstrate with a marquess spoke well for the groom's standing as an equestrian.

"I would see the mare given into her ladyship's keeping, lad. I'm asking about Mrs. Bonaventure's pride."

Sebastian knew Pamela as a society escort knew a woman. Biddle was in her employ, though, and his carefully blank expression conveyed volumes.

"She'd sell to a marquess," Biddle said. "I'd miss Arty, but she'll be happier with a lady who appreciates her."

"Then I'm off to ramble in the woods. I won't need my parasol, my lord."

"Best not walk in the woods right now, my lady." Biddle occupied himself untangling the horse's sweaty forelock from the bridle. "What with the inquest and all, you might not be the only person wandering about there."

That was an extraordinary observation for a groom to make to a guest, also quite sensible. Truly, the local populace had no respect for St. Sevier's rights as a property owner.

"No woods, then. I'll find someplace else to enjoy some peace and quiet."

Biddle led the gelding away, and I was reminded that he had not been among the crowd at the inquest. Somebody had to stay and mind the horses, and Biddle seemed to have the horseman's true calling.

"Shall I buy the mare for you?" Sebastian asked, ambling with me out of the stable yard.

"Yes, please. I will, of course, reimburse you, and cost is no object. That mare is going to waste here."

"You won't be able to ride much longer, Violet."

"For a time I will, and eventually I will be able to resume normal activities. The mare knows she's resented and tolerated at The Gauges, while I appreciate her. I will look forward to riding her when my confinement has passed."

He took my hand as we walked along, a presumption we'd grown comfortable with as adolescents. "You are determined to rescue somebody."

"I am determined to see justice done." I wanted to be away from the house as I recovered from my bout of the weeps, and I wanted time to think over the day's developments. Sebastian seemed content to wander hand in hand with me down the rhododendron path, past the clearing, and on to the fairy cottage.

"Hugh rescued me," I said as we settled on the steps to the cottage porch. "I was in a bad way, Sebastian. My family had no idea how bad, much less what to do about me." They had *never* known what to do about me, not even when I was being biddable and as well behaved as I knew how to be.

"I'm sorry you needed rescuing." He set aside his hat and looped an arm around my shoulders. "We might not be able to save St. Sevier, Violet. He seems damnably resigned to martyrdom."

I leaned against Sebastian, having at some point made the adjustment from familiarity with the contours of a tall, sturdy Scottish boy, to the more muscular frame of the adult Sebastian. He was an imposing specimen, and a good friend.

Could we manage as husband and wife? At one time, I'd fancied him madly, as a girl fancies a youth—the only youth—to show her respect and liking.

I let myself sigh, as that tired horse had sighed. "St. Sevier thinks that by resisting enclosure, he is standing between a dozen families and slow death in London. He is not wrong."

"He's not, which is why my family has had nothing to do with the clearances," Sebastian said. "We saw all too well what the result would be. The land overrun with sheep, the only wool we could sell of the coarsest quality, and our people scattered to the four winds. If those hardy breeds of sheep thrive in Scotland, they can thrive anywhere."

"Meaning the wool market was only a short-term source of profit?"

"Worse than that. The rest of the world was bound to start raising its own sheep, and those places that could raise better-quality wool would soon be shipping their product wherever demand for it was greatest. Scottish landowners would be left to once again make do on the orts and leavings of commerce, so we've shifted into shipbuilding, or those of us who can have made that shift."

"And those of you who can't?"

"Our land, which once boasted endless forests and the best fishing streams in creation, is now fit only for the rapine of sheep breeds that can tolerate our winters. Then the manufactories put even the cottage weaver out of business, and if our young people don't take the king's shilling, they emigrate to places where the land hasn't yet been ruined by stupidity and greed."

This was a discussion such as an engaged couple might have, about the situation occupied by the fellow's family and his outlook on the future. I found the change in topic a relief from the day's challenges, and even interesting.

"So how do the MacHeaths go on?" I asked. "If you did not sink your fortunes into wool, what does that leave?"

He gave me a one-armed squeeze. "I can support you, Violet. Have no fear on that score. My great-grandfather well understood that the only benefit to Scotland for giving up our sovereignty was access to English ports. He started building ships straightaway and was careful to replant all the timber he harvested. Wood grows slowly in the far north, but that makes it hard as hell and worth a pretty penny. My grandfather and uncle invested wisely, were prudent in their politics, and married wealth. We'll manage."

That *we* might have meant we MacHeaths, or we—you and I.

"St. Sevier begged me to marry you."

"Are you amenable to begging now? You never were as a younger lady."

"You were never very adept at groveling, was the problem. St. Sevier admonished me to think of the child, the same point I made to him as he prepares to die for children whose families are hanging on by a whisper in a good year."

"We should always think of the children," Sebastian said, "but if marriage to me will make you miserable, then it's not a solution. You've already endured one bad marriage, and it nearly killed you. Your happiness is important to me too, Violet."

Sebastian had never been one for fine speeches or lofty declarations, but he was unfailingly honest. Marriage to Freddie *had* become a tribulation, the magnitude of the burden obvious to me only when I'd finally set it down.

I had grieved for Freddie, taken too young, and so forth, but I had grieved as well for my innocence, for five years wasted trying to be a good wife to a bad husband. Not a terrible husband—I could have hated a terrible husband—but a selfish, heedless, faithless husband.

"Did St. Sevier tell tales out of school?" I asked, because Sebastian and I had been estranged during my mourning years.

"He did not, though your brother Felix has made some pointed remarks. St. Sevier worried for you, over a few brandies late at night. He worries for you still, as do I."

At that precise moment, my own worries were slipping from my grasp. I felt a catnap coming on and closed my eyes.

"And now we worry for him. I'm missing something important, Sebastian. Something obvious, something so obvious we don't notice it. Freeman has the means to buy Belle Terre, doesn't he?"

"Freeman has no need for more acres. He's doing splendidly on what he already has. I have wondered if our hostess doesn't covet Belle Terre."

~

I opened my eyes and sat up. "What makes you say that?" Sebastian's speculation about Pamela's possible involvement in St. Sevier's troubles had the ring of truth to it.

"Mrs. Bonaventure is the grand lady of the shire," Sebastian said, "with her pretty footmen, lovely estate, and London town house. She is invited to all the house parties and knows everybody. At the opera, her box is never without visitors, most of them single men. She married one of the few good catches in the shire and has lived comfortably ever since. If anybody in these surrounds would know how to go on at Belle Terre, she would."

I could well envision Pamela amid all that grandeur and elegance, and The Gauges's deer park marched with Belle Terre's woods.

"She would enclose the common acres, Sebastian. I believe Pamela buried her finest sentiments with her husband, and she would capitulate to Bellamy's carping for an enclosure act before the ink was dry on the deed."

My mind, drifting toward slumber a moment before, began to hum with questions. Did *Pamela* have the money to buy Belle Terre? Handsome footmen came dear, and a truly wealthy widow might be more inclined to entertaining, to holding house parties as opposed to frequenting them. She would at least entertain her neighbors, and yet, I had heard no mention of Pamela's reputation as a hostess.

Her wine cellar did not recommend her as such, and her menus were unremarkable. But then, I was a guest she'd not been expecting and would probably not bother impressing.

"Enclosing the commons would be expensive," Sebastian replied. "Miles of wall don't build themselves. Land doesn't clear itself. I'd be surprised if Mrs. Bonaventure could both buy Belle Terre and enclose the remaining common land. Her house is not... There's thrift, and then there's neglect. The public rooms are maintained, but other than that, the carpets need beating, the windows could do with a scrubbing. I suspect our hostess is somewhat short of coin."

I well knew what enclosure cost because my father had cited that factor as part of his reason for leaving some of his own land as common ground. I had not bothered snooping about Pamela's house, but now that Sebastian brought up the dust, the faded carpets, the dingy windows, my imagination seized on possibilities.

"If St. Sevier were hanged," I said, "and the jury was in the mood to deny the crown a prize, Belle Terre might well be available for a *chanson*. Ann would want to get rid of it, the sooner the better." I rose from the steps. "I need to get my hands on Pamela's riding boots."

Sebastian got to his feet as well. "Violet, have a care. You can't storm Pamela's dressing closet."

"What if it was Pamela in the cheese cave? We already know St. Sevier was there when he showed the place to Fiona and Ann. What if one day, he was lounging against that far wall, waiting patiently while Fiona counted all the cheeses, and the next, Pamela was in there for reasons of her own?"

"Then Mrs. Dorrance lied when she said it was Holly Faraday trysting in that cave."

"Why lie? Who has paid that housekeeper or threatened her, such that she all but put a noose around her employer's neck?" I began to pace, reminded once again that Belle Terre's housekeeper owed some allegiance to The Gauges's owner. The two households were in league. Were they in league against St. Sevier or simply prone to the rural sport of malicious gossip?

Sebastian took me by the wrist when I would have gone hotfoot for the house.

"Violet, don't go off half-cocked. Pamela will attend divine services tomorrow, and if you plead a headache, the house will be all but deserted for most of the morning. I will escort her and play the pretty in the churchyard while you will have a discreet look at her dressing closet."

I did not want to wait one hour, much less one day, to compare Pamela's boots with my own.

"Get a look at Mrs. Dorrance's boot prints too, Sebastian. I will give you my boot tonight so you can get a sense for the dimensions of my tracks. The prints in the cave were slightly wider but of the same general contour and length."

"And the left and right foot were the same size. I am not an idiot, Violet."

He was humoring me, which suggested he wasn't entirely of sound mind either. "I would not marry an idiot. As you noted, I tried that once. It did not end well."

He cocked his head, and I was abruptly aware that I was alone, in a secluded clearing, with a man who had proposed to me. A healthy, attractive, shrewd, determined man whom I had known and esteemed for most of my life.

"You fear that marriage to me will go as badly as marriage to your late fop of a spouse did."

Well... No. I feared marriage to Sebastian could go even worse than marriage to Freddie had. "Freddie Belmaine and I were never friends, Sebastian. I had hoped... but my hopes came to less than nothing. If I marry you, and we do not suit, I will lose..."

He waited, my hand in his.

What precisely was at stake should a marriage between me and Sebastian become unendurable? I could barely wrap my mind about the intimacies such a union entailed. I esteemed Sebastian, and in a general sense, I could appreciate that he was desirable, but the next step in the progression—allowing myself to desire him—utterly flummoxed me. He was desirable, certainly, but desirable *to me*, as a spouse?

And was I desirable to him?

All of that notwithstanding, if he played me false as a spouse, no matter how discreetly, I would be devastated, nor could I conceive of taking up with another man while I was married to Sebastian.

"What will you lose, Violet, if we become friends married to each other? Do you want a white marriage?"

A marriage without physical intimacy. I ought to leap upon that offer—if Sebastian was making an offer. And yet, I had thought myself absolutely through with intimate congress when my husband had died. Through with it and relieved to have my freedom from it.

Then St. Sevier had come strolling by, exuding endless patience and no little allure. When I had finally realized that we were attracted to each other, I had stipulated that I was willing only to dally with him. He had stipulated that he was pursuing me in hopes of winning my hand.

The ensuing *discussions* had been luscious and, for me, revelatory.

"I don't know precisely what I want." I wanted my freedom, and I wanted respectability for my child. I wanted independence, but I was no great fan of loneliness. "If I knew that..."

He stepped closer and framed my face in his hands. "I want to kiss you. May I?"

My heart began thumping, and not from lightheadedness. A kiss would tell me much, for better or for worse, as it were. We had kissed before. As a schoolgirl, I had recruited Sebastian for kissing practice. More recently, he'd surprised me with affectionate kisses in parting and greeting. Once last summer, when facing deadly peril, he'd given me a proper smacker on the mouth.

He was asking permission to kiss me now, and while the setting was bucolic, I still had a sense of facing peril. "You may."

A kiss could be nothing—a peck on the cheek, a perfunctory commonplace—or it could be the prelude to cataclysms. Sebastian began by slipping an arm loosely around my waist. I stood passive and abruptly all at sea.

Sebastian was a grand specimen, taller than Freddie, more muscular than St. Sevier. He bore the scents of cedar and sandalwood overlaid with a hint of leather. His touch on my cheeks was

light and warm and not like any other touch that had passed
between us.

"Close your eyes, *mo chridhe*."

"What does that mean?"

"My heart. Close your eyes, my heart."

"But you've been calling me that for..."

"Ages." He stroked his thumbs over my brows, a curious caress,
both relaxing and intimate. "Ages and ages. I'm nervous too, you
know. St. Sevier was doubtless a vast improvement over Belmaine,
and now I'm to contend with your memories of both. The one you
grieve for, the other who won your heart."

Sebastian pressed his lips to my cheek, slowly. I took in that
sensation while my mind tried to grasp the significance of having
been *my heart* to Sebastian for *ages and ages*.

"This isn't kissing, Dunkeld."

He ignored me, kissing the other cheek with the same madden-
ingly slow deliberation. By degrees, I realized that Sebastian would
not be hurried, and he would not allow me to simply endure his kiss.
We were to attempt this experiment together and without restraint.

Oh, very well. I sank my fingers into the hair at his nape, got a
good grip on him, and kissed him full on the mouth.

∼

I left Sebastian a good ten minutes later. He remained by the cottage,
pleading a need to think through the day's events in solitude.

The *day's events* would doubtless include our kiss. That kiss had
proved that in the years he'd been away, Sebastian had learned about
more than how to make war on the French. I stopped at the edge of
the clearing to behold him as he resumed his seat on the cottage steps.

His kisses were languid and bold, and his caresses... Blessed Saint
Andrew, when Sebastian smoothed his hand down my arm or along
my shoulders, I yearned to arch and stretch like a cat. The immediacy
of my physical response stunned me.

The man lounging in the summer sunshine was Sebastian MacHeath, companion of my youth and friend of longstanding, but he was also a stranger to me. A handsome, intriguing stranger who had handled me with confidence, skill, and—this flummoxed me endlessly—*tenderness*.

He regarded me across the clearing, his smile slight. "Nobody will know, Violet, and I'm not about to tell them."

So self-possessed, and I realized that was part of what troubled me. Sebastian the youth had been shy, perceptive, and playful. Sebastian the man was still perceptive, but nothing of shyness or boyish playfulness remained.

There would be no managing him. Absolutely none. "If I wanted a white marriage, would you agree to it?"

His smile became wistful. "With any other woman, I might, but not with you, *mo chridhe*. We have a real marriage or none a'tall, for the sake of all concerned. The decision is yours. I will see you ensconced at one of our island estates, I will stand as godfather or guardian to any child you bear out of wedlock, but I'll no' be a pretend husband, not to you."

And what Sebastian MacHeath said, he meant. He made a curious picture, bareheaded, at his ease, sitting before the humble dwelling, and yet, he still exuded lordliness, a formidable quality. Regardless of whether he and I married—and that question had grown only more fraught in the past quarter hour—I would long recall the sight of him in that pretty, peaceful clearing where we'd kissed.

I turned to go, intent on a bath, a tray, and a lie-down, when something caught my eye. I regarded Sebastian more intently, trying to deduce what specifically had gained my notice.

"Don't move, my lord." I remained yards away, letting my gaze simply take in the whole scene.

Handsome Scotsman perched on the steps.

Grass in what passed for a yard, overgrown, in want of a few hungry sheep.

Half-timbered cottage looking both cozy and deserted on a pretty summer...

"The curtains."

Sebastian rose. "What curtains?"

"When we were last here, every curtain was closed, which makes sense if the cottage is unused. Sunlight is hard on upholstery, carpets, and wallpaper. But if you look on the second floor, directly above the rose trellis, somebody has tied the curtains back."

"So we aren't the only people to use this as a trysting spot. One of those handsome footmen has tempted some house maid off the path of strict propriety. Are you surprised?"

"No, and one kiss does not a tryst make." The young ladies of the shire were without male companionship for the most part, and footmen were an accommodating and canny lot of necessity. "Do you suppose the footmen spy on the woodland sirens?"

Sebastian sent me a wry smile. "If, immediately after kissing me, you can shift your focus back to the woodland sirens and their possible admirers, then my kissing needs practice."

"No, it does not."

His smile became a grin. "Then I am content for the nonce. I might as well walk you back to the house. Whom do you suppose occupies the cottage?"

I considered the overgrown grass, the lack of smoke from any chimney, the absence of even a pot of violets on the porch.

"Nobody occupies it, but it's in use." I ought to ask Pamela about the place, but what if Pamela did her frolicking in that bedroom above the roses? Then again, whatever she got up to with her devoted staff was no business of mine and not relevant to St. Sevier's situation.

Sebastian and I made our way to The Gauges's formal garden, and he stopped me at the foot of the terrace steps. "Were you appalled, Violet?"

At first, I thought he meant by the inquest, or by somebody

holding assignations in The Gauges's backyard, but he studied the rear façade of the manor with particular casualness.

"Appalled by that kiss?"

One nod.

"I was impressed, if you must know." Also agog and bewildered.

"And that's a problem?" He left off studying the house to study me.

"I'll see you at supper." I swanned past him, head held high, expecting to hear smug male laughter in my wake. When I reached the house, I again turned to regard him.

Sebastian stood at the top of the terrace steps, an imposing figure exquisitely turned out in the first stare of rural fashion. It occurred to me that he was off to investigate some aspect of the situation he'd not shared with me, and he would wait until eternity for me to enter the house.

I offered him a curtsey and left him to it. Whatever Sebastian discovered, whatever evidence he sought to reexamine, he would share the results with me. I might not know how to deal with desire as it related to Sebastian MacHeath, but I trusted him absolutely.

And that mattered.

CHAPTER FOURTEEN

Dinner was a quiet affair. Our hostess seemed withdrawn and once again fatigued, suggesting the results of the inquest had given her a turn. I had little appetite, and Sebastian eventually left off trying to engage either of us in conversation.

"They will hang an innocent man at the assizes," I said when the fruit and cheese had been served. "They will trot out Mrs. Dorrance's perjury at a trial on kidnapping charges. Squire Bellamy will recall St. Sevier threatening murder, and some other self-serving local will remember St. Sevier meeting with Barbary Corsairs by moonlight and accepting money from them."

"Have some more wine," Pamela said. "St. Sevier will not be convicted of kidnapping." She sounded tired rather than confident.

"How can you say that?" I shot back. "Half the shire frequents his woods, any number of young ladies have cause to be jealous of the supposed victim, and half their papas covet Belle Terre's riches. And yet, only St. Sevier has been considered a suspect in any wrongdoing."

"Holly Faraday is very much a victim," Pamela said, rising and tossing down her table napkin. "You will excuse me. I must make an early night of it. Given the day's developments, I think it would be best if you returned to London on Monday. I'm sure you understand my reasoning."

She glided from the room, the footman on sentry duty at the sideboard staring straight ahead the whole while.

"You may clear the dishes, Maitland," I said in Pamela's absence. "No need to stand on ceremony." The wine bottle was nearly full, and by custom, the rest of the contents would be consumed in the kitchen—or the footmen's dormitory. I wished them the joy of their libation, for the vintage, like many Pamela had served, was unremarkable.

Maitland looked to the marquess.

"Do as her ladyship suggests," Sebastian said. "You endured a hard ride earlier today and are doubtless longing for your bed."

Maitland withdrew a sizable tray from the sideboard cabinetry. "I am that, my lord. Dry roads in summer are a blessing, though the heat and dust are tribulations."

"You travel to visit family?" Sebastian asked, slicing himself off another bite of cheese.

"Family?" Maitland set the tray on the table and began collecting the dishes at Pamela's place setting. "Aye, my lord. My old granny and my mum. They miss me something fierce, but The Gauges pays well, and London ways are a bit more formal than I'm used to. I like it here, and Mrs. Bonaventure doesn't mind if I put my half days together for an occasional jaunt home."

He was good at his job, moving china, crystal, and cutlery without making a sound. He spoke well, though not quite Mayfair drawing room English, and his appearance alone recommended him for his post. Though, like many rural servants, his grasp of decorum was rather loose.

"I admire a son who bothers to look in on his mother and grandmother," I said. "You can take the wine, Maitland, and our compliments to the kitchen. The, um, fowl was quite good."

The fowl had been partridge, unless I mistook the matter, served a bit ahead of the legal season. Perhaps Pamela's gamekeeper had mistaken a rustling in the undergrowth for a grouse, grouse season being in the offing.

"I'll let Cook know, my lady. She'll be that pleased."

Maitland was that pleased to collect the wine bottles. He disappeared with the tray full of bottles and dishes, and I contemplated having another serving of cheese and raspberries. That thought led to the memory of raspberries and cream drizzled with honey.

While Sebastian looked on, I dumped half the bowl of raspberries onto my plate. "Not a word, Dunkeld, and I am not going back to London until St. Sevier's situation is resolved. I will send a note to Ann at Belle Terre first thing tomorrow morning. Quitting The Gauges, with its handsome, mendacious footmen, musty carpets, and sly, gossiping staff will be quite honestly a relief."

"What of Mrs. Bonaventure? I thought you considered her a friend?"

I savored the raspberries, which all too soon would be available as only preserves and cordials.

"Not a friend, an acquaintance for whom I once performed a favor."

"Do you have friends, Violet?"

The question deserved an honest reply, because I suspected Sebastian was asking who would stand by me if I bore an illegitimate child. I had not thought through that particular inquiry, so I gave it my attention.

"My sisters-in-law are my friends. Since I've put off mourning, they have proven steadfast and amiable, and they will see to it that my brothers treat me decently. The ladies and I are regular correspondents, and their cordial company makes the thought of time at Derwent Hall less oppressive."

"Who else?"

Maitland returned with a tea service on his tray. He set the pot and teacups near my elbow and put the cream, honey, and sugar in the middle of the table.

"St. Sevier is my friend," I retorted, somewhat testily. "In her way, I suspect Ann is also a friend. We have interests in common and a certain compatibility of character."

Lucy Hewitt, my lady's maid, was, in fact, more of a friend than a subordinate. She could have left my employ for a more prestigious post anytime and had chosen not to. Her wages were scandalously generous, and I would have done anything for her short of casting myself into the Thames.

I waited for Maitland to depart again before dumping cream and a drizzle of honey over my raspberries. The result was an exquisite pleasure, a craving satisfied.

"The look on your face..." Sebastian said as I slipped the spoon from my mouth. "What did you mean about mendacious footmen?"

"I referred to Maitland." I lowered my voice because the door was open. "Biddle said he was off to visit his auntie and cousins. Maitland said the visit was to his mother and granny. Perhaps they all live together, but it's more likely Maitland is visiting a young lady, and he doesn't want Pamela to know."

"Busy fellow," Sebastian murmured. "No wonder he looks dead on his feet. I might ask Freeman to put me up. Fellow officers and all that."

I paused between bites of my ambrosia. "That is brilliant. Make him squirm. I'm convinced he knows more than he's told us."

"Just as St. Sevier knows more than he's told us, as does the fair Pamela, and Mrs. Dorrance, and the footmen... Though once St. Sevier has been formally charged and bound over, Freeman's role is complete. He might testify as a witness, but his authority over the case will be at an end."

"Then he must not charge St. Sevier until we have a better sense of what's afoot." And then Freeman must charge somebody else, or go back to brooding about the injustices of fate.

"Violet, we've spent a week poking about and have learned nothing of value. We are outsiders, and nobody will talk to us. Holly

Faraday is still missing, at best, and nobody speaks on St. Sevier's behalf."

Sebastian was trying to prepare me for the next step in this protracted tragedy, but as I spooned up more raspberries, I recalled Pamela's parting shot.

"Mrs. Bonaventure said that Holly Faraday *is* very much a victim. Not that Miss Faraday *was* a victim or *has been* a victim. Present tense—*is*. I have wondered how Holly fares, if she's injured and has no physician to attend her. She must be in a bad way, and yet, nobody is searching for her."

"A passing word choice is little to go on, Violet. Did you speak of Belmaine in the past tense from the moment of his demise?"

To consistently adopt the past tense when mentioning Freddie had taken me weeks. "Pamela waited until the inquest had concluded to toss us out. She wanted us where she could watch us until the jury returned a verdict."

"Or she put up with our imposition until St. Sevier's situation turned hopelessly scandalous."

"It's not hopelessly scandalous yet."

"Stubborn," Sebastian said, finishing the last of his wine and making a face. "Mrs. Bonaventure needs to consult a new sommelier."

"Maybe her inferior wines were chosen in an attempt to get rid of us. Where did you get off to after the inquest?" *After kissing me witless?*

"Paid a call on Hannibal."

I finished my dessert and debated making myself a second serving. "You visited your horse?"

"The very one."

"And how fares dear Hannibal?" I decided not to indulge in more sweets. I'd eaten a few bites of the partridge to be polite, but adhered to my father's theory that game tasted best in season. I was satisfied for the present and could ask for more berries and cream in the morning.

"Hannibal is homesick for Scotland, as am I, but the point of the excursion was to inquire as to where Maitland's family resides. I was told they dwell outside Eltham."

"That is a good thirty miles in the direction of London." On good roads, changing horses, Maitland could travel home one day and back to The Gauges the next and still have time to visit with family. "Why is that of interest?"

Sebastian poured some berries from the bowl into his hand. "I rode dispatch."

This again. "And survived, thank the Deity and the poor aim of the French. Do go on."

"The key to successfully completing a mission was often keeping my canteen full. Much of Spain is hot and dry much of the year. If my horse and I were to make good time over hard terrain, thirst had to be kept at bay. Before I'd part with my canteen, I'd part with my guns or knives."

I thought back to Maitland's arrival in the stable yard. "No canteen, no change of clothes bundled behind the saddle, not even a cloak lashed to the cantle in case we got more rain. No sack of biscuits and bread from Mama's kitchen..." Nothing consistent with Maitland's stated reason for travel. "That makes little sense."

Something else teased at the edges of my awareness, some fact or observation that also did not make sense, that had to do with Biddle, or—

Maitland returned, this time carrying a plain silver salver on which sat a sealed missive. "For my lord. We can send a reply tonight if necessary, sir. Won't take but twenty minutes to deliver, cutting through the wood."

Sebastian slit the seal, scanned the contents, and passed the letter to me. "No reply this evening, thank you."

Maitland collected more plates and departed while I read Freeman's note.

· · ·

My lord,

On Monday, St. Sevier will be formally charged with kidnapping Miss Holly Faraday. Her sisters have provided new evidence which confirms his role in Miss Faraday's disappearance. I have informed Madame St. Sevier of this development, and I'm sure she will appreciate the support of her friends at such a time. Monsieur will be transported to secure facilities at some point after the noon meal. The matter will then be out of my hands.

I remain your obed serv,

Freeman

I tossed this vile communication at Sebastian and tore from the room. I made it as far as the landing before Sebastian caught up with me, but I was in no mood to listen to reason. I marched for my apartment, and when he would have followed me inside, I simply shook my head and gently closed the door in his face.

∼

I refused to come down to breakfast on Sunday morning, too sick at heart to start my day with another tense meal. I sat at my vanity, arranging my hair in a simple braided chignon, failure staring me in the face.

Failure and grief.

A soft tap on the door heralded Lucy's arrival, a tray at her hip. "The lot of them are off to services. Told 'em you were resting in preparation for the journey back to London." She set a bowl of raspberries, cream, and honey on the vanity, the spoon already nestled among the fruit. "At least try to eat."

I jammed another pin into my bun. "How do you know we're returning to London?"

She put the tea tray on the cedar chest and started making the bed. "Word came from the magistrate last night that St. Sevier's to be bound over on Monday. What's done can't be helped. You did try, my lady."

"Word came in a sealed missive. How could you possibly know?"

"Had it from Belle Terre. One of Monsieur's grooms all but announced the news in the servants' hall last night."

"And you said nothing to me about this?" An accusatory note had crept into my voice that Lucy did not deserve.

"You need your rest, milady, and I'm saying something now, though I do wonder how a groom got news that Madame had likely just received herself. I can't see her confiding in that Dorrance creature."

"The Dorrance creature is a lying, spying busybody whose stupid games will see St. Sevier hanged." That wasn't quite fair. As best I could deduce, Mrs. Dorrance was protecting somebody. She could have told a complete fabrication and placed Holly Faraday in the cheese cave with St. Sevier, but she hadn't.

She'd let innuendo and prejudice do that work for her. Why?

"You have a letter, my lady." Lucy took a folded, sealed missive from her skirt pocket and passed it to me, then drew the quilts up over the bed and smoothed them flat. "From Derwent Hall. I recognized the rider."

"When did this arrive?"

"Not a quarter hour ago. The groom left the Hall at dawn. He's eating his way through the larders and waiting for your reply."

I expected to see the letter's direction rendered in a feminine hand, but the missive was from my father. Now was no time for a summons to the family seat, but then I recalled that I had written to Papa regarding St. Sevier's situation.

"Please ask the groom to wait. I might well have a reply. And, Lucy, I am not at my best. I apologize for my short temper."

Lucy finished making the bed and departed after admonishing me to eat something, which I hoped was her way of expressing forgiveness for my rudeness.

I took Papa's epistle to the window, prepared to read that my brother Felix had come to grief training some fractious colt. But... no. The letter wasn't bordered in black, so the news within could not be tragic. Then too, I had written to Papa when I'd first arrived at The Gauges, and he was an experienced magistrate and a peer of the realm.

Papa would not have responded so quickly to my query unless he had something of substance to convey. I slit the seal with a shaking hand.

Dearest Daughter,

The case you describe piqued my interest, so I did a bit of research before replying to you. No magistrate worth his salt (many are not, alas) would bring murder charges without a body. If there's one case pounded into the heads of our squires and celebrated in the magistrate's manuals, it's the Campden Wonder. Ask Freeman about it, though the particulars are simple enough. Some fellow's servants were hanged for murdering him, though no body could be located. The supposed victim turned up, right as a trivet, months later.

English justice got a rare dose of humility that has resounded down from centuries past.

I was more interested in the notion that your friend had been detained without charges for a period of days in a situation where murder could not be alleged. That is not the done thing. Our magistrates can decide petty cases, bind over alleged felons, and generally poke their noses into the odd corner if it relates to a crime, but to detain a man for any length of time for questioning is a grave insult at best—particularly when the gentleman served with distinction on the Peninsula.

English law takes the liberty of the commoner seriously, and a magistrate is to ask his questions and let witnesses go about their business, not drag them into confinement without charge or conviction. If the magistrate fears a witness will not appear for trial, the old laws allow that a surety—a recognizance—be demanded of the witness.

The statute is often honored in the breach, I know, and detaining material witnesses has been the subject of legal debate. In such a delicate case, with such serious consequences for both victim and offender, Freeman really ought to be minding the letter of the law more conscientiously.

I tell you in confidence, Violet, that I have on more than one occasion made quite a to-do over questioning a party whom I knew to be guilty, but could not prove had committed the crime. My questioning was intended to warn him to take himself off so he no longer troubled my neighbors with his thievery or drunkenness. The crown was saved the bother of a prosecution that could go nowhere, and the shire was restored to peace and safety, which ought to be considered a worthy object of any criminal proceeding.

I cannot fathom what Freeman is about, but if he'd like to consult me on the case, I am at his disposal. The aunties send their love— might you please invite them up to Town, Daughter?—as do I. Your brother Ellersby and his lady appear to be in immense charity with one another of late, though I refrain from speculating about the cause for their newfound marital accord.

I remain your devoted father,
Derwent

I was the Earl of Derwent's *only* daughter, hence the salutation struck me as an example of Papa's dry, often abrasive wit, but the rest of the letter gave me much to think about. Freeman had arguably lacked the authority to detain St. Sevier in the first place, much less for days on end.

And yet, Freeman was not stupid. He was the only legal authority in the shire, his competence unquestioned by his neighbors and his character above reproach. His handling of the inquest had been professional and disinterested, and he appeared to genuinely regret charging St. Sevier.

The most interesting aspect of my father's letter was near the closing. He offered to *consult* with Freeman. When a wealthy and wily old earl offered to consult with a mere country squire on the particulars of a serious case, the country squire was being reprimanded, if not threatened with scandal.

I did not always like my father, and I even more rarely understood him, but at that moment, he was the best father in all creation. He'd read my letter as the plea for aid that it had been, and he had offered to ride into St. Ivo, guns blazing, as it were.

Would he have come to my assistance as readily if he'd known I had conceived a child out of wedlock?

I poured myself a cup of tea, ate my raspberries and cream, and remained at the window, thoughts whirling. My view looked out on the tree line that formed the boundary between Belle Terre's woods and The Gauges's deer park. I stared at that pretty vista, all the while reviewing what I knew of St. Sevier's situation and racking my brain for anything that would preserve him from being bound hand and foot and tossed into the back of a cart before noon on the morrow.

When half an hour of serious pondering had yielded no alternative, I penned a reply to my father, thanking him profusely for the information he'd provided. I asked him to attend me at Belle Terre posthaste—underlined twice—and admitted to him that I feared for St. Sevier's life.

For Papa to arrive at Belle Terre before St. Sevier was sent away would require that the earl heed my summons at once and travel on the Sabbath. I could not see Papa bestirring himself to make that effort, but I implored him for further aid anyway.

I was begging mostly for the sake of my child and also on behalf of St. Sevier, but I was begging in no small measure on my own behalf as well.

~

I left my room and found a footman to pass my reply to the Derwent Hall groom. My next destination was Pamela's dressing closet.

Finding her apartment took a bit of poking about, but many country houses follow a similar design, and I soon located what I sought.

Pamela's rooms occupied the southern end of The Gauges's second floor. From her sitting room, she had a fine corner view of the front drive, while her bedroom took up another corner and overlooked the garden and deer park. A balcony wrapped about the bedroom corner, from which she could easily monitor the path to the stable and carriage house.

The roof of the half-timbered cottage peeked from among the trees, and the formal garden spread out in a lovely expanse that gave way to the wilder beauty of the park. Truly, The Gauges enjoyed a lovely situation.

The apartment walls were hung with faded silk of a green, blue, and lavender paisley design—no murals here—and even the dressing closet boasted a window. I found Pamela's riding boots, which were in want of a good cleaning, oddly enough.

Comparison with my own footwear revealed that Pamela's boot was as close a match for those in the cave as Miss Bellamy's had been. My first thought was that both women might have frequented the cave, but my next thought wasn't half so encouraging: Neither the length nor width of the boot prints in the cave had been unusual.

Half the shire might have tromped through that location, and matching a foot to a footprint was probably a doomed undertaking.

I left the dressing closet, eager to be done with my snooping. Pamela's bedroom was unremarkable, save for the portrait of what I assumed was her late husband hanging opposite the bed. The painting was predictably rendered, considering the subject. Mr. Bonaventure, attired in shooting jacket, field boots, and riding breeches, had been posed with a pair of handsome lurchers panting at his feet and a brace of hares dangling from his hand.

He was not handsome so much as he was masculine, in a lanky and slightly windblown way. He had wheat-blond hair and sparkling blue eyes, and the manner in which he held his long gun broken open over his arm suggested complete ease with a sportsman's accoutrements.

Pamela had loved him madly, to hear her tell it, but nothing in the portrait reminded the viewer that this man had had a wife who adored him. No cameo propped on a table, no smiling portrait of that lady hanging on a shadowy back wall, no bouquet of flowers full of romantic symbolism.

Freddie had sat for a portrait with me in the first year of our marriage. His painted image beamed husbandly joy, and mine... I could no longer bear to look upon the hope and innocence my own likeness had revealed. The portrait was packed away in my attic, where it would remain indefinitely.

My intention was to leave without any further intrusion into Pamela's privacy, but in my haste to leave the sitting room, I brushed past Pamela's escritoire and sent half a stack of correspondence cascading to the carpet.

I gathered up the letters and found that I held a dozen invoices, some from London, some from what appeared to be local establishments. Most included several months of arrearages, and one for a set of lace curtains was more than a year old. The bills remaining on the desk were arranged in date order, so I tidied up the mess I'd created as best I could.

Pamela was a commoner. She could be jailed for unpaid debts, and while shopkeepers typically extended credit to regular customers, Pamela's arrearages constituted a small fortune. Why run that risk when the stable had good horses going to waste, and the carriage house included at least one vanity conveyance?

I sorted those questions onto my increasing heap of vexatious puzzles and made my way to the stable. I was surprised to find that Biddle was in conversation with Thetis Faraday. They stood quite close to each other off to the side of the stable yard beneath the shade of a towering oak.

Her mare lounged at the ladies' mounting block, a hip cocked and eyes closed, suggesting that Thetis had been on hand for some time.

To hack out on the Sabbath was not exactly blasphemous, though it appeared to me that the young lady had taken some trouble with her appearance.

"Good morning," I said. "I see I am not the only person avoiding divine services today. Miss Thetis, that is a fetching habit."

She bobbed a curtsey. "My lady, good day. After yesterday's excitement, Mama said we might have a restful morning at home. The verdict has upset us all."

Thetis looked upset. A trifle pale, a little fatigued. Perhaps she was one of those women who, when feeling daunted, took extra trouble over her appearance. While her riding habit wasn't precisely fashioned *au courant*, it was less out of date than the one I'd seen her wear previously.

"Are you upset because the jury believed your sister came to a bad end," I asked, "or because the result will be further charges and possible hanging for Monsieur St. Sevier?"

Biddle frowned at the mare, and I'm sure he did not like my question.

"Both, I suppose," Thetis said, smiling uncertainly. "I love my sister, and I hope the jury is in error, but whether Holly has been murdered or kidnapped, justice must be served."

The riding habit was red, a fine military hue, but not one that suited Thetis's fair coloring. Her older habit, in dark blue, had been a more flattering choice. I had not been raised with sisters, but I had spent several years at finishing school. I drew on those years as I posed my next question.

"Was that one of Holly's habits?"

Thetis's smile faded. "One of her castoffs from the Season before last. Holly and I are the same size from top to toe. Mama says we might pass for twins, except that Holly is fairer-haired. We share everything, or almost everything. I would never ride Holly's mare."

"Shall I fetch Artemis for you, my lady?" Biddle spoke a little too hopefully.

"No, thank you. I'm attired for riding, but now that I'm out of doors, I find the heat gathering more quickly than I'd realized. I will greet the horses and enjoy the cool and quiet of the stable. Miss Thetis, good day, and like you, I hope the jury—and the magistrate—are in error."

I sauntered on my way, my mind full of questions. Freddie had not been dead twelve hours before the staff had been dyeing my plainer dresses black and hanging the mirrors with crepe. Every lady I knew with any coin to spare kept a set of weeds at the back of her wardrobe, because aunties, cousins, and grandparents had a habit of going to their rewards without warning. One did not want to be unprepared for such eventualities.

Thetis could have gone abroad in dark blue, but she'd chosen bright red. She'd chosen to hack out the day after her sister had been pronounced dead at violent hands. She'd spoken of Holly in the present tense—Holly is *fairer-haired, we share everything*—and Thetis was already aware that St. Sevier was to be bound over on the morrow.

I considered these facts while I offered Artemis a lump of sugar and found the precise spot on her neck that she most enjoyed having scratched.

"What is going on?" I murmured. "What on earth is going on?" I stepped from the stall, and the mare went back to her pile of hay. At any moment, the carriages would be returning from Sunday services, and I would be expected to share a meal with Pamela and Sebastian.

I was not ready to face my hostess, whom I suspected was playing a role in St. Sevier's ruin. She could have put a stop to the gossip between neighboring estates, but she had not. As the shire's grand lady, she could have put a stop to the young ladies cavorting like pagans in St. Sevier's woods, but she had not done that either.

As Mrs. Cooper had pointed out, Pamela had done nothing to solve her neighbors' most pressing problem—a lack of suitable bachelors for the local ladies to enchant—when matchmaking should have been her privilege, honor, and fondest diversion.

I left the stable and on a whim crossed to where I'd been

conversing with Thetis Faraday. I put my boot down beside the imprints she'd left in the stable yard and stared at the two depressions side by side in the sandy earth.

Thetis's footprint dwarfed my own, in both length and width. If Thetis and Holly were alike enough in build to be twins, then Holly Faraday had never been in that cheese cave, and Mrs. Dorrance's testimony was entirely untruthful.

I wanted to shout for Biddle to saddle Artemis so that I could convey my insight to Freeman, but Biddle was nowhere to be found. Moreover, before I bludgeoned Freeman with Mrs. Dorrance's perjury, I wanted to confer with Sebastian.

Lest I be found in the stable yard when the churchgoers returned, I started down the path between the rhododendrons. Peace and quiet were in order, as was some solitude and some hard thinking—more hard thinking. I reached the first clearing only to see Biddle and Thetis departing from the opposite side.

They walked with their arms about each other's waists, Thetis's head on Biddle's shoulder, and their destination was clearly the secluded cottage.

CHAPTER FIFTEEN

To my great relief, Pamela pleaded a megrim, and I was left to enjoy a quiet meal with Sebastian on the side terrace. I asked him to stroll with me in the garden when we'd finished eating rather than risk that my hostess would eavesdrop through an open window.

"The ladies don't wear riding boots to Sunday services," Sebastian said, frustration making his burr more pronounced. "Heeled slippers for the gentry women, half boots for the rest. I marked my own boot with charcoal so I'd know precisely how long a track I was looking for, but most of the churchyard is grass. I was faced with the prospect of placing my foot directly against the ladies' and could not see a way to do that without giving offense."

"Pamela might well have been in that cheese cave, but I can assure you Holly Faraday was not." I explained how I reached that conclusion and further elucidated the contents of my father's letter.

"What was your reply?"

"I begged him to come at once. Freeman, the king's man, has arguably broken the law."

Sebastian gazed out across the tidy gravel walks and fragrant lavender borders. "I would have said the magistrate was a decent man, if a bit fixed on his objective. Not the sort to blatantly pervert justice, for all he's also been less than forthcoming with us. I'm not as familiar with English law as I am with Scottish law, so I didn't think to question..." He scrubbed a hand over his face. "This is not good, Violet."

"Could Freeman have killed Miss Faraday?" To have this discussion on such a pretty day in such pretty surrounds felt obscene, and yet, across the deer park, the edge of the wood took on the prospect of an enemy army. Birnam forest, making a stealthy advance on the unsuspecting denizens of high Dunsinane hill.

"Might her death have been an accident?" Sebastian asked. "Freeman is a landowner. He could have been out after game."

We walked along in silence, and I developed a whole new appreciation for the magistrate's role in upholding justice. If the king's man was corrupt, then he held the power of life and death over every man, woman, and child in the district. Society could be cast back into the lawless dark age of war lords and blood feuds, one shire at a time.

Silence, perjury, or faulty recollections would be a small price to pay for staying in the magistrate's good graces.

"Freeman essentially told Ann to go back to Scotland," I muttered, "when she's one of few supporters St. Sevier has. A wife deserting her husband would make him look only more culpable. Freeman did not reexamine the crime scene before the rain washed away the bootprints I found. I don't believe he's interrogated the gamekeepers, who are often abroad in the woods."

Sebastian turned with me at the foot of the garden so we faced The Gauges's back terrace.

"Freeman is also a former amour of our hostess," I went on. "She'd keep on an eye on us at his request." To think that our every move had been reported to the magistrate... I took a seat on the nearest bench.

"And then," Sebastian said, coming down beside me, "Pamela is trying to send us back to London now that the inquest is complete, lest we keep poking about... Except I still don't think Freeman capable of murder."

I considered what I knew of the magistrate, which wasn't nearly enough. "My instincts say he's honorable, Sebastian, but he has clearly abused his authority. He dealt in ciphers and subterfuge during the war, and that, too, suggests a less than forthright code of honor."

Sebastian scraped his boot over the crushed shells of the walkway. I could see the little slash of charcoal where he'd marked the leather to indicate how long the prints in the cheese cave were. I would not have thought to do that, but it was the sort of practical, commonsense measure typical of Sebastian.

A cool, prickling sensation accompanied my next thought. "We've been looking at the wrong boots."

"I beg your pardon?"

"We've been looking at ladies' boots. We need to compare St. Sevier's boots to the prints in that cave. I can prove that some woman other than Miss Faraday was in that cave. If the larger prints don't match St. Sevier's boots, then he wasn't in there either."

"But, Violet, *he was*, when he showed the place to his wife and daughter."

"Then we find his prints and the prints of whoever Miss Bellamy or Pamela was meeting as well. We create doubt, and we do it today. For all we know, Thaddeus Freeman buys his boots from Dern."

I was still in my riding habit—Sebastian and I had eaten outdoors, after all—and he was also attired for riding, having traveled on horseback to and from St. Ivo's. I marched directly for the stable and asked Biddle to saddle Artemis for me.

Sebastian dealt with Hannibal himself, which presumption Biddle did not protest.

"Out for a hack, my lady?" he asked, leading the mare to the ladies' mounting block.

I saw no reason to dissemble when the domestic spy network would keep him informed of our every movement.

"We're calling at Belle Terre and hope to uncover further evidence of Monsieur's innocence."

Biddle took up Artemis's girth and walked around the mare's quarters to check the balance strap. "You'll use the bridle paths?"

Why was he asking? "The woods should be cooler than the lanes, also a shorter ride."

"Better footing on the lanes, if you mean to let Arty have her head again."

Not appreciably better. "You are trying to keep me out of the woods *again*, Biddle. Why?"

He patted Artemis's shoulder. "Best for all of us to keep out of those woods."

Perhaps his comment related to the ladies' use of the stream for their sunset frolics, or perhaps he referred to Holly Faraday's murder by person or persons unknown.

"I have concluded that the magistrate in these parts holds his neighbors in thrall," I said, climbing the steps and settling myself on Artemis's back. "I have sent for my father, the Earl of Derwent, because I cannot believe justice was served at the inquest. At least one witness committed perjury, and your magistrate has exceeded his authority. I'll not have it, Biddle. Whatever is afoot here has gone on long enough, and I mean to get to the bottom of it."

I arranged my skirts and gathered up my reins. Biddle handed me a lady's whip from the assortment propped against the mounting block's rails.

"Stay on the bridle paths," he said. "It's worth your life to keep to the paths, my lady."

As Sebastian led Hannibal out, Biddle stalked back into the barn.

"What was that about?" Sebastian asked as we turned the horses in the direction of the deer park.

"Biddle warned me to stay out of the woods, and if I must ride through them, to keep to the paths. He said it was worth my life not to leave the paths."

"To do otherwise would be to trespass. You make a fine picture on that mare, Violet."

I glanced back at the stable yard and saw Biddle standing in the doorway to the barn, monitoring our progress toward the tree line.

"Why do I get the sense that it's worth *his* life to keep his mouth shut, Sebastian?"

"Because we have tarried too long in this blighted shire, where nobody is honest, and everybody is hiding something."

In deference to the heat, we cantered through the woods rather than galloped. On another occasion, I would have explored side paths and game trails and simply enjoyed the forest primeval. I nearly hated the woods now, which was not rational.

I had less than twenty-four hours to see St. Sevier's name cleared, and when we arrived at Belle Terre, I was curt with Mrs. Dorrance.

"We're here to see Madame, at once if you please."

Mrs. Dorrance offered us a brittle smile. "Madame is out. I don't know when she'll be returning, nor where her errand took her."

How I longed to smack that pretty, lying face. "We will wait for her in her private sitting room."

Fine blond brows drew up. "I'm sure the formal parlor would be more suitable, my lady."

Sebastian loomed at my elbow. How exactly he went from being a brooding presence to an imposing one, I did not know, but the effect was impressive.

"You will comply with her ladyship's request," he said. "Her loyalty is to the owners of this house, as is my own. Unlike present company." He had not raised his voice, but Mrs. Dorrance's smile winked out like a candle in a gale.

"This way."

She led us abovestairs and showed us to a room decorated in blue and cream with touches of gilt. The wallpaper was sky-blue flocked with cream fleur-de-lis. The escritoire and chairs were in the style of Louis Quatorze. Savonnerie carpets covered most of the parquet floor, and Brussels lace curtains filtered the summer sunshine.

All was light, airy, and peaceful. Despite the elegance, a wicker workbasket beside the love seat, and a bound copy of Voltaire's essay *Upon the Civil Wars of France* proclaimed this to be an intimate space, a private space. A pair of St. Sevier's slippers sat by the hearth, slippers I had at one time—in another life, it seemed—appropriated for my own feet.

"You do it," I said. "If Mrs. Dorrance sees me absconding with a pair of Monsieur's boots, she'll have me arrested for theft. You're a peer."

Sebastian doubtless knew that I was loath to enter the bedroom shared by husband and wife, and he wasted no time moving to the next room. He returned a moment later carrying a pair of gentleman's riding boots. Brief inspection confirmed that they had been made in Dern's shop.

"I would feel more comfortable leaving Ann a note," he said, "but the staff will doubtless read it."

"She should sack the lot of them and without characters." I all but fled the apartment, and we passed no one on our way to the front door. "Where do you suppose Ann has got off to?"

"Possibly visiting her husband, perhaps calling on the Coopers."

"Or maybe she simply wanted to be away from the people who are sending her husband to the gallows."

We collected our horses from the stable and rode back to The Gauges by way of the cheese cave. I dreaded what we might find within, but my fears were misdirected. We entered the cave, the slanting afternoon sunshine providing a significant amount of light beyond the opening.

Enough light to see that every blessed footprint and track had been swept from the floor.

Sebastian swore softly in Gaelic, while my rage exceeded the limits of mere profanity.

∾

As we rode back to The Gauges, I tried to make a mental list of every lie, question, and inconsistency Sebastian and I had uncovered. Perjury and abuse of authority had now been joined by destruction of evidence, and the whole foul miasma swirled in a filthy haze over Belle Terre's woods.

"I want to confront Pamela," I said as we crossed the deer park at a walk. "I want to shake her until her teeth rattle."

"Then you'd be as guilty of intimidation as Freeman might well be. Shall I fetch Derwent for you? If he's willing to leave Derwent Hall at moonrise, I can have him here before noon tomorrow."

I hated the notion of running to Papa, but I was out of both time and options. "Yes, please do fetch him, if he's willing to come."

"Shall I fetch him if he's *not* willing to come?"

"Lay hands on a peer, Sebastian?" Assault of a peer was an exceedingly serious crime, one Sebastian contemplated with apparent relish.

"If there are no witnesses," Sebastian replied, "then who's to say the earl didn't lay hands on my exalted personage?"

"Will Freeman's corrupt example turn us all into criminals, then?"

"Criminals or lunatics. Promise me not to take any unnecessary risks in my absence, Violet."

What Sebastian deemed a necessary risk and what I deemed a necessary risk might vary slightly—or a lot.

"I promise," I said as we approached the stable yard, "and you likewise, Sebastian. Rest your horse, read the signs at each crossroad twice—all of the signs—take your cloak, and carry a knife."

His lips quirked. "You are telling me how to ride dispatch?"

"I am telling you to be careful."

His smile faded, and he ran a gloved finger along my cheek. "You will never lose me, *mo ghràidh*. A jaunt over to Derwent Hall barely qualifies as an outing to this old soldier. Send a note to Ann telling her to expect to host a guest or two, and I'll see you in the morning."

I tarried in the stable yard while Upjohn brought Sebastian a cloak, saddlebags, and two canteens. Biddle watched these preparations in silence, and I purposely did not disclose where the marquess was off to or when he'd return.

Sebastian gave Upjohn some last-minute instructions, which occasioned glances in my direction and nods from Upjohn. Upjohn stepped back, and Sebastian led Hannibal to the gentlemen's mounting block.

"You are not to worry about me," he said, giving the girth a tug. "I studied the route earlier this week, in case I had to send Upjohn to Derwent Hall. The weather is fair, and Hannibal is a seasoned campaigner."

I glowered at Sebastian. "You are not to worry about me either. Lucy and Upjohn will literally guard my door if I ask it of them. I am a decent shot and utterly determined to prevent further injustice."

"And that," Sebastian said, "is precisely what I do not want to hear. Please hold your determination in check until tomorrow, Violet. We can't be certain what fate has befallen Holly Faraday, but I know I don't want it to befall you too."

He would have turned to leave on his mission, but I put a hand on his arm, then pulled him into an embrace and hugged him tight.

"I cannot lose you again, Sebastian."

"You won't." He pressed a swift, businesslike kiss to my mouth, mounted up, and cantered down the drive.

"Will he be back?" Biddle asked.

"Where is Holly Faraday?" I retorted.

Biddle's expression went from resigned to bleak, and he shuffled into the barn.

"I'm to escort you anytime you leave the house, my lady," Upjohn said. "My lord's orders."

And Upjohn would never disregard my lord's orders. "Can you ride?"

"Aye." His tone was less than enthusiastic. "If I must."

"I intend to call upon St. Sevier before he's hauled away in chains on the morrow, Upjohn. I intend to put some very pointed questions to the magistrate, and I will want you on hand as a witness, if not as a bodyguard."

"Aye, milady. His lordship said as much. I'm to go wherever you go and do as you say, short of leaving you alone. I'm to enlist Miss Hewitt's aid if necessary."

"Miss Hewitt is doubtless busy packing for our remove to Belle Terre tomorrow." That fact reminded me that I had a note to write to Ann. I set off for the house, Upjohn at my side, and realized that I would need my note delivered to Belle Terre and could not assign that job to Upjohn.

Nor would I entrust it to a member of The Gauges's staff, not when I was alerting Ann that a belted earl, duly sworn magistrate, and nuisance at large was about to descend on Thaddeus Freeman.

Lucy was my only other option as a messenger, and she'd had a village upbringing. A short jaunt through the woods on a sunny afternoon should pose no challenge to her at all. I promised Upjohn I would remain in my room while he served as her escort.

Despite all, I was abruptly in need of another nap.

~

Dinner was a tray in my sitting room—more partridge. Pamela's megrim was apparently to beset her until the moment I stepped into the coach that would take me off down The Gauges's drive.

I spent my evening making long lists, of inconsistencies, lies, and frustrations.

The young ladies hunting for morels that were not in season.

Giles Bellamy showing me the crime scene that was not the crime scene.

Mrs. Dorrance testifying to an assignation between Holly Faraday and Hugh St. Sevier that had never happened.

Thaddeus Freeman, an apparently upright man, exceeding the authority of his post by detaining a witness for questioning instead of charging a suspect with a crime. Beginning a murder investigation when no charge of murder could be laid in the absence of a body.

The crime itself shifting—*after* the inquest—from murder to kidnapping because of a case my father claimed even the most dimwitted Squire Lumpkin knew of.

My list expanded to include seemingly irrelevant details that nonetheless would not leave my mind.

Anthony Bellamy, who had all he could do to manage his own acres, insisting that St. Sevier enclose the last patch of common ground in the area. Why? What St. Sevier chose to do with his property was his business and his alone.

Biddle, warning me to keep to the paths in a wood half the shire apparently considered public land.

Thetis Faraday, engaged in an apparently doomed romance with a groom and happily borrowing her "deceased" sister's clothing.

Elizabeth Bellamy stopping by "water her mare," and in so doing, creating silent enmity with Biddle.

Somebody destroying evidence, Belle Terre staff spying on Hugh and Ann, and most vexing of all, *no body*. No body, no victim, and no more time to investigate.

And bracketing the whole, Pamela Bonaventure, a young widow, quite well-to-do to appearances, and well liked by her neighbors. She claimed to miss her late husband terribly, but had done not one thing to assist the young ladies of the shire to find husbands of their own. She did not host the young ladies in Town. She did not reproach them for imprudent self-indulgence. She'd not held a house party or a shooting party, nothing.

She had funds enough to maintain a large stable and hire Town footmen, but she wasn't paying the trades. She pleaded the need to retire early, then apparently hopped into her coach and went off into the night on some errand known only to her.

I'd thought myself too anxious to sleep, but I was wrong. One minute, I was staring at my bedroom curtains fluttering in the night breeze. The next, I heard robins singing their morning odes. I was not exactly brimming with energy, but I was full of determination.

I resumed studying my list, and Lucy found me at the escritoire when she brought up the tea tray.

"Morning, my lady. Looks like another scorcher. If we must endure summer's heat, at least we're not stuck in London while we do it. I brushed out your riding habit, though I can tell you Upjohn does not enjoy time spent in the saddle. Are you sure you won't take the coach to see Monsieur off?"

Lucy's chatter had a forced cheerfulness that in my present mood sat quite ill. "St. Sevier is not jaunting over to Paris for a few weeks."

"They'll take him to Maidstone, Upjohn says. Things are not looking good for Monsieur, are they, my lady?"

I poured myself a cup of tea and downed half of it. The bowl of raspberries and cream had no appeal. *Things*, for St. Sevier, were looking abysmal, and my digestion felt abysmal too.

"Monsieur should in theory receive a fair trial," I said, "but if fairness pertained, he'd be home with his wife and daughter, complaining of the infernal heat."

If I took my coach to call on Freeman, my trunks could be sent over to Belle Terre by wagon, and I could spare Upjohn the ordeal of time in the saddle.

"Have you packed my dresses?"

"I have," Lucy replied, pulling the quilt from the bed and draping it over a chair. "I can unpack a carriage dress, if you like. Your habit is quite fetching, though." She stripped the linens from the bed, which made the fact of my removal to Belle Terre real to me.

I was leaving The Gauges under a cloud, but then, I'd more or less invited myself, and I hadn't been an easy or gracious guest. Nor had Pamela been a gracious hostess. The inferior wine, the game out of season, the constant admonitions to stay out of the woods that held the key to the entire mystery...

I would not miss The Gauges. At all.

"I'll wear my habit," I said, finishing my tea, "and take the coach. If the locals think my wardrobe behindhand, that doesn't begin to compare with what I think of them. Do you know how to swim, Lucy?"

I rose and began dressing while Lucy disappeared into the bedroom and emerged with my riding boots.

"I do, some. Enough not to drown, though I haven't gone swimming in years."

"Children swim, schoolgirls paddle about or go wading and think themselves quite daring. Women staring spinsterhood full in the face do not swim, and if they do swim, they don't announce their eccentricity to the entire shire."

I had gone for a swim earlier in the summer, careful to wait until full darkness, and to remain unobserved as I'd departed for my indulgence. I'd also been at Derwent Hall at the time, and I was a widow with much less of a reputation to protect.

Lucy tossed the pillows into a chair. "The young ladies hereabouts are apparently headstrong. Biddle says nobody in their right mind would go frolicking in Belle Terre's woods."

I wiggled into the short corset designed to be worn when riding. "When did he say that?"

Lucy began folding up the quilts, sheets, and blankets she'd removed from the bed. "He drove me and Upjohn over to Belle Terre in the pony cart yesterday."

"I thought you walked through the woods?" I'd sketched her a crude map, and she'd assured me the fresh air would be welcome. Doubtless, some time alone with Upjohn would have been more welcome still.

"Biddle saw us setting off and wouldn't hear of our using the bridle paths. I passed the note directly to Madame, as you instructed, and Biddle brought us back here. Not the chattiest fellow, but I gather he's pining for a young lady whose parents won't let her marry a groom."

I held still while Lucy took up my laces. "No tighter than necessary, Lucy. If I'm not to be in the saddle, I should at least be free to breathe. Did Madame St. Sevier say where she'd been?"

"Visiting. She went to see some of the poor families. Took them letters signed by Monsieur saying they had his permission to gather the nuts and berries and so forth from the woods. They are allowed to collect the deadfall and the mushrooms and I forget what else. The man is that kind, and he's the one we're sending to the dock."

Truly, I would need to let out the seams of my habit or soon give up riding. "Was he allowing those families to run tame in his woods?"

"Apparently so. Makes Biddle's fussing hard to understand. If the Grant children are berry picking in the woods, and the young ladies go bathing there, and anybody who pleases can use the bridle paths, why shouldn't I have been allowed to daunder over to Belle Terre on foot with Upjohn as my escort?"

"Because we are supposed to believe that Holly Faraday ended her days in those woods." Though half the shire apparently still came and went as they pleased on St. Sevier's land.

Lucy resumed swatting pillows and folding blankets. "Then why has Miss Thetis Faraday come trotting out of the hedgerow nearly every day since we arrived? Why has Miss Bellamy used those bridle paths?"

I normally enjoyed Lucy's volubility, just as I enjoyed birdsong in the morning, but today I wanted to clap my hand over her mouth. Her questions belonged at the top of my list: If the wood was so dangerous, the scene of a murder or kidnapping, why were the local folk, *including the victim's very sisters*, larking about there without a care in the world?

Why were children gathering berries there?

Why were young ladies supposedly looking for mushrooms there?

Why was Biddle all but forbidding me to set foot in the wood?

"I am glad to be leaving this place," I muttered, fastening the skirt of my riding habit about my waist. "I am not at all pleased with the course of events here, but I will be exceedingly relieved to remove myself from The Gauges."

"I will not be pleased to have to deal with that Mrs. Dorrance. Dreadful Dorrance, the footmen call her."

"What do they call me?" I tied a cream linen stock about my neck and secured it with a plain gold pin.

"They don't talk about you much at all, not in front of me. They like Hannibal. Sit down, my lady, and I'll braid your hair."

I complied, because Lucy's efforts always looked sleeker than my own, and if Lucy secured a chignon at my nape, that chignon did not unravel, flop, or otherwise betray my dignity, no matter how hard I rode or how brisk the wind.

"Why are a lot of footmen discussing his lordship's horse?"

"I guess these footmen aren't too high in the instep to socialize with the outside help."

I thought about Maitland, who'd clearly ridden a distance and did so regularly. In Town, a footman on horseback was nearly unthinkable. In the country, distances demanded commonsense compromises.

"You should eat something, my lady," Lucy said when I was as tidy and presentable as I could be in riding attire.

"I'm not hungry."

"You will be."

Lucy was wrong. The idea that I must bid farewell to St. Sevier, that I had let him down and might truly—truly—lose him to the hangman's noose, had stolen any hint of an appetite.

"I'll be back before noon," I said, "and then we will quit this place once and for all."

"I'll be ready to go. Upjohn is waiting for you at the foot of the stairs."

I had hoped I'd waken to find my father strutting around The Gauges, announcing that he'd taken St. Sevier's situation in hand and arrested Freeman for some sort of malfeasance. I'd hoped that Sebastian at least would have returned from Derwent Hall so my farewell visit to St. Sevier need not be undertaken alone.

But Papa was not one to forgo a good night's sleep merely to meddle in another man's jurisdiction, and Sebastian would deliver Papa to my side, even if that meant putting up with Papa's dithering and delays.

"Shall I go with you, my lady?" Lucy asked, gathering up my nightgown and slippers.

"No, but thank you. Thank you for so much." I slipped out the door rather than indulge in a fit of the weeps. I was not giving up. The London solicitors were preparing for the trial to be held in Maidstone, and I would continue to investigate to the extent I could do so from Belle Terre.

But I was grappling with the real possibility—the probability—of defeat and all that would entail.

CHAPTER SIXTEEN

I collected Upjohn at the foot of the steps. He was attired for riding, but the ensemble did not fit him well.

"Borrowed finery, Upjohn?"

"One of the footmen is about my size. It will have to do."

We headed directly for the stable, where Biddle offered me a sullen greeting. "We're taking the coach," I told him, "but if you would have Artemis ready for a remove to Belle Terre by noon, I would appreciate it."

"I can take her there for you, my lady," Biddle said. "See her settled in. His lordship apparently discussed particulars with Missus after services yesterday."

Did he seek to gather the morning's gossip, or did he truly care for the horse? I was debating that question when a bay gelding trotted into the stable yard, both beast and rider dusty and sweaty.

"My bad luck," the rider said, sliding to the ground. "The constable's wagon up from Maidstone would not let me pass for two entire miles. They couldn't pull off for one minute to let me by." He took off his cap and swatted it against his thigh. "Biddle, you'll need to cool Bacchus. He's put in a hard night's work."

The rider was attired as a groom, and yet, he was another of Pamela's comely footmen. He patted the horse on the neck, then stepped back to allow Biddle to loosen the gelding's girth.

"The constable's wagon is already on the way?" I asked, a chill gripping me despite the morning's heat.

"I finally passed it on a curve, my lady, but yes. They apparently left at first light. Magistrate's orders."

Freeman had told me I had all morning to pay this call. Another lie. "Biddle, give me Bacchus's reins and please saddle Artemis for me."

"You're not going to ride through the woods, are you, my lady?"

Good God, I wanted to backhand him. "Saddle the mare *at once*. I will take the fastest possible route to Freeman's property, and that does not necessitate cutting through the bedamned woods."

I snatched the gelding's reins from Biddle. He scowled, but did as I demanded.

"I can walk the horse, my lady," Upjohn said.

The footman who'd ridden in on Bacchus had bowed and disappeared up the path to the house. What had he been doing traveling the road down from Maidstone and at this hour of the morning?

"Upjohn, I am going to ride like the demons of hell are after me. That might well mean hopping stiles and gates and anything else in my path. Can you acquit yourself at that level of skill in the saddle?"

"I... cannot."

"Your honesty is appreciated, also refreshing. Dunkeld would be very wroth with us both if you broke your neck trying to impersonate a steeplechase jockey."

"You could visit St. Sevier in Maidstone."

"No, I cannot. Freeman has no authority over the case once St. Sevier leaves this jurisdiction, and no innocent man should have to spend one night behind bars. Walk Bacchus, though I vow and declare, I have never met such a lot of saddle weary footmen."

Upjohn took the reins from me. "I've never met such a lot of footmen for riding the shire at all hours either. They don't seem to observe a regular half day, don't have a darts team at the local posting inn, don't do much besides lounge about the servants' hall, dicin' and talkin' rot about the grand posts they got sacked from in London. His lordship would never stand for that much idleness, and I doubt your ladyship would either."

Just as Maitland had arrived from his *family visit* at an early hour, dusty and road-weary. Now this other fellow came dragging into the stable yard looking as if he'd ridden the whole distance from London in... one... night.

Because he had. As Bacchus's tired hoof beats echoed through the morning air, I caught a wisp of an explanation for the strange goings-on in Belle Terre's woods.

Biddle emerged from the barn with Artemis.

"You're off to see the magistrate?" he asked, taking up the girth.

Did he intend to *argue* with me? "I'm off to see justice done. I know why you've tried to keep me out of the woods, Biddle. I assume your motives are at least partly honorable, but if somebody on this blighted property had passed along even a scintilla of the truth, that would have been appreciated far more."

He looked miserable, as if he was about to cry.

"Don't say a word," I went on. "If you admit what you know, you might well be charged as an accessory. If Thetis's parents turn up their noses at a groom, they will send her to a nunnery before they allow her to marry a felon."

I led the mare to the mounting block and got situated in the saddle. "If Dunkeld arrives, please send him on to Freeman's posthaste, and don't despair, Biddle. If you are an accessory, so is Thetis, so are her parents. This whole perishing shire is one great big criminal conspiracy, and I will happily leave you to it, but first, I will snatch St. Sevier from your snares."

I gathered up my reins and trotted from the stable yard. When we reached the foot of the drive, I turned Artemis for Freeman's hold-ing, tucked low, and gave the mare her head.

~

I overtook the constable's wagon as it approached the turn to Free-man's drive. The vehicle was a dilapidated greenish black monstrosity that looked to date from German George's day. The windows were barred and a deadbolt secured to the single door.

The idea that St. Sevier was to be shut up in that dog cart for humans inspired me to urge Artemis into a flat-out, thundering gallop as we crossed a grassy park to reach the manor house. I was terrified for St. Sevier, who was caught up in a desperate and potentially lethal scheme, but I was also angrier than I could ever recall being.

I'd been disappointed in my husband, wroth with him, and resentful of his peccadilloes, but Freddie had never put the innocent in harm's way for his own gain.

Artemis cleared the last stile and cantered up to the circular drive before the house. Freeman and his prisoner stood on the front terrace, along with Giles and Anthony Bellamy. I brought the mare to a heaving halt, slid from the saddle, and passed her reins to a startled-looking groom.

"How dare you?" I began marching up the steps, my whip in hand. "How dare you send an innocent man to be tried for a capital crime?"

"Now see here, my lady," Anthony Bellamy began. "You cannot... cannot *trespass* in a fit of hysterics and interfere with the king's man."

"Hush." I spoke softly, ready to stripe his pontificating face with my whip. He must have sensed the depth of my ire, because he took a step back. I turned to the victim of this deadly farce. "St. Sevier, one question: When did Freeman explain to you the ramifications of the Campden Wonder?"

St. Sevier, who looked utterly self-possessed if not bemused, bowed to me. "Good morning, my lady. Monsieur Freeman discussed that case with me on the second night of my detention over a game of chess."

I whirled on Freeman. "*You knew he was innocent,* and you all but arrested him, hoping the real crooks would reveal themselves in a fit of overconfidence. You thought to lure your miscreants into thinking themselves safe, and you put St. Sevier at risk of death to do it."

"Yon Frenchie is the real crook," Anthony Bellamy sputtered. "He allows the local rabble free rein in those woods, where they are doubtless helping themselves to all manner of game. With him gone, the poaching will stop."

Bellamy was nearly frothing at the mouth and pointing at St. Sevier with a shaking finger. Giles, by contrast, was pale and still.

"The poaching," I said, "is a well-established ring of felons, and the poor of this parish do not participate in it. Would they be all but starving if they did?"

Freeman watched me with a brooding intensity that suggested he was unraveling a particularly difficult cipher.

"St. Sevier owns the land," Freeman said. "He's either involved in the poaching, or he's tacitly permitting it."

"Precisely," Bellamy snapped. "There's no ring of anything, just the usual crooked gamekeepers, tenant farmers with their snares, lazy slackers, and their naughty boys."

"St. Sevier." I tried to moderate my tone. "Were you attempting to identify the poachers?"

He wrinkled his nose. "I was."

"Did you succeed?"

"I have only the most disturbing suspicions. I am more concerned with the fact that Anthony Bellamy trespassed on my land for the purpose of laying mantraps. I saw him about that vile mission on two occasions, but had no witnesses with me."

Giles sank onto the terrace steps. "Papa, you didn't."

"I told you I would. If nobody else will do anything to uphold the king's laws, I will."

I felt as if I were in a labyrinth of lies, for another insight befell me as I beheld Giles, all but collapsed on the steps.

"Giles, remove a boot, please."

Bellamy senior took a step toward me. "Are you daft? A gentleman does not disrobe in public at a lady's command."

"Do as she says," Freeman murmured. "Do it now."

"My lady?" St. Sevier turned a curious smile on me. "The benefit of your thinking would be appreciated."

"Giles jaunts up to Town regularly, but he must watch his pence and quid and supplement his funds at every opportunity. I suspect he frequents Dern's boot-making establishment and was engaged in an assignation in your cheese cave with Mrs. Bonaventure."

Freeman peered at the bottom of Giles's boot. "Dern. How did you guess?"

"Because that maker's mark was apparent on the tracks left in the cheese cave—tracks Mrs. Dorrance obliterated. She's not stupid, but she is a criminal."

"I've known Hecate Dorrance for years," Anthony Bellamy said. "A finer woman you will never meet."

"She perjured herself," I retorted, "claiming Holly Faraday met with St. Sevier in the cheese cave. Holly Faraday's tracks would be much larger than the ones we found in the cave, though Elizabeth Bellamy and Pamela Bonaventure are both arguably the right size."

"I suspected Bellamy *père* of fabricating his testimony," St. Sevier said. "When I had my altercation with Miss Faraday, no other rider was visible on the path. If we were overheard, the witness was lurking in the undergrowth, as a poacher might."

"Then why would Bellamy set the mantraps?" Freeman asked as the constable's wagon lumbered up the drive.

"To warn off his competitors?" St. Sevier suggested. "A mantrap is only a threat to those ignorant of its location, and my woods attract trespassers like a fat hound attracts fleas."

Another missing puzzle piece snapped into place. "Holly Faraday ran afoul of one of Anthony's mantraps." I shuddered to think of the pain she'd endured, cruel metal teeth snapping closed about her foot or leg. The larger mantraps could sever a foot, or cause death by exsanguination. Worse, the mantrap was usually securely staked to prohibit its victims from escaping.

And these murderous devices were considered a legal means of protecting a property owner's right to shoot his own hares.

"Who else is involved?" I asked St. Sevier, for surely he had some clue. My first thought was the Grants and Williamses and their ilk. They had the greatest need for food. They lived proximate to the wood and had the owner's permission to travel through it freely.

St. Sevier would protect them with his life if need be, because they were facing a looming and lethal injustice if the land was enclosed. He watched as the nasty old wagon with the bars on its windows came to a halt near the ladies' mounting block.

"I have no proof, my lady."

He was being honorable, damn him. "Pamela Bonaventure is not worth your life," I snapped. "I know her involvement, Monsieur. She has her little army of footmen, who take the game up to London by night. To get the best prices from the clubs, Giles doubtless negotiates for her. It's done all the time, but a woman is not usually behind it."

Freeman swore in some language I did not recognize. Anthony Bellamy sank onto the steps beside his son.

"Oh God. Oh, Giles..."

"Don't say anything, Papa. Please, not a word. St. Sevier admitted it himself. There's no proof."

Oh, but there was. "Pamela needs the money." I paced across the length of the terrace, my whip still in my hand. "You will find her accounts in arrears, her wine cellar all but empty. She does not entertain because she cannot afford to. She does not encourage the young ladies to marry or leave the area because *they are part of her scheme*. The young women set the actual snares and patrol the woods for her." At dawn and sunset, when they were least likely to be observed.

And their mamas and papas, having perhaps some clue where the extra money was coming from, turned a blind eye.

A portly, sweaty man in plain attire climbed down from the box of the police wagon and unlocked the single door. He stood by the open door, along with another man who'd traveled on the boot.

"Holly would know how to set snares," Freeman said. "She was the son her father never had, and no English boy from the shires reaches the age of twelve without snaring a hare or two."

Unless that boy set his snares on land owned by his father, he risked serious, even capital consequences for his actions. Even selling the meat could result in transportation, and yet, poaching was a thriving rural industry.

I was about to expound on the role of the footmen, some of whom would likely confess to their involvement in the hopes of leniency, when a heavy traveling coach rolled up the drive through the dust plume left by the police wagon. The more elegant coach steered deftly around the shabby wagon and halted at the foot of the terrace steps.

"Who could this be?" Bellamy senior muttered, getting to his feet. "Giles, look sharp. That is a crested coach."

As Giles heaved himself to his feet, the Earl of Derwent, in full morning splendor, emerged from the coach, followed by Sebastian.

"My lady." Papa bowed to me cordially. "You are in great good looks as always, though it's a sorry moment when the gentlemen of England must be schooled with a whip so early in the day. St. Sevier, greetings." Papa sauntered up the steps, a tired-looking Sebastian at his side.

"You must be Freeman," Papa went on, peering at the magistrate. "Dunkeld tells me you've decided to impose martial law on rural Kent. While I realize the peasantry can become fractious, they are English peasantry. We're to read them the Riot Act and consult our watches when they get too rumbustious. No martial law allowed. Who might these fellows be?"

Papa struck just the right note, half-imperious, half-bored curiosity.

Giles rallied first. "Giles Bellamy, my lord, at your service." He bowed. "My father, Mr. Anthony Bellamy." Bellamy senior managed a bow as well.

"And I have the pleasure to be Derwent," Papa said, nodding regally. "My lady, have you sorted matters to your satisfaction?"

"I am not the victim here, my lord. St. Sevier has been incarcerated, slandered, separated from his wife and child, and put in fear for his life. He submitted himself to those abuses because he did not want to see a group of young and foolish women hanged for poaching and because Freeman told him the charges against him could never be proven. He is to be commended for his chivalry and castigated for his misplaced trust."

St. Sevier nodded to me. "But I have the most excellent taste in friends."

I felt a foolish urge to cry. "As do I."

We shared an impossible, incongruous smile, and for the first time, I felt as if the whole mess—the poaching, St. Sevier's situation, the baby, everything—had a prayer of coming right.

But only a prayer.

"You lot," I called to the constables. "Take yourself around to the kitchen and see the horses watered and fed. Mr. Freeman will be withdrawing all charges against the present suspect, but he might have need of your wagon by the day's end."

Assuming he, himself, wasn't among those shackled and bound over for trial.

~

"I hadn't taken St. Sevier for the trusting sort," Papa said as the constables climbed back onto their vehicle and departed for the stable. "But then, gallantry is no respecter of reason. Freeman, are you asking for my assistance as a fellow magistrate with a legal matter in which your impartiality might be compromised?"

Oh, that was lovely. I hadn't realized a magistrate had that option.

"I am, my lord."

"And do you withdraw any and all charges lodged against Monsieur Hugh St. Sevier?"

Freeman had the grace to look chagrined. "I do, my lord. I would have testified at the trial, made certain the jury was aware of myriad factors that weigh against—"

Perhaps my whip hand had twitched. Most assuredly, Sebastian had done that business of adding several inches of menace to his posture.

"Anthony Bellamy trespassed on St. Sevier's property," Sebastian said. "Bellamy lset a deadly weapon on St. Sevier's land where it could and did harm the unsuspecting. Pamela Bonaventure has conspired to violate the king's game laws, as have at least four young women of this shire along with Hecate Dorrance and a platoon of footmen. Giles Bellamy has doubtless also fomented the whole disgusting undertaking, and he said nothing to the proper authorities while an innocent man was bound over for trial."

At some point, I'd taken Sebastian's hand, and I could feel the anger vibrating through him.

"Ann St. Sevier," Sebastian went on, "has been subjected to violations of her privacy and her peace and deprived of the company and protection of her husband, all so a lot of ruralizing hoydens could have new bonnet ribbons. Meanwhile, you try to throw the struggling families of this shire off the land while smiling graciously at one another in the churchyard. Is this what passes for law and order in England?"

Giles cleared his throat. "It's not like that."

St. Sevier considered him. "What is it like, Mr. Bellamy?" The question appeared sincere.

"We're all struggling. If Elizabeth hadn't taken over the books, Papa would have had no choice but to sell the property years ago. The Faradays aren't doing any better, nor are most of our landed neighbors. Pamela is hanging on by a thread, but she conceived this scheme to spread around a little of the wealth St. Sevier does not need. The woods are overrun with game. The gamekeepers turned a blind eye in exchange for the occasional coin, and I handled the dealings with the clubs. We all get a little bit to help make ends meet, and there's no harm done."

"I see." St. Sevier packed a world of irony into two syllables. "And what of Holly Faraday? As the field marshal of this little enterprise, is she kicking her heels at Mrs. Bonaventure's London town house, ready to miraculously reappear once I'm hanged?"

Giles looked anywhere but at me. "I don't know, and Pamela won't tell me. I came upon Holly and honestly believed she was dead. I went for the magistrate, thinking the worst, but then Holly's sisters found her, cut off her boot... and you saw the blood. Pamela says Holly pried the mantrap off her foot, crawled to the stream bank, and fainted, but she is recovering."

"A young woman was seriously injured nearly a week ago," Sebastian said. "You have no idea where she is, this shire has no physician, and we're standing about here, pointing fingers, and—"

"I know where Holly is," I said. "She's in the cottage near The Gauges's stable in an upstairs bedroom."

"She's not," Giles said, looking puzzled. "We use the cellar of that cottage to hang the game because the foundation is stone, and the cellars are quite cool, but the upstairs..."

"Thetis comes by every day to check on her sister," I went on as if Giles had not spoken. "Elizabeth has also visited the patient, and Selene has doubtless done so as well. They, along with Pamela, are probably taking shifts in the sickroom—hence Pamela's fatigue and muddy boots—but I fear the worst. Somebody had best get St. Sevier's medical kit."

"I'll fetch the kit," Sebastian said, "Freeman, I'm borrowing your fastest horse. Derwent, might we prevail on you for the use of your coach?"

"I'll ride Artemis," I said, "and see you at the cottage."

"Dunkeld," St. Sevier called, "ask my wife to join us at the cottage. She is an extremely competent nurse, and if anybody is owed an apology for this debacle, she is."

Sebastian bowed, jogged down the steps, and took off at a lope in the direction of Freeman's stable.

"Into the coach," Papa said, "the lot of you. I have never kept such close company with a criminal in my life, young Bellamy, unless you count my compatriots in the Lords. Daughter, you will doubtless arrive at the scene before us. Temper your wrath with compassion. St. Sevier will come to no further harm. My word on that. The same cannot be said for his enterprising neighbors."

"To the coach," St. Sevier said. "A young lady is in need of medical attention, and that is what matters at the moment."

I mentally applauded Hugh's savoir faire—and his compassion—but as Artemis cantered back in the direction of The Gauges, I was assailed by how narrowly he'd escaped a dire fate. Had I dawdled in the stable yard, waiting for my coach to be hitched up. Had I slept another thirty minutes...

But I had not, and Sebastian had delivered Papa to me, and in another hour or two, I could quit The Gauges and never return. I let Artemis trot the last quarter mile, though she was sweaty and winded when we reached the stable. Biddle took her reins as I dismounted.

"You're back already?"

"And off to the cottage, Biddle, where I expect I will find a seriously injured young woman in need of immediate medical attention. *Dr.* St. Sevier will soon be on hand, so the situation is not without hope."

He closed his eyes for a moment, then speared me with a look. "Missus is having her coach hitched up as we speak, and her pretty boys were carrying trunks down to the carriage house. One of them told me I'd best scarper if I know what's good for me."

"If you scarper, you arguably leave Thetis to face a dire situation without the support of the man who loves her."

"If I stay, I could swing with the rest of them."

Pamela came down the path with what could be characterized as unladylike speed. In the normal course, the coach would have pulled up before the house, and she would have departed in plain view of her staff.

She was scarpering, to use Biddle's words, and making a poor job of it.

"Lady Violet, you will excuse me. Urgent business requires that I—"

I held up my whip. "You are not going anywhere. You could have helped these young women find suitable husbands, and instead, you led them down the path to criminal wrongdoing. You have much to answer for."

Pamela stared at me, hatred of breathtaking intensity radiating from her gaze. "You don't know what it's like to love a man to the point of madness while he lives only to tramp his acres and regale his friends with tales of hunt meets past. I adored him, and he adored his sporting life. The money—the money I brought to our marriage— went to an endless progression of hunters and fowling pieces and race meets. He spent more time on the grouse moors than he did with me, and I have nothing, not even a child, to show for my years as his wife."

And this, somehow, justified the creation of a lucrative poaching ring?

"Right now, your bitterness does not matter, and my rage does not matter. Holly Faraday matters, and competent medical talent is on the way to do what can be done for her."

"Let me by," Pamela snarled. "You can't do this me." She would have shouldered past me, doubtless to hop into her coach and catch the next packet for Calais, but Biddle stepped in her path.

"Not this time, missus. Her ladyship says you will bide here for the nonce, and that's what you'll do."

"Good man." I passed Biddle my whip as Papa's traveling coach came tooling up the drive. "I'm for the cottage."

I dodged down the path at a fast trot, glad my corset had been laced so loosely. The door to the cottage was unlocked, but the place had the still, stuffy air of an unused dwelling.

"Holly!" I called, climbing the staircase. "Miss Faraday!"

No reply. I navigated to the door of the room that sat above the rose trellis and knocked. "Miss Faraday, a physician is on the way. I'm coming in." I pushed the door open. "I am Lady Violet Bel..."

The stench was overpowering. I took two steps back and sank to the floor against the far wall. Had I consumed any breakfast... but I hadn't. I was still on the floor, breathing through my mouth and sending up silent prayers, when St. Sevier arrived five minutes later.

CHAPTER SEVENTEEN

Never had I heard such cursing in French or any other language. St. Sevier spoke softly, though, and interspersed his invective with gentle English conversation directed at a patient apparently incapable of replying.

I remained in the corridor, while Freeman and Giles Bellamy joined St. Sevier in the sickroom. I heard the sound of a window sash scraping open, and an eddy of less foul air reached me.

"Violet, come away." Papa extended a hand to me. "St. Sevier will do for the woman what can be done. We are in the way here."

With Papa's assistance, I struggled to my feet. My head swam slightly, so I kept hold of his arm as we descended to the cottage porch. Papa saw me settled into one of two rocking chairs and took the other.

"St. Sevier and Freeman have been to war," Papa said. "They are the best possible source of aid in a situation this dire." Papa had been to war, too, as a much younger man. If he said the situation was dire, he spoke knowledgeably.

"All week," I said, closing my eyes to the pretty summer morning, "every day while I have been sipping Pamela's bad wine and arguing with her grooms, that young woman has been in torments. She needed help, she needed medical attention and constant care, and she's been stashed away to die in that—"

"Violet, stop. Even with the best of care, we might be measuring Miss Faraday for a shroud. She *was* poaching, and St. Sevier would have been within his rights to resort to mantraps. You found her, you've cleared St. Sevier's name, and you've cleared his woods of poachers. Cease your dramatics."

I opened my eyes and beheld the man who'd known me longer than any other person, save my mother. "It won't wash, Papa. You cannot scold and annoy me back to a sanguine outlook. What happened here was a monstrous wrong. To St. Sevier, to Ann and Fiona, to the poor families who'd be deprived of St. Sevier's aid... Evil was done here."

"So somebody must pay?" Papa sounded half amused. "Your mother had a fine sense of justice, too, and she lamented my more pragmatic outlook on human foibles."

"I miss Mama." The words came out plaintive and weary.

"You are very like her, and she would be immensely proud of you, as I am proud of you."

I had needed to hear those words, and from Papa. I also needed to test them. "I am unconventional."

Papa sighed and set his chair to rocking. "Society does not move forward because of those who uphold convention, Violet. The people who can think for themselves, who can see past customary existence and dream of better worlds are the people who move us forward. Convention has its place—somebody must hoe the peas and raise the children—but your disdain for convention has upheld the cause of justice and truth here and elsewhere."

Was my father *approving* of me? I sat up and peered over at him. "Papa, are you well?"

He gave me his signature charming-rogue grin. "I am in my prime, Violet Marie. How dare you suggest otherwise?"

"I am not in my prime. I am hungry, tired, angry, and worried for that poor young woman." I was also expecting a child, and realizing as I sat in that comfortable rocker on that prosaic little porch that my life had already changed because the child was on the way. I had gone for my last wild gallop for some time, among other things.

"You should also be relieved. Freeman resorted to desperate measures in an effort to solve what to him was a puzzle. He suspected Anthony Bellamy, but had no proof. He suspected the poorest families, but they had every reason—and permission—to be in the woods. He did not see the evidence right before his eyes, or did not want to see it. Freeman's gamble went badly awry, and the outcome could have been even worse."

Sebastian and Ann rode into the clearing, each with a bundle tied behind their saddles.

"She's alive," I said. "Upstairs, second door on the right. It's bad."

Ann slipped from the saddle unassisted. "We brought both bags, medical and surgical. Dunkeld, come along. The patient might well need to be restrained if Hugh has to operate."

She took the bundle from behind her saddle and jogged up the steps and into the house. Sebastian tarried long enough to secure the horses and untie the second bundle, then climbed the porch steps more slowly.

"Violet, are you well?"

"Managing. Papa has been assigned the job of talking sense into me."

Sebastian stood peering down at me, a question in his eyes. No, I had not told Papa about the baby. Yes, I probably should. I rose and hugged Sebastian.

He hugged me back and took his time about it. "If anybody can bring medical matters right, St. Sevier can, and Ann has spent many an hour in the surgery tent. No effort will be spared."

"You have to go," I said, keeping a snug hold of him. "Biddle has prevented Pamela from catching a packet to Calais."

"First, we see to Holly Faraday, then we sort out the rest." Sebastian kissed my cheek, gave me a squeeze, and let me go. He collected the second medical bag and disappeared into the house.

I sank back into my rocking chair, feeling marginally better. I had always loved Sebastian's woodsy scent, and that alone had quelled a slight queasiness.

"The problem with poaching," Papa said, as if my exchange with Sebastian had not taken place, "is that proving the offense requires catching the culprits with the goods, or finding one of them willing to give evidence against another. Proving that Bellamy set a mantrap on St. Sevier's land will be equally difficult."

Fine, then. We would discuss legalities, because those might be adequately vexatious to distract me from what was happening inside the house.

"Difficult because we have only St. Sevier's word that Bellamy is responsible?"

"And because St. Sevier did not come forward at the time he first noticed Bellamy trespassing. He arguably condoned the trespass by keeping silent. The lawyers would have a fine time debating the subtleties."

"We will probably find a dozen brace of hares very unsubtly hanging in the cellars of this cottage." Pamela had not allowed Holly's circumstances to interrupt regular deliveries by the footmen to London's clubs.

"And Mrs. Bonaventure will claim she had no clue that an unused building had been taken over by a ring of female felons."

"How does she explain a young woman half dead in an upstairs bedroom?"

Papa gave an airy wave of his hand. "Clearly, that young woman was the mastermind behind the whole nefarious scheme. Mrs. Bonaventure will deliver protestations of innocence worthy of Mrs. Siddons at her tragic best. Assuming Holly Faraday survives, Holly will make the same claim. She was having an innocent stroll in the woods—heeding nature's call while out on a hack, no doubt—when tragedy befell her."

I began to understand—though not approve of—the steps Freeman had taken to rid the shire of its poachers. The usual methods hadn't worked, the unusual methods weren't working, so he'd resorted to questionable methods.

Arrest a plausible suspect and hope the real felons mis-stepped badly enough to be caught.

"What's to be done, then?" I asked, my frustration mounting. "While the poorer families of the shire watch their children sicken season by season, the squires and their daughters play lethal games in St. Sevier's woods. Freeman must resign at the very least."

"He will doubtless offer to. If I read the man correctly, he will first arrest himself for malfeasance and bind himself over for a trial at the assizes."

"Is that a jest?"

A loud moan floated down from the second-floor window.

"Partly. Freeman was a code breaker and code maker during the war, Violet. I gather he was famous for unorthodox solutions to military problems. He had some French general's sheets washed in a tincture of an itching weed from Canada, for example. The fellow's vastly inadequate subordinate led in battle the next day, with happy results for His Majesty's forces. A contest that might have been lost after a day's carnage was instead won in less than an hour."

Papa's point was clear: Did a man who'd distinguished himself to that extent deserve to be ruined by scandal now? A man who had been wounded and maimed in service to his country?

"Holly could well die, Papa. I understand why Freeman took desperate measures, precisely because he knew how dangerous poaching can be, but Pamela has no such excuse." And it was at Pamela that most of my ire was directed. "She could have simply admitted the truth: Holly stepped on a mantrap while, as you say, making a necessary stop in the woods. She could have sent Holly to London, where physicians and surgeons abound. She could have sold The Gauges and lived on the proceeds."

Papa ceased his rocking. "But she had to have her fine house, her handsome footmen, her pretty carriage. Nobody holds a grudge like a woman scorned, and I suspect Mrs. Bonaventure was not a happy wife. This estate is hers by virtue of her marriage. By perpetrating her crimes, she exacts a sort of revenge on her husband's memory."

That Papa would so easily deduce Pamela's motives astounded me. "I should then entice my maids to go to work at the brothel Freddie frequented and have them set fire to the place? I'm having trouble following the logic, Papa."

He rose and perched on the porch's wooden balustrade. "You would not grasp the connections, because you are not bitter. St. Sevier, I gather, is most of the reason why that malady did not befall you. How are you managing, Violet?"

His gaze was on the rhododendrons ringing the overgrown yard. The blooms were magnificent, and in his way, Papa was magnificent too. He could be petulant, selfish, sly, and difficult, but that was not the whole of him. Not nearly. He was also wise, often kind, and—this amazed me—capable of shyness.

"Dunkeld proposed to me."

"One wondered what all that brooding Scottish silence was about. He has fancied you since he was a lad, but please don't marry him to spite me."

Ah. Spite. Papa's admonition gave me the tiniest sliver of comprehension regarding Pamela Bonaventure's scheme. A woman scorned, Papa had said. Scorned, betrayed, and abandoned, and that was before her *adored* spouse had gone and died on her of an ague contracted in the hunt field.

"I am not in a position to indulge myself with tantrums, Papa. I am with child."

Papa studied the rhododendrons as if he expected a sixteen-point buck to emerge from their depths. "Are you well, Violet?"

Somebody—Freddie?—had informed Papa of my disappointments, though Papa and I had discussed those losses only briefly in the past.

"I am in more robust health than I have enjoyed in years." The best health I'd had since marrying, in fact.

"See that you stay that way." A paternal command, rendered with dry imperiousness. "Dare I ask who the father is?"

"St. Sevier. We were in contemplation of marriage, then Ann showed up with Fiona."

"Once a Deerfield, always a Deerfield. You do not seem upset with your situation."

Papa was not upset. Now, when I truly, truly needed him to be my father and not some spluttering peer bent on self-serving machinations in the Lords, he was behaving with impressive aplomb.

"I have been... bewildered. I don't want Dunkeld marrying me out of pity. I do want my child to be at least nominally legitimate."

Papa pushed off from the balustrade. "If a Scottish marquess with more pride than Scotland has scenery offers for you, when he knows your child could be his legal heir, then that man is not in the grip of pity. He's making a bid to win by opportunism what my intervention denied him years ago. The man is mad for you, Violet."

Papa bent to kiss my forehead. "You will always be my daughter, and I will always be proud of you. I might wish you were less outspoken or headstrong—for your sake as well as my own—but you are your mother's daughter too. All she and I would want for you is a long and happy life."

He descended the steps, took up the reins of the horses tied in the yard, and led them back up the path to the stable. I watched him doing a job that might have been delegated to the lowliest groom and felt tears spilling hot and heartfelt down my cheeks.

"Papa!"

He turned.

"I love you!"

"As I have ever loved you." He blew me a kiss and went upon his way.

~

"I could have saved those toes had somebody called for me at the time of the injury." St. Sevier propped a hip against the porch railing in the same spot Papa had occupied. "But no. A young woman must fight for her life and go about permanently disfigured—if the good God allows her to live—so some fat London lordling can dine on hare or partridge at his whim. And you English call the French a savage race."

Ann, who occupied the other rocking chair, smiled. "He's always like this after a successful operation. What matters a few of toes compared to a life cut short by stupidity and bad luck? St. Sevier would have us all bounding about with Olympian immortality."

"The toes," St. Sevier began, "are more important than we realize. Balance, posture, speed, power, these all depend on the lowly toes, and now Miss Faraday is short three of the usual complement because of arrogance and greed. That same arrogance and greed could well cost her her life, because the wound became infected."

"Some of that arrogance and greed," Sebastian said, "must be attributed to the young lady herself." He sat beside my rocking chair on the planks of the porch floor. I had the strangest urge to pet him, to stroke his hair or brush my finger across his nape.

His presence soothed me, and I suspected he'd been of great help to St. Sevier in the sickroom too.

"True," St. Sevier said. "The young ladies are not blameless, nor are their parents, nor are the Bellamys, nor is Freeman himself. Violet, have you decided what's to be done?"

He was asking me about the whole poaching business, and maybe about the baby too.

"Dunkeld and Lady Violet will be our guests at Belle Terre," Ann said.

We all looked at her, though nobody spoke.

"First, we are not enemies," she said. "Far from it. We four are privy to some unique truths, which are a lighter burden for being shared. We need not dissemble before one another for the sake of appearances. Second, Lady Violet will need a respite before she undertakes more travel. She has had a trying week and must consider her health, though I'm sure she's eager to be quit of The Gauges. Third, we must find a way forward, for the sake of our children, and a cordial display now will do much to thwart gossip in the coming years."

I thought back to Papa's little homily, about progress depending on the unconventional thinkers. He'd been referring to steam engines and hot-air balloons, to men who had the courage to sail around a supposedly flat Earth, but his reasoning applied in other spheres as well.

"Violet and St. Sevier were visiting friends in Perthshire earlier this year," Sebastian said. "Then she and I met up again in the Lakes. The child could be mine, in theory."

"*L'enfant n'est pas...* The child is *not* yours." Hugh had spoken with some exasperation. "I will support my offspring, not only because that is my duty as a gentleman, but because that is my honor and privilege. I cannot be expected to waltz along, ignoring a life I created with every intention of... *Bon Dieu, sauve moi.* Ann, I mean you no insult, but the situation is vexing."

"My baby and I will be fine," I said. "Derwent made it plain that my family will support me regardless of the choices I make in this instance. I suspect he's atoning for past meddling, but his goodwill will mean much to the child. St. Sevier, if your conscience troubles you on the matter, rest assured I would not do anything different had I the chance to do it all again." If anything, I might have taken him as a lover sooner and more often, a sentiment I saw no reason to air.

"My lady is being honorable," St. Sevier retorted. "Honor has its limitations."

Ann folded her arms. "Who was willing to risk the gallows for the sake of a lot of rural schoolgirls bent on wickedness?"

"*Un point valable,* but the young ladies were not the only parties whose welfare depended—"

"Don't argue with your wife," Sebastian said. "Ann is Scottish, and more to the point, she's right. You got in over your head, as did Freeman, and only Violet's persistence saw the whole scheme unraveled."

"And your persistence too, my lord," Ann said, "for which I thank you both. I honestly care not if anybody is arrested for anything. I would like to see Miss Faraday make a complete recovery and see the local young ladies steered to pursuits more likely to lead to happiness than a hangman's noose."

"You are too kind," St. Sevier retorted. "You saw the state of Miss Faraday's foot. Another few days, and her situation would have been hopeless. She is in wretched pain and will face, at best, a long convalescence, which is entirely—"

"I was once a young girl," Ann said, "bent on following my sweetheart to war. A very good man tried to come to my aid when I became a widow, but I would have none of that. I got a second chance when I deserved none, Hugh St. Sevier. I am in no position to cast stones."

A look passed between husband and wife that I need not decipher. Whatever else was true, Ann and Hugh St. Sevier were a couple, a committed union, capable of dealing with each other honestly and courageously.

That realization had a subtle and profound effect on me. I did not need to look after St. Sevier, to guard him against unforeseen perils, or protect him in any regard. He'd told me that, but I could see with my own eyes that Ann would protect him, and if Ann needed reinforcements, she would send for me. If I needed reinforcements, I could send for her, and she would similarly put herself—and her husband, to the extent she could—at my disposal.

I had family, *and I had family.*

"Violet," Sebastian said, "shall I escort you back to Town, or shall we tarry for a few days at Belle Terre?"

He left the decision to me, and the last of my bewilderment fell away. "We will visit with our good friends, because Ann is right, I do need to rest. We have also yet to sort out what's to be done about the poaching, but I have some ideas."

"I will ensure that my patient is resting as comfortably as possible," St. Sevier said, "and give her sisters instructions for her care, then I will—"

"You will come up to The Gauges manor house with us," I said, "and we will deal with Pamela, Freeman, and the footmen. You have doubtless lectured Thetis and Selene at length. Then we can repair to Belle Terre and commence a peaceful respite from all the drama of the week." And all the drama of the year.

I thought perhaps Hugh would get offended or remonstrate with me. He rose, bowed, and smiled. "To the manor house, then. A gentleman does not argue with a lady."

Ann snorted as she took his arm. Sebastian assisted me to my feet, and we returned to The Gauges for what I hoped was the last time. We had not climbed to the top of the terrace steps before I heard Pamela shrieking like a banshee about false imprisonment and slander and the respect a widow was due.

"We can put this off," Sebastian said as Hugh and Ann continued on into the house. "She'll calm down eventually."

"She has had years to calm down. This is not about a poaching ring, Sebastian. This is about a wedding ring. She put her whole heart and soul into her marriage and was treated at best as an afterthought. Before her husband could outgrow the error of his ways, he died and left her without much in the way of means. I do not know what would make her happy—some women hold to grief as tightly as they ever held to love—but punishment will only make her that much more bitter."

"St. Sevier is leaving this up to us," Sebastian said, "which is shrewd of him, innocent little French émigré that he is. What do you suggest?"

Ann was leaving this up to us as well, and I had the sense she was simply not interested in sorting out the rest of the problem.

I leaned into Sebastian, so grateful for his steadfast calm I nearly started weeping again. "The problem is one of coin and common sense, and Pamela is in a position to rectify at least one of those issues. Anthony Bellamy can do his part too. Come along, and then you will escort me to Belle Terre, where I will take a spectacularly long nap."

CHAPTER EIGHTEEN

Upjohn and one of Sebastian's grooms escorted a fuming Pamela into The Gauges's library. She refused to sit when offered one of the reading chairs, until Sebastian patted the back of the chair.

"The discussion could be lengthy," he said, "and your petulance would force every gentleman in the room to remain on his feet for the duration. Sit down and know that my men will stand guard just outside the door."

Never had a Scottish burr rung with more authority.

Pamela flounced into the chair. "Ordering me about in my own house, Dunkeld. Is that really necessary?"

"This will not be your house for long." I situated myself in another wing chair. "With the exception of Maitland, your footmen have abandoned ship, and only Biddle's good example prevents your outside staff from doing likewise. You have much to answer for, Pamela."

"Then send me to trial, but explain how you will accuse me of violating the game laws when I set not one booted foot in Belle Terre's woods."

"Conspiracy is a separate crime," Papa said, settling himself at the library's venerable desk. "All it takes is one person's testimony to implicate you, madam, and whether you are convicted or not, you will be ruined by the charges."

Freeman and the Bellamys had drawn up chairs from those at the reading table. The St. Seviers occupied the window seat, and Sebastian lounged against a corner of the desk. I had chosen a seat near the windows, the St. Seviers on my right and the others ranged about me in a semicircle.

Freeman's pretty wall paintings made this an unlikely courtroom. I wanted to be done with the whole business, though, and the library was large enough to house our proceedings. The only servant on hand was Maitland, standing by the fireplace, and he was not present in his capacity as footman.

"What could any witness say that would implicate me?" Pamela retorted. "My hands are clean."

"Meaning," I said, "that you never handled the game itself, or bothered to set a single snare. No matter. You were seen conferring with Miss Selene Faraday as she held a half-dozen dead hares at the back door of the cottage. She went inside with her catch—ostensibly to hang it in the cellars—while you went off to the stable to order your carriage brought around for Sunday services. You had incontrovertible proof of poaching and did not notify Freeman of the crime."

According to Papa, Biddle had witnessed that little vignette with Selene, among many others. Pamela instructing the footmen as to destination and expected remuneration. Pamela passing out payment to the young ladies. Pamela collecting the coin from the footmen returning from London...

"Mrs. Bonaventure had nothing to do with this," Maitland said. "The whole thing was my idea."

Papa looked amused. The other gentlemen in the room winced.

"Maitland loves you," I said to Pamela. "He is willing to *give his life* for you. I suggest that rather than commending him to the gallows, you accept his offer of marriage, and take advantage of the cheaper accommodations to be had on the Continent."

"Marry a footman? I'd be ruined just as effectively as if I..."

I stared at her. She was an angry, selfish woman, but not stupid. "That is the point, Pamela, to ensure you are ruined and banished. If Maitland must suffer marriage to you as his penance, I consider that a bit of retribution for his role in your scheme. Perhaps you will come to appreciate him as your late husband never appreciated you."

"I cannot marry a footman."

"Maitland." Papa turned a very severe eye on Pamela's swain. "If Mrs. Bonaventure is willing, would you speak your vows with her?"

"Absolutely, my lord. I would live anywhere, do anything, take any post—"

Papa held up a hand. "You have made your point, and may God have mercy on your heart."

I suspected another part of Maitland's anatomy was doing at least some of his thinking. "Marriage to Maitland," I said, "solves only part of the dilemma you've caused, Pamela. You will sell The Gauges and put the proceeds in trust to serve as dowries for the young ladies whom you inveigled into your scheme."

"I didn't inveigle anybody. Those women are of age, and they were bored witless. I gave them an idea, a means of..."

Sebastian cocked his head. "Do go on. Gave them a means of becoming criminals instead of wives or aunties? Gave them tasks that resulted in serious injury to one and will lead to the ruin of all of them? What exactly did you give them?"

"I have nothing more to say."

"Good," I retorted, "for I have much to say. You doubtless hinted to the misses that you would invite them up to London, hold a house party brimming with eligible bachelors, and otherwise advance their marital interests. All they had to do to earn those precious boons from you was take enormous risks for your enrichment."

Maitland took a step forward. "They were paid. We were all paid. Nobody was forced to do anything."

"They were paid a pittance," I said gently, "as you were. Giles

Bellamy doubtless saw some coin, too, as did the gamekeepers, but most of the money went straight into Pamela's hands."

She sat silently twitching at her skirts, while I watched Maitland grapple with a sobering dose of truth.

"We found the books," Freeman said. "She kept them in her late husband's estate office. Mrs. Bonaventure has accumulated a tidy little fortune from the illegal efforts of others."

"But, Pamela," Maitland said, his handsome face a study in consternation, "you said... the wages had to wait... And the wine... the... *A tidy fortune?*"

"Sufficient," I said, "to modestly dower a few misguided young women, or see them with a comfortable competence should they prefer not to marry." I was insistent on that last provision, particularly for Holly who had likely been poaching on Pamela's behalf for years.

"That is my money," Pamela said, rising abruptly. "I am owed that money. I brought *wealth* to my marriage, real wealth, and now I cannot afford even to paint over the damned flowers Bonaventure commissioned for the walls. Those commissions went to you"—she pointed an accusing finger at Freeman—"and this is the thanks I get?"

"According to English justice," Papa observed mildly, "you deserve a noose, ma'am. Violet, might she be permitted to keep a bit of coin with which to establish her Continental household?"

I thought of the compassion Ann had shown for the young women and of the bitter disappointment my marriage had become.

"One-third of the ready cash," I said. "And one-third of any coin raised by the sale of fungibles and livestock." Pamela's stable was ample, and The Gauges was elegantly furnished. The wheeled vehicles alone would bring in a substantial sum. "I trust Mr. Freeman can act as factor overseeing those transactions."

"A dower portion," Ann murmured. "More than I would have done."

"This is all subject to the approval of Monsieur," I said, "who might wish to see Belle Terre sold before The Gauges is put on the market."

Hugh took Ann's hand and kissed her knuckles. "Sell The Gauges as soon as may be and give Mrs. Bonaventure her remittance. What will you do with the proceeds from the sale of her real estate?"

I had given that matter some thought. "Clear her debts first, which are considerable, despite the money she made. The rest should be added to the dowries. I would like to see Giles Bellamy established on his own small property, provided he marries Miss Holly Faraday. Thetis is in anticipation of a marriage proposal, and a few acres would make her situation much happier."

"Selene is in anticipation of a marriage proposal as well," Freeman said. "Assuming I am not in the constable's wagon when they leave for Maidstone."

"You should be," Pamela spat. "I would have married you." Failing to propose to her, rather than any ill-advised legal bungling, was clearly Freeman's greater offense.

"We would not have suited," Freeman replied, in what had to be the grandest display of gentlemanly forbearance in the history of gentlemanly forbearance.

"I'll marry you, Pamela." Maitland stood very tall. "Despite everything. I'll marry you and live with you in France or Italy or Portugal. We can be happy. I know we can."

I saw in Maitland all the foolish innocence of the young and naïve. Pamela would break his heart, which was an unavoidable shame. Perhaps, before it was all over, he could break hers, too, and then they could get on with salvaging their marriage.

"What of Papa?" Giles Bellamy said. "He meant well, but his plans went awry."

Anthony Bellamy stared straight ahead, probably ready to climb into the constable's wagon and roast all the way to Maidstone.

"St. Sevier?" I asked, because he alone of all of us could assess Holly Faraday's injuries and prognosis.

"Trespassing is wrong," St. Sevier said. "Half the shire apparently feels free to use my woods as their personal royal forest, so I am prepared to overlook that disrespect. Leaving a mantrap, though, in my woods was a heinous presumption that has resulted in the very predictable outcome of grievous harm to another. Bellamy's own daughter might have come to a bad end because of her father's meddling."

Bellamy's gaze shifted to the pretty carpet. "I wanted them to stop. I had no idea young women were involved, but I suspected Giles had a hand in matters along with those wretched families scraping by on the common land. I told Giles exactly what I planned. I've traveled those woods my whole life. I know the game trails, the salt lick, where the deer ford the stream. I know that whole woods better than St. Sevier does. Giles grasped the seriousness of my warning."

"I did not!" Giles shot to his feet. "You are always maundering on about selling our property, about sending Elizabeth to the aunties as a companion, about taking Mama to Bath for her rheumatism, but you never *do* anything. You ride about your acres by the hour, enjoy your pint at the posting inn, and come home full of more talk."

He paced the length of the library, a caged beast. "I am twenty-three years old, Papa. I have no trade, I have no prospects because my brother will inherit the estate. I missed out on the war lest I break Mama's heart, and I have only a scintilla of education. I cannot sit by... oh, just hang me. I will take responsibility for everything, but leave my family out of it. Tell Holly I love her, assuming she lives, and I will die content in the knowledge that I meant well."

Papa's eyes were dancing as Giles concluded his tragic monologue, and Sebastian had turned to the sideboard to pour a round of brandy—or something.

"Miss Faraday is young and strong," St. Sevier said. "That she has not already expired is proof of a very vigorous constitution, but if you should end your days in disgrace on the scaffold, her chances of recovery plummet."

"Heed him," Freeman said. "When serious injury diminishes our physical powers, it can diminish our spirit as well. When my hand was rendered all but useless, I considered taking my own life. Fortunately, my ability to load, aim, and fire a handgun had also suffered. By the time I had regained those skills, my outlook had improved, but it was a very near thing."

Something in his recitation led me to believe that in low moments, it might still be a very near thing for Thaddeus Freeman. Perhaps Selene could encourage him to resume painting, because his talent was formidable and unique.

"I set that mantrap," Anthony Bellamy said. "I am to blame for the worst harm here. I meant well—"

"You did not mean well," I said quite firmly. "You suspected Giles might be handling the London end of things, with his periodic trips to Town and unexplained income, but you believed the poor families were setting the snares or netting the fish. You did not care if one of them suffered the fate Miss Faraday did."

Bellamy had the grace to keep his stupid, arrogant mouth shut.

"What shall we do with you?" Papa mused. "Freeman has agreed to step down as magistrate and to refuse the post should it be offered to him again. That leaves this matter in my capable and thoroughly disgusted hands."

Papa did have a flair for drama, so I let his taunt—his threat— hang over Bellamy's head for a moment.

"I have a suggestion," I said when nobody else spoke up. "Have Mr. Bellamy deed his property to his oldest son. If it's entailed, the entail can be broken, as that son is his heir. Giles and Holly might consider buying the largest tenant property, which should result in a dose of cash to treat whatever ails the Bellamy estate. If Giles feels frustrated and useless, I can only imagine his older brother feels worse yet."

"There's nothing wrong with Nigel's mind," Freeman said. "And if he owns the property, then he can take over the magistrate's post, for which he is well qualified."

"But he's..." Bellamy looked to Giles. "Your brother has spells. He grows morose. He doesn't speak but four words in the course of a day."

"He doesn't set mantraps on his neighbor's property," I said, "and he hasn't clung to the wool trade until his acres were all but ruined. Give your sons a chance and take your wife to the seaside. She can doubtless use a change of air."

Bellamy wanted to argue, clearly. He glowered at me, then he tried glowering at Giles, who remained blessedly silent.

"You will not get a better offer," Sebastian said. "Giles is contemplating marriage to the woman whom your foolish scheme saw maimed and nearly killed. You might consider a permanent remove to Bath, assuming Mrs. Bellamy doesn't toss you out on your ear."

"Mama could do it too," Giles said. "But I do fancy the idea of the property deeded to my brother. Nigel is smarter than I will ever be, and he reads everything. He's the one who suggested Elizabeth take over the books."

"You lot *schemed* to give Lizzie the books?" Bellamy retorted.

I was out of patience with him and abruptly quite tired. "Be grateful that they did. Will you relinquish the title to your land or not?"

Bellamy drew himself up and again glowered at Giles, then he rose. "I will deed over the land, I will take Mrs. Bellamy to the shore, and I will apologize to all for my role in these goings-on. Am I free to leave?"

"You need to work on your apologies," I said. "Mrs. Bellamy might well accept your escort to Bath. It remains to be seen whether you'll be permitted to return home with her."

The squire all but dashed from the room.

"Am I free to leave as well?" Giles ran a hand through hair that was for once disheveled. "I played a role in all the wrong that has been done, and I don't regard marrying into a comfortable position as adequate to the punishment I deserve."

"Holly hasn't said she'll have you," Ann pointed out, "and she will have to learn again how to walk. She will know significant pain, even once the fevers have passed, and she—who used to gallop unescorted at all hours, or tramp at will through the woods—will need much patience and care."

"She will consider herself disfigured," St. Sevier added, "and she might blame herself, or blame her father, *or blame you*. You knew the mantraps might have been set in the woods, and you did not dissuade her."

"I tried to."

How hard had he tried, given that he claimed he did not believe his father's threats and he, too, benefited from the poaching?

"Suffice it to say," Papa replied, "that your road will not be easy, and very few tenant properties are kept in first-rate repair, assuming your brother will sell you the best of the lot. Away with you. Your beloved will want to see you when her latest dose of laudanum wears off."

Giles looked a little sickly, but he left the library quietly, and I watched through the window as he made his way across the terrace and in the direction of the cottage.

"Which brings us back to you," Papa said, considering Mrs. Bonaventure. "You can either heed her ladyship's suggestions and use your ill-gotten gains to put right some of what you've put wrong, or I will arrest you on the spot and see you bundled off to Maidstone—unless Monsieur or Madame St. Sevier have something more to add?"

❦

Ann and Hugh had been mostly quiet during this whole unusual proceeding, but Ann rose now. She crossed to stand before Pamela and delivered a sharp slap to the widow's face. The sound reverberated through the library like a thunderclap and I daresay woke up the assemblage.

"That is not for my husband," Ann said, "who would never wish harm on another. That is for the Grants and their neighbors. They desperately need the services of a physician. For want of a bottle of cod liver oil, their children are growing up with painful deformities, which my husband knows precisely how to treat. But you and your damned scheming neighbors tried to run us off, tried to disgrace a good man.

"That is no matter," Ann went on, pacing away when she doubtless longed to deliver a backhand to Pamela's other cheek. "My honor is my own, and my husband is a man well above reproach. But you thought only of yourself, only of your pitiful little vanities. Your most obvious offense is not against my husband and me, it is against the young women and against Miss Faraday in particular. She will never be whole. She will never know if Giles married her out of pity or guilt. She has been maimed by your greed, but you have been a blight on this whole shire."

I saw precisely where Ann's reasoning led and agreed with her wholeheartedly.

"Your neighbors, all of your neighbors, are desperately in want of a physician in their circle," Ann said, "from Mrs. Bellamy with her rheumatism to any woman facing childbed. You did everything in your power to stop a highly skilled physician from settling in here and relieving what suffering he could.

"You and Bellamy and his ilk,"—she gestured in the direction of the village—"believe that your hunger for coin is more important than a mother's hunger to see her children grow up straight and strong. For shame, Pamela Bonaventure. I wish you had seen what I saw in Spain, what I still see in Scotland, and what Monsieur has doubtless seen in London. You are a greater disgrace than you can even fathom. I have nothing more to say to you. Monsieur, please take me home. We have a housekeeper to turn off without a character."

At some point in this excoriation, Pamela's bravado had wavered and collapsed. She began to cry, and Freeman passed her a handkerchief.

"My wife and I will take our leave," St. Sevier said, rising. "She speaks more eloquently on my behalf than I ever could. My lady, Dunkeld, we will expect you at Belle Terre shortly."

He bowed over my hand and kissed my cheek. Ann gave me a

fierce, tight hug, treated Sebastian to the same display, and withdrew with her husband. The library door clicked softly closed in their wake, and the only sound remaining was Pamela's soft weeping.

~

"Maitland," Papa said, "pack your things and have your intended on her way to Dover within the hour. I will instruct the coachman to return with the vehicle directly, so don't think you can sell the carriage and team before leaving the country. When you are settled on the Continent, send Freeman your direction. Mrs. Bonaventure, where is your strongbox?"

"In the coach, packed beneath my underlinen. Lady Violet said I was to have some coin, so I don't see why—"

"I'll tell you why," I said. "Because your staff—the maids and cooks and grooms—all deserve to have their wages brought up to date, and they must be paid to maintain the place until another owner can take possession. Lord Dunkeld's grooms will fetch the strongbox, and you will tell Lord Derwent the combination. Then you shall wait in your coach for Maitland to join you."

Pamela sniffed into her handkerchief. "You have grown very good at giving orders, *my lady*."

"And you have much to learn about following them," Papa said. "Dunkeld, if you would dispatch your groom."

Sebastian complied, sending the groom to the stables and tasking Upjohn with escorting Pamela to the estate office.

"Will you bide here tonight?" I asked Papa when Pamela had gone sniffing and muttering on her way.

"I will impose on Freeman's hospitality. He'll need to prostrate himself with remorse before somebody, and I am on hand to oblige. He truly got carried away, but then, Miss Faraday could have died, suggesting that Freeman's concerns were justified. Ironic, that a man known for original thinking did not fathom that women could form a poaching ring. Diana the huntress is hardly an obscure fable."

"Freeman's method of flushing the criminals from their covert was anything but conventional," Sebastian observed. "And his departure from convention has been vindicated: The poaching continued while all fingers pointed at St. Sevier, and thus Violet could unravel the puzzle. Thank you for your assistance, my lord. Your standing and knowledge of English law have also helped see the matter efficiently resolved."

"A pretty speech, young man." Papa looked like he wanted to say more, to launch into a lecture of some sort, but he merely bowed over my hand and admonished me to visit at Derwent Hall before the summer was over.

I was left alone in the library with Sebastian, and though the day was only half over, I was exhausted.

"Brandy?" Sebastian asked. "I cannot vouch for the quality. I can also offer a nip from my flask."

"A nip will do. I am astonished, given the severity of the situation, that nobody has been charged with anything."

Sebastian produced a silver flask from his inside breast pocket. "St. Sevier was charged with kidnapping, lest we forget."

I settled on the window seat and took a cautious sip of Sebastian's whisky. "This does the nerves a power of good. The charges against St. Sevier were dropped, and thus the whole situation is tied up with a more or less tidy bow."

"St. Sevier plans to remain in the area for a time," Sebastian said. "At least until a competent physician can be enticed to move here. Ann seems determined to take the whole shire in hand, and St. Sevier appears to support her ambitions."

"Two tidy bows, then, because somebody with as much talent and skill as St. Sevier has should use his gifts." Ann saw that, while I hadn't given the matter of Hugh's vocation much thought until late in our association.

Sebastian came down beside me. "That leaves one last loose end. Will you marry me, Violet?"

I handed him back his flask. "Yes, I will marry you."

He tucked the flask away without sampling the contents. "But? With you, I am always mindful of a possible but."

"I have reservations."

"You think I don't, *mo chridhe?*"

"I like it when you call me that." Had liked it even before I'd known what it meant. "I need time, Sebastian. I care for you greatly, though if I marry you, I am also giving up something I care for greatly." I had worked this out only as the morning had progressed.

"You're giving up St. Sevier?"

"Not him. He was never mine to have." Though he would always be mine to esteem, for many reasons. "I had to steel my courage to permit him to court me. After making such a miserable job of being a wife and a grieving widow, I was just beginning to find my balance as... as myself. Hugh was determined that we should marry, but he respected that the decision would be mine."

"He had better have grasped that much."

"This decision is mine too."

"With reservations. What do you need from me, Violet?" He slipped an arm around my waist, and I let my head fall to his shoulder. "Tell me your reservations, and I will tell you mine."

I was reminded once again of why I had long loved Sebastian. Even as a youth, he'd had the gift of listening to me, of knowing when my words mattered and when I was simply in the mood for a rousing debate.

With me, he was patient, kind, and loving, and if that wasn't enough—I would admit this to no one save myself—he was also a very accomplished kisser. In the course of a long union, such a skill and all it portended was not insignificant.

Our marriage would not be built along any of the usual patterns, but if we always showed each other patience and kindness, we could be happy together.

Very happy, in fact.

We remained on the window seat for more than an hour, the sun warm at our backs, the quiet of the library surrounding us. Sebastian described for me a small manor house for sale on the Surrey side of the county line, about ten miles distant from both Belle Terre and Derwent Hall. Sebastian, who had been sent away from family at a young age, argued eloquently for St. Sevier's child to grow up where some sort of relationship with Hugh, Ann, and Fiona was possible.

I was touched and comforted to think that Ann and Sebastian were invested in the child's welfare already. I owed them both much and knew St. Sevier would share my sentiments.

Sebastian and I agreed to visit that small manor later in the week and to send to London for a special license—a document valid for six months—as well. By the time we sent word to the stable to saddle Hannibal and Artemis, Pamela and Maitland had departed, the rest of the staff had been informed by my father of the situation, and Papa had left for Freeman's house.

The situation at The Gauges, to use my words, had been all wrapped up, and the adventure of a life as Sebastian MacHeath's wife and marchioness had just begun. We would solve more puzzles in the future, of that I was sure, but for the nonce, I was at peace.

I was grateful that the situation had resolved in favor of those I cared about. I was in good health, with much to look forward to, and I was ready for a very, very long nap.

TO MY DEAR READERS

But wait! How do Hugh and Anne get on, and was their marital rapprochement really as precipitous as Violet believes? (Pretty sure that's a nope.) Will Violet and Sebastian get married, or will mischief arise on the way to the altar, as mischief is ever wont to do? (I'm guessing yes and yes...)

I don't see the Lady Violet series as complete, but six titles was as many as I was willing to backlog before hitting publish. I hope you've enjoyed every one so far, and that you will forgive me for bouncing over to my romance writing for a bit while Hugh, Anne, Violet, and Sebastian take a short respite.

The next novel-length happily ever after in the queue is ***Never a Duke***, an addition to my **Rogues to Riches** series (excerpt below), though I'm also working on another **Mischief in Mayfair** story, tentatively titled **Miss Desirable** (June 2022). Monsieur Xavier Fournier and Miss Catherine Fairchild have no intention of falling in love, or falling into bed. None whatsoever, at all, in the least... Oh, sure they don't.

Excerpt below. Ordering links should be available on ***Miss Desirable's web page*** soon if they aren't already. I'm also working on a novella series for release this spring with Erica Ridley, **The Siren's Retreat Quartet**.

Yikes, that's a lot to keep track of! If you'd like to stay up to date on all my releases, discounts, and pre-orders, following me on **Bookbub** is probably the easiest way to do that. I also have a **Deals** page on my website, which I update about monthly, and that lists any sales, early releases, or freebie, especially those happening on the **web store**. If you're inclined toward **newsletters**, I publish one about every month or so, and I promise that unsubscribing is easy, and that I will never sell, spam, or swap your addie.

However you prefer to keep in touch, I wish you always...

Happy reading!

Grace Burrowes

Read on for an excerpt from **Never a Duke**!

NEVER A DUKE—EXCERPT

*Ned Wentworth, de facto manager of His Grace of Walden's banks,
has been summoned from his duties by note from an anonymous lady
claiming to need his aid...*

So what could a well born lady have that would make troubling on
her behalf worth Ned's while? He gathered up the dog's leash, bowed
a farewell to Lord Stephen, and strode off for the park.

When he arrived, he was reminded of Burns's admonition about
the best laid plans, for on the third bench along the bank of the
Serpentine sat none other than Lady Rosalind Kinwood in all her
prim, tidy glory.

She was the farthest thing from a damsel, and a stranger to
distress unless she was instigating it. Her devotion to various causes
was both articulate and unwavering. Her ladyship of course occupied
the one bench in all of London she should not occupy at the one hour
when Ned needed her to be elsewhere.

He bowed and touched a finger to his hat brim. "My lady, good day. Might I join you for a moment? The water makes a lovely prospect and the dog could use the respite."

She twitched her skirts aside. "We haven't much time. I sent my companion off to purchase corn for the water fowl, and she'll be back any minute."

Doom yawned before Ned, the same sensation that had enveloped him when as a boy, he'd been grabbed by the collar after a bungled attempt at snatching a purse. One blunder, and he'd been tossed into Newgate, his life over, his prospects forever ruined.

Lady Rosalind wasn't nearly so dire a fate, but not for lack of trying. She was the scourge of fortune hunters, the worst nightmare of climbing cits, the subject of witty pub songs, and the despair of the matchmakers.

Ned unfastened Hercules's leash, and let the dog go nosing off along the bank. "You sent me that note?"

"Don't you dare sit," she snapped. "Your presumption will be noted by every busybody in the Home Counties and the gossips will have us engaged before Monday."

Clearly, an awful fate as far as her ladyship was concerned, and Ned agreed with her. "I heeded your plea for help out of an abundance of gentlemanly concern. Say your piece and nobody need fear Monday's arrival."

She huffed out a sigh, and because Ned was studying the curve of her resolute jaw, he noticed what half the bachelors in London had noticed late at night after a few philosophy-inducing brandies: Lady Rosalind, for all her tart tongue and waspish opinions, was well formed, and her features would not have been out place on a Renaissance tapestry. Features like that could entice otherwise wary unicorns to have a closer look.

The Almighty was nothing, if not perverse in His generosity.

She watched the dog, who snuffled about the reeds near the water's edge. "My lady's maid has gone missing."

"So you summoned a banker? Did she go missing in a Wentworth establishment?"

"Don't be odious. Bad things happen to young women who go missing."

"Elopements?" Ned replied. "New posts? A return to village life and the adoring swain who pined away in silence when his beloved left him for the blandishments of the capital?"

Lady Rosalind rose. "You trivialize a tragedy. I thought you would understand. Arbuckle is a village girl, but she's been in London long enough to know its dangers. She needed her wages, and believe me, the post paid well."

And she had the effrontery to leave your employ without notice? But no, Ned could not say that. He might never be a gentleman in the eyes of Mayfair society, much less a duke, but he could be civil to an obviously upset woman.

"What exactly is it that you expect me to do?"

Lady Rosalind gave him a brooding perusal. She was neither tall nor short, but she carried her ire before her like regimental colors. Her temper directed itself to bumbling younger sons, drunken baronets, the monarch's extravagances, and countless other targets. In the main, Ned agreed with her exasperation, as most of her peers doubtless did.

But a young lady did not remark on such matters until she was safely married and presiding over her nursery, and then she mentioned them to only her closest friends and in strictest confidence.

"I had hoped you could find her," Lady Rosalind said. "I cannot. I have tried, but the grooms and crossing sweepers won't talk to me, my brothers won't listen to me, my father is threatening to send me to take the waters with Aunt Ida. Arbuckle has nobody else to worry for her, and she could be in very great danger."

Ned whistled for the dog, who trotted to his side like the well-trained beast he was. "And you believe the crossing sweepers and such will talk to me?" He'd been managing the Wentworth banks since finishing that purgatory known as university studies. He had some wealth of his own; he spoke French, German, and Mayfair passably well, and he was accounted a competent dancer.

But Lady Rosalind had sought him out because his native language was Cockney and his home county was the stews. *Still.* Society never flung his origins in his face, but they never flung their marriageable daughters at him either.

"Arbuckle is pretty," Lady Rosalind said, gaze fixed on the mirror-calm surface of the Serpentine. "She has lovely features and a quick mind. She's sweet and quiet, not like me, and that means she's at greater risk of harm."

Ned sensed in Lady Rosalind's words an admission of sorts, an insight into the woman whom most of society invited to their gatherings out of unwillingness to offend her titled father.

"You fear for her."

"I do, terribly."

The calm façade wavered, as Hercules panted gently at Ned's side. For an instant Lady Rosalind looked not affronted, not impatient, not any of her usual repertoire of prickly expressions, but *desperate.*

Ned knew desperation well and hated it in all of its guises. That Lady Rosalind, termagant at large and spinster without compare, was in the grip of desperation affronted him.

"I'll see what I can find out."

"Thank you." Two words, though like all of Lady Rosalind's other pronouncements, Ned believed she meant them. "There is more to the situation than I can convey at the moment, and I am so worried."

"I apprehend that your companion approaches." At a good clip, just shy of a trot. "I will shop tomorrow at Hatchards among the biographies at ten of the clock. Prepare to recount for me all you know of the situation."

He snapped the leash back onto Hercules's collar.

"Thank you, Mr. Wentworth. Thank you so very much."

Ned tipped his hat and sauntered on his way, though some dim back corner of his heart put those words of thanks in a special hiding place, where they would be well guarded and much treasured.

Order your copy of **Never a Duke** and read on for an excerpt from *Miss Desirable*!

MISS DESIRABLE—EXCERPT

Catherine Fairchild has attired herself as a widow the better to ensure discretion when she's intent on buying some wine. She has eyes of a distinctive lavender hue, which most of polite society takes as confirmation of her status as a legitimate by-blow....

Veils were stuffy and they made one's spectacles steam up, but Catherine appreciated the privacy afforded by thick black netting. Monsieur Fournier had been so charming, so... easy to be with, that the moment when he'd caught sight of her eyes brought more than the usual disappointment.

In the instant when a stranger first met her gaze, Catherine could discern who *knew*, and who had yet to be disabused by the gossips regarding her situation.

Fournier clearly *knew*, but then, he was reputed to be a man of varied interests and wide connections. The émigrés had to be, if they intended to thrive in the London marketplace of products and influence.

"Shall I tell you about the wines?" he asked. "I warn you, I am as effusive as a doting papa when it comes to my vintages. This verbosity is pointless. You will make up your own mind based on your experience of the drink itself."

"One suspects you enjoy airing your opinions, Monsieur, and I know next to nothing of fine wines. Why are all the clarets in green bottles, for example?"

Her observation pleased him, if the crinkling of his eyes was any indication. "Most people don't notice that. Sunlight can affect the flavor of the clarets over time, just as it can wash out certain gems and fade many fabrics. The green glass protects the wine. Then too, some wines are not so lovely to look at in the bottle. Sediment, clouding, a color other than the customer expects for that vintage, so the tinted glass provides the wine a little privacy. One cannot begrudge a vintage that small boon, can one?"

He was reassuring Catherine in some regard, about her own privacy. His perceptiveness both comforted and unnerved.

"So what have you chosen for me to sample?" The question could have been vaguely flirtatious, coming from another woman. Too late, Catherine had learned how make questions simply questions and answers simply answers.

Monsieur Fournier launched into a little homily about how to blend clarets, how each strain of grape had particular strengths, though any wine he offered would be well above reproach. One bottle was more affordable than the others because the product was more plentiful—the curse of a good harvest, *non?* Another—the Cahors—was darker and carried more of a plum flavor from the malbec grapes.

Fournier's native French gave the recitation a lilting cadence, decorated with the occasional charming cognate. The Cahors was too *audacieux* for delicate palates. *Le merlot* occasionally too *arrogant.* A flourish of humility here and there—*comment dit-on ce mot en Anglais?*—added a self-effacing quality to his patter, as if his opinions truly were an offering Catherine was free to accept or reject.

She let the mellifluous current of his voice wash over her as the rain washed down the shop winders, creating a barrier between the elegance of Fournier's office, and the grit and coalsmoke of the city beyond. Catherine knew exactly what she needed from Monsieur Fournier's wineshop—a high quality, hearty, claret with strong flavor and a rich color.

She also knew that Monsieur Fournier had no need to ask her for this or that word in English, because despite his polite question—how does one say this word in English?—he always sailed right along, finding the exact right turn of phrase himself.

To a woman who loved books, such a skill merited notice.

A quarter hour later, Catherine noticed something else: She instinctively *liked* Xavier Fournier, which made no sense. He was handsome, which should have put her *off*—dark hair, dark eyes, height, athletic frame—and he was nonetheless *interesting*.

Steak and potatoes affronted him, the new process for making a clear champagne fascinated him. English winters were a trial to his spirit. Unlike the usual lordling, Xavier Fournier did not resort to irony, understatement, and sarcasm to make his points. He was both subtle and forthright, blunt and deft.

Catherine had learned to her sorrow that beauty was easily mistaken for goodness in both men and women. While Fournier's looks warned her to keep a distance, everything else about him—the charm, the little personal confidences, the fine manners, the passion for his wine, for good food, for English newspapers—beckoned her closer.

Which would not do, though where was the harm in appreciating the man from a safe distance?

Look for **Miss Desirable** in June 2022, book four in the Mischief in Mayfair series!